D0553614

white lies

white lies

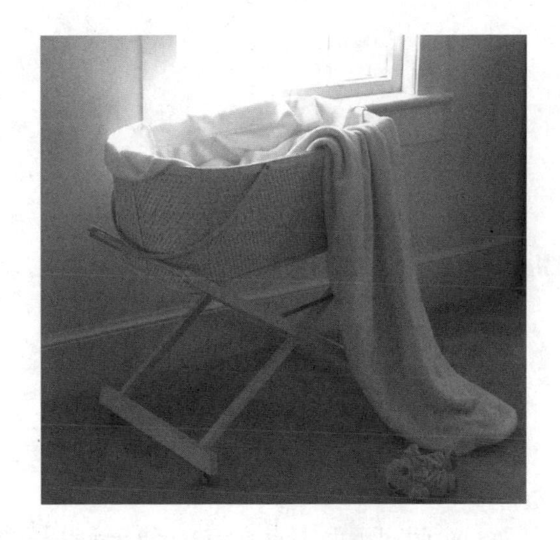

A Tale of Babies, Vaccines, and Deception

SARAH COLLINS
HONENBERGER

Cedar Creek Publishing
Virginia, USA

Although this book was inspired by actual places, people and events, it must be read as a work of fiction. The characters, places, details and dialogue are invented. Certain very real incidents or characteristics have been altered or re-imagined.

First Printing, 2006

First published in the United States of America by
Cedar Creek Publishing, Virginia, USA 2006
www.cedarcreekpublishingservices.com

Library of Congress Control Number 2006935678

ISBN-13: 978-0-9790205-1-3
ISBN-10: 0-9790205-1-4

Printed in the United States of America
Set in AGaramond Text

Dedicated to the babies who never grew up
and the parents who dare to ask why

Chapter One
LACY

In the shadowy place of my memories Danny stays small and blue-eyed, sweet and happy. I've been over it and over it a thousand times. There's always something missing, some piece of the puzzle I can't quite figure. That June morning in 1969 I remember how he grabbed the spoon with his fingers, tugging eagerly. You'd have hardly known he had a fever except for those little crying fits like someone was pinching him. When I'd called Doc Snowden's office the day before, his nurse Mary said if Danny wasn't back to his old self in the morning, call again.

Although the days blur together—in 1969 he spent weeks on end in the hospital—the day of that first seizure is the one day I can't forget. He was three months old, his hair already starting to curl like Scott's. I remember thinking when he grew up, he would be handsome and smart, thanks to my brand new college-graduated husband. And brave and kind because I'd make sure of that. Was I nutty about that baby? Oh, yeah. A baby of my own was the one thing I'd wanted since I was a little girl.

I know what they say about infants and gas, but that morning when Danny raised his head, he was definitely smiling. I only left him for a minute—to mix his cereal—maybe not even a minute. He sputtered a little bit, coughed. But after the cough there was no noise at all and when I rushed back to the living room, he was gasping for air, his legs sticking straight out from his knees like a broken jackknife. His face had gone all white. And he was making scratchy sounds as if he were scrabbling up a boulder.

Just as he started to slide out of the baby seat, I grabbed him. Pounded his back. Yelled for help. But when I put my finger on his tongue to keep him from choking like they showed us in baby class, he clamped down and wouldn't let go.

On the landing I banged on doors. Out came George, the apartment manager, half-dressed, looking for the fire. I'm standing there in my nightgown, screaming like a lunatic. He grabbed my elbow and pulled. When my finger popped loose, Danny wheezed as if there weren't enough air in the world. George drove us straight to the hospital. Ran every light. On the median strip. Honking the whole way. And right before the emergency doors he scraped a parked car, but that didn't slow him down any.

Weird, isn't it, how a person's brain works? Despite all that panic, I can see the color of his car. And the slippers I was wearing. Twenty-one years later that's what sticks. That yellow car and those red slippers. Like a hand in front of the sun, they keep my mind from the rest of the memory; the feel of Danny's legs dangling against my stomach and the sight of his eyes rolled back and his skin turning blue. His eyes were open, but he never blinked. The nurse grabbed him right out of my arms and walked away without saying a thing.

You'd think in a big city hospital there'd be a ton of people. Ambulances and doctors rushing around. But that hospital was like a funeral home. No noise, nothing moved. And on the floor there was a single line of black tile. One line in a great wide ocean of white, winter everywhere. Not a real color, just cold, cold enough to drown in. It was July in Virginia for God's sake and I was frozen.

Over and over I mixed that stupid oatmeal and heard that sound when he stopped breathing. But I couldn't step across the damn line.

Chapter Two
JEAN

In my line of work I hear too many secrets. People in failing marriages do incredible things, and in twenty-two years of divorces I've heard them all. Most of my former clients, when they see me, hurry in the other direction. No one likes to be reminded of bad times. And I know things they'd rather not remember.

The first time I met Lacy Stonington she came for a no-fault divorce from a man she hadn't seen in a decade. Matter of fact and practical, she knew it had to be done. She didn't talk much about her heart's desires, but neither did I. Fresh out of law school, I was consumed with my professional image.

Twelve years later when she came back I'd discovered that clients rarely tell their lawyers the whole truth. Perspective changes truth, so truth becomes relative. And once you bend the rules about something as definite as truth, it's hard to keep to any standard. If clients didn't recognize the truth and judges didn't want to hear it, how futile my role as purveyor of justice became. After years of clients' stories that all sounded the same, practicing law had become a business.

On that early spring afternoon in 1990 when Lacy told me her secret, she said a mother's love ought to count for something. I laughed at first, thinking she meant it as a joke, because, other than her divorce case—long completed and filed away—motherhood was the only thing we had in common. But the intensity of her gaze made me pause. I thought of my own children. Defensive about the career that limited my time with them, I wondered if she knew something I didn't.

I didn't understand what exactly she meant until much later. Later, in the thick of things, my lawyer's mind decided that nothing would have changed if I'd understood from the beginning. In the cold, hard light of hindsight—I lecture myself—it wouldn't have made a difference to her son or mine. Or to the thousands of other children like them.

Lacy convinced me that it did. And should.

This is Danny's story, but it's the story of his mother, too.

April 1990

Shoving the door with my briefcase, I elbowed through the milling spectators in the hallway outside the courtroom to reach the foyer. I felt like punching someone. It was getting to be a regular feeling.

Only in a small farming community would the divorce of the local veterinarian draw such a crowd. In the entryway the witnesses from the two day hearing lingered; two accountants—ours and the husband's—Doctor Stanley's partner, his golf buddy, and the latest girlfriend, conveniently sporting a diamond engagement ring for the court hearing. Most of the others were spectators, primarily female, dressed in their finest blue jeans, complete with pressed creases, pastel button-down shirts, and polished cowboy boots. Their necks and hands glittered with gold. Doc had some well-heeled lady friends. I could just imagine their pets.

Determined to show the world they were on the side of right and justice—and not my client's—they turned their faces away as

I passed. Their comments, too low to distinguish much more than their dislike of Ursula Stanley. And me by association. I wondered how they would've behaved if Ursula had hired a male attorney with as much charisma as her gregarious husband.

"D'you win, sweet baby Jean?" Chase Taggart asked from the corner. Even though he was ten years older, he and I had been buddies since my early days practicing law. Unorthodox and outspoken, he didn't fit in with the good old boys. As the only female attorney in six counties and a transplanted Northerner to boot, neither did I.

Chase, with an habitual offender at his heels, was perpetually waiting for his allotted twenty minutes to plead for a restricted license so his client could get to a job he'd already lost because of the court appearance.

"Hell, no, I didn't win," I said under my breath. "That fancy lawyer from the big city pulled every trick he knew."

"You complaining about the rules of evidence again?"

I nodded, frustrated and willing to settle for any sympathetic ear. Chase put his arm around my shoulder and whispered.

"Was he high?"

"The other lawyer or Doc Poochy-Goochy-Goo?"

"Rumor has it the good doc dispenses bovine medicine to two-footed creatures."

"You should have testified."

"I also heard that he performed an abortion on one of the girls who cleans the animal hospital. Did you put that into evidence?" Chase meant for me to laugh.

As bad as Ursula's husband was, I didn't think he would risk his license. Tax fraud I could believe. And had almost proved until his accountant testified that my client had propositioned him for a look at the books.

I ranted under my breath to Chase. "You know the system stinks. The Judge never gets to hear what really happened between the couple. Anything to do with the kids is hearsay and if you have a real psycho for opposing counsel, he can make any sane person look ridiculous just by fabricating events. The old 'When did you stop beating your wife?'"

When Chase's client shuffled over to the water fountain, eyeing the clock with devotion as it approached cocktail hour, Chase leaned closer to me. "That woman in the red dress, is that Doc's current honey?"

"Fiancée," I spit back at him.

"Hey, were you at the altar?" Chase tweaked the back of my neck affectionately, then straightened his tie in the reflection of the glass door. "You win the ones you're supposed to win and you lose the ones that were pro bono."

I frowned. "That isn't even funny."

Winking, he grabbed his client's collar and sat him back down on the bench.

"Wait here," Chase said, "It might finally be our turn." He disappeared into the courtroom.

Outside on the courthouse steps the last of the simpering March day was slipping away. Long dull shadows stretched between storefronts on Main Street, shooting fingers of dark across the street to where I stood waiting for Ursula Stanley. Post-trial reassurances were not my favorite part of being a lawyer.

Eventually she trailed out, her own shirt unbuttoned too far to command much respect. The mini-skirt revealed athletic legs. Her chest was belligerently thrust forward to make more blatant yet her protest against the injustice of having to defend the doctor's accusations in front of an audience. Unlike most of my clients, she carried her own briefcase. Calfskin, with gold fittings, probably Gucci.

I tried to remember how much during our pre-trial prep sessions I had admired her organizational skills. I tried to think positively.

"That was not fun," she said. "But I did okay, didn't I?"

I was tempted to say; *No, you blew it. You let yourself be suckered into admitting your male friend is more than a friend and you should never have described your son's drug use in such detail. It indicates your own familiarity. And even if he did get the stuff from his father's office, the judge is bound to blame the parent at home.*

Instead I mumbled, "You did fine," and stepped down to the sidewalk.

She followed me. From the daggers in her eyes I guessed she was calculating how many of these women had slept with her husband. Even in the cooler air out here she was perspiring enough to leave large semi-circles on her shirt. It made me feel ten degrees warmer.

She tapped her cigarette against the briefcase before lighting it. "When will the judge decide?"

"About the kids or the property division?"

"You told me he wouldn't change custody if the kids were doing fine in school."

"Jeffrey's drugs are a problem. I warned you about that."

"But he's honor roll," she whined.

I couldn't argue with her anymore. We'd been through it a hundred times, in a hundred different ways. No matter what I said, she was smarter, she had the angle all figured out, she'd tell the judge a thing or two.

I picked up the briefcase. "I'll call you next week."

"Don't we need to plan our strategy if he appeals?"

"He isn't going to appeal." I said. He was going to win.

Back at the office my secretary Jillian handed me a stack of messages. "How did it –"

"Don't ask. It's like that damn running weed in the grass. You keep yanking it out, but you know it'll be back in the morning. Only worse because you know the truth is underneath where the Judge can't see it for all the . . . ah, fertilizer the other attorney keeps dumping."

Jillian looked a little shocked. I was not usually so graphic. "Peter called and said he'd make dinner. He figured the trial would go late." She smiled and I smiled back. "Your husband's a nice guy," she added.

"Mmmm," I murmured, shuffling messages. "He knew we'd be hours with the accountant over the business valuation."

"You didn't forget Mr. Reams' appointment at 5:30? Maybe I should move it."

I shook my head. "It'll take my mind off this wasted day."

Leaving the briefcase for her to empty, I moved through the narrow hallway that connected the string of rooms, end to end, on my half of the building. The old bowling alley, converted to office space a decade ago, housed two of us, me and a bookkeeper who worked odd hours, mostly under cover of darkness. I'd never seen him with anyone or anywhere else. I wondered if he had a family who missed him when he was here, late into the night, night after night.

The puzzle of the veterinarian's son using drugs resurfaced. Had that happened because his father left his mother? Or because, as my client insisted, the veterinarian worked every weekend? Why did the son falter when the daughter moved skillfully through the same minefield? It occurred to me the seeds of division that led to divorce might spring from the same failures of communication that made a child substitute fantasy for reality. It had to be more than mere absence that started the unraveling. Lots of parents worked long hours and their kids thrived from the example they set. Or maybe in spite of it.

While I'd been gone, files had sprouted in unequal piles on the corners of my desk, Jillian's attempt at prioritizing. She was twenty and working hard at being professional. Too tense to sit, I stood by one corner and read the letter on top without really paying attention. After I shook out my hair and rotated my shoulders, I was still fuming over the other attorney's insinuations when I heard raised voices.

Jillian spoke fiercely. "Hey, wait. You can't just barge in there."

Chapter Three
JEAN

Lacy Stonington, with mascara running in streaks down her cheeks, moved through the open door toward my desk. "I have to talk to you." She spoke with barely contained control as if she were one more distraught wife here for a divorce conference. Her hands fluttered at her side.

"I told her you were busy," Jillian said, trying to position herself between the desk and this intruder.

Oblivious, Lacy smiled weakly through the tears. Mascara spotted her white T-shirt. After wiping her hand across her cheek, she laid her palm against her jeans and drew it slowly across the faded material. The gesture hinted at stubborn, but I missed it then.

"It's okay, Jillian," I said, actually relieved at the distraction. "Give me a buzz when Mr. Reams arrives for his appointment."

She shrugged, an apology for failing as my line of defense, and retreated. Lacy froze. Her eyes darted from the window to me, and back. Finally she cleared her throat. That's how they all start, needy and insistent. I listened with one ear.

At a fraction of her initial volume she spoke. "I have a son I never told you about."

This was a line I hadn't heard before. I wondered how she would work it around to the stories I knew so well, the husband with the heavy fist or the ex who refused to send money. Closing the open file, I shoved the paperwork to the far side of my desk and pointed at the empty chair. "I only have ten minutes."

After examining her hands where the make-up had left more small dark splotches, she dug around in her purse for a tissue. For several long seconds she rubbed the skin until the tissue shredded. Noticing the mess suddenly, she gathered up the scraps. Her timidity caught me off-guard. She was unnerved, I suppose, by having to admit whatever she'd been hiding. She took deep breaths the way you do when you stand on the high diving board.

"That looks so official," she said, nodding in the direction of the legal pad in front of me.

"Just pretend we're old friends. Pretend we're chatting on your front porch." I had no idea whether she had a front porch, but I wanted to get this over with. My divorce clients delivered a regular dose of histrionics. I didn't need more of that.

In the last ten years I'd only seen Lacy at the grocery store where she worked the register or on the sidewalk in front of the post office. If I appeared in her check out line, she always sang out, "I love you." A little embarrassing for me, in my business suit, with clients and neighbors in line around me. But you have to admire someone who's that open with her feelings. It's unusual.

Before grocery checker, she was a school bus driver and she always honked her horn in front of my office. If Peter was with me when we met on the street, she would admonish him to take good care of me while she was hugging me. She treated everyone in our little town the same way. I didn't think much about it.

Sometimes she'd refer in passing to her ex-husband, Scott Kellam. His third divorce, another change of employment. She'd offer up his latest failure of character as if our complicity in her no-fault divorce case meant we shared this interest. She'd immediately chase the gossip with how lucky she was to have found her second husband, Moss.

Moss's real name was Henry. She explained this to me in great detail in one of our random sidewalk conversations. More than once she told me how her sweet Mosste had ridden into her life on a motorcycle when she was at her lowest point and she was never going to let him go. She'd never revealed her lowest point to me. And no matter how she saw our relationship, I honestly didn't know her well enough to ask.

Although I didn't meet Moss until long after my part in this story began—I'm not a motorcycle fan—the fact that she was still madly in love after all those years tickled me. Good news from one of my divorce clients was rare.

This troubled Lacy, weepy and floundering, was a stranger. In our earlier conferences the only negative emotion she'd displayed had been disgust over Scott and even that rarely displaced her cheerful self.

Once the door shut behind Jillian, Lacy stopped shifting her weight between feet and sat down. With one hand resting on each knee, she propped her sneakers on the front rung of the chair. When she finally spoke, she still sounded misty-eyed. "I thought we were friends."

I was mystified. "We are."

"You said, 'pretend.'"

"Oh," I swatted the air between us, "That was just a figure of speech."

"I don't know figures of whatever. My little high school diploma from Twyman's Mill can't stand up to all your fancy degrees." Her arm swept across my wall, where Peter had helped me measure and hang the documents that spring immaculately from law school graduation.

I smiled as kindly as I could manage after a day of examining accountants and adulterers. "You started to tell me something about your son?" I began signing the letters in the nearest pile, perusing each one superficially as I turned the pages.

She missed the innuendo or ignored it. "I saw a show on television this morning."

Morning television was not high on my list of reliable sources. I checked my watch, nine minutes until the 5:30 client was due.

"They showed these babies like Danny. Before and after." As if she'd practiced the speech, she spoke distinctly, "The bottom of the screen listed an eight hundred number."

Staring into the darkness under the old oak desk, I rolled my eyes where she couldn't see me do it. Crazy people called television talk shows. Crazy people thought lawyers could perform miracles. She was not headed anywhere I wanted to go. There was a good reason why they advise you never to ride with your clients when they offer to drive.

"In a very few minutes," I interrupted her, "An anxious client will appear in my front office for an appointment he scheduled weeks ago, impatient to tell me why he deserves a divorce." I tried to keep my voice even and pleasant. "I only have eight minutes. You have to summarize. Or reschedule."

She blurted out, "What they showed on television, that happened to my son. But they never told me why. They made me give him up."

"They?" Fiddling with the buttons on my jacket sleeve, I felt like the cartoon psychiatrist whose client would momentarily admit to hearing voices. I was not trained to deal with this. And I didn't have time.

Startled, she looked up, as if she hadn't expected me to doubt her. She appeared to be struggling for the right words or perhaps willing me to understand instantly so she wouldn't have to set it all out in black and white. On the verge of speaking her lips parted and remained apart for several long seconds, long enough for me to shift in the chair and un-wrinkle my jacket where it had bunched up in the back. It was hard to tell which of us was more uncomfortable.

With other clients I'd seen that the admission of a long held secret creates an almost physical pain, deep and unidentifiable and disconcerting. The teller, despite knowing all along, has to justify what seems like a lie all of a sudden, usually when no such intent existed. When the minute hand ticked by the five, I checked the closest stack of files to see if the folder for the upcoming appointment was there.

Lacy stood up, mashing the tissues from her lap into her pocket. She stared woefully at me. "I thought you'd understand."

"I'm trying, but what you've told me doesn't make sense. Ten years ago when you were here, your children were the same age as mine. They're teenagers now. Today you burst in and tell me you've seen something on television about another baby. In the next breath you imply a connection with an unnamed conspiracy. And you're here talking to a lawyer so you must think there's a legal claim somewhere in the mix."

She winced at each sentence. "Until today I never knew what happened to Danny."

"What? What happened?" The tone exposed my exasperation before I could call it back.

After an interminable silence with her face turned away, she sat back down, dry-eyed, ignoring the tissue box I offered. My watch said twenty-eight past five.

"You'd think," she said, "After all these years, I'd have learned how to deal with losing him."

The vision of a dead baby in Lacy's arms—with her same shock of black hair and Crayola cheeks—sprang full-blown in my head. Time scrolled forward and I imagined her kneeling in a rainy graveyard and flinging herself on the matted grass by a miniature tombstone. A lone red tulip shuddered in the wind. It had been a long day.

"He died?" I asked with dread.

"He had a really bad seizure. He stayed sick. They ran tests, but never found anything. At least they never said what they found."

"They must have said something."

"They told me to put him in the state hospital where there were people trained to care for babies with his kind of problems."

"Did you do that?"

"Would you? When I argued with them, they thought I was crazy." She shrugged as if craziness were a minor character flaw. There was a long pause before she spoke. "Maybe they were right, and I was a little crazy." She looked up from her lap. "Maybe a lot crazy." At least she could admit her story sounded more than a little implausible.

"So what did you do?"

"I kept him with me. But then I got sick and no one would keep him, not even for a few days. I realized when I died, no one would be there to take over for me. Plus the state people promised to teach him stuff. I had to let him go."

"So the state doctors diagnosed his injuries?"

"I'm not sure what you mean by injuries. He was healthy and then he wasn't."

Nothing she'd told me had a shred of legal relevance. My five-thirty appointment would be pacing in the front room.

"The doctors had no idea what caused his illness?"

Her perplexed expression disappeared. "The television doctor says they did know. Even though kids were getting sick, the drug companies were getting rich, so, they didn't tell anyone. They just kept using the same medicine."

I sat up, awake instantly, my lawyer's brain ticking. "What medicine?"

"PDT or DPT or something like that. It's what they gave Danny just before his first seizure."

As I scribbled on the blank pad, the intercom buzzed.

"Mr. Reams is here for his five-thirty appointment," Jillian announced.

I never hesitated. "Reschedule him."

Chapter Four
LACY

Thirty-five years . . . it's a long time to lose. The lies changed everything, and the truth changed everything. So who decides which is better? Or which is right?

Here on the porch, looking out over the mountains where Moss brought me to forget, I think about my Danny a hundred miles from here. In his wheelchair he looks out on these same mountains, but he doesn't know I'm here. Jenny's with him, the nurse who tried to teach him how to feed himself. The good mother, I tell her. She's the one who calls me when he gets pneumonia or has worn out the ankle padding on his sneakers. She sits next to him all day while his gnarled hands twitch at the lap blanket, his feet knocking at the wheelchair footrests. She listens to his soft moans echo in that cement room with the metal windows that only open in inches.

The place where he lives is called a training center. Not that they aren't kind and patient, but he's the same today at thirty-five as he was at three months, only bigger. When I visit, Jenny walks with us and I push his chair. Every time I go there she points out the cafeteria, his room with the dolphin comforter I replace every few years, worn from industrial washing, and the music studio where he listens to tapes and wags his head in a slow uneven nod for an hour twice a week. She swears he smiles when he hears my voice. I spend half the visit thanking her. She's doing what I can't bear to do.

Still, if Danny hadn't gotten sick, Moss wouldn't have found me. I wouldn't have my other children, Carson and Diana. None of us would have had the chance to work with creepy old Lawyer Fine with his fancy shoes and his cut glass taste. And Jean would've gone on like she was.

During that awful time when Danny was in and out of the Fairfax hospital, Doc Snowden used to tell me to make the experience count for something. And Mary his nurse, she'd rush to hold Danny when everyone else just stared and held on more tightly to their perfect children. Snowden and Mary were like the mountain folks I knew from home. They'd worked together forever, from way back, umpty-ump years since his medical school graduation. Like my Gram, Mary was a tough old girl. She grew up on a peanut farm with a whole bunch of brothers and cousins. Lots of love and not much more. Her nursing scholarship was her ticket out.

As much as I loved babies, nursing's what I should've done, although I'm not sure about all that book learning. Back then I wasn't thinking that far ahead. Getting away from Twyman's Mill was the most important thing. And I was dealing with a lot of other stuff: a mother who acted as if she'd like to give away all three of her children if she could have. And her second husband, John Thompson, with his creeping hands and his begging eyes. As soon as I could get a work permit, I started making plans.

I was waiting tables and saving my money for bus fare when Scott Kellam came along. He ate at the restaurant with his college buddies, but he'd talk to me before they came or after. It didn't take me long to see how different he was from the boys I'd gone to high school with. Really smart, not just smart-mouthed. Shy with me, but mad at the world and itching to get back at it and his parents. He must have figured marriage to a mountain girl would show them. Of course I didn't see it that way back then. He used to take me driving and talk about the buildings he was going to build. Without a close family himself, he loved to hear my stories of Gram taking all of us cousins to the parades—she had ten children—or teaching us how to make applesauce. When he offered so politely, his hands poised on the steering wheel, to take me with him to Virginia, why would I say no?

For almost a year we had a perfect life. He engineered parking garages and bridges for the company that had hired him right out of school and I found a job from the newspaper, sorting mail at the post office. Our apartment was clean and quiet, no more lewd comments by John Thompson, no mother dragging in late from work, ignoring us and fussing over him. It didn't matter that Scott and I went out less and less with his new friends or that he was furious when I turned up pregnant. He'd change his mind as soon as he saw the baby, I was sure about that. Everyone loves babies. Other than getting away from John Thompson, a baby of my own was the only thing I'd ever wanted.

You would think, after not knowing what went wrong for so long, the truth would be enough. But sitting here, with the sun on my face, I wonder. Would I trade it all to have my baby back, to be eighteen again with Danny in my arms, blue sky reflected in his eyes, to know that he was mine?

Chapter Five
JEAN

The vaccination Lacy named was familiar to me, though not as a lawyer. All three of my children had started the series as infants. Vaguely I recalled periodic boosters required for public school. My children had had them all. I tried to remember what our pediatrician had said about the shots, but nothing specific came to mind. Certainly I would have paid attention to a danger warning that could send a child to the hospital.

While I hung up my jacket and filled two glasses with water, Lacy expounded.

"The telephone lady at the disease place said she wasn't allowed to give legal advice. But I asked her, what would you do if you had a perfectly healthy baby and right after his three-month check up, after that shot, he got sick? She told me I should hire a lawyer."

I cringed. Most legitimate attorneys think television lawyers are quacks. They work people into a frenzy to sue someone, anyone, and leave it to the real lawyers to explain why there's no legitimate claim.

"Listen," I said with forced patience, "those shows . . . they exaggerate on purpose . . . to create a controversy. You know what I mean? To agitate people, to get them upset, for the entertainment value to other viewers. The Center for Disease Control's pretty conservative. It's run by the government. What you're describing sounds like science fiction."

"Yeah, okay, if it's nothing, I can live with that. But before Danny had the shot, he was fine."

"There are a thousand things that can go wrong with a baby."

"But it happened right after the shot," she mumbled. Her jaw and shoulders were rigid, and she winced, as if disagreeing with me hurt her physically.

"Lacy, what do you want me to do?"

"Moss said you'd know what to do."

"Whoa, whoa, I'm a divorce lawyer. Until two minutes ago I didn't even know Danny existed, much less anything about vaccinations and seizures. It's not an area of the law I deal with."

"You can look it up in your books." Grinning, she waved her hands at the bookshelves, confident that the mere ownership of law books could make things right.

There was an indefinable moment when I saw through her smiles and her universal friendliness to the center of her, to the real Lacy who'd picked herself up from some place dark and rocky and managed to find the open air and the sunshine. The distress, the fear, the treacherous path she'd traveled, she'd left all that behind. She'd packed it up, stored it away, and shut the door so she didn't have to see it.

Yet here she was, standing at that threshold and offering to open it up for that secret son. Somehow she'd convinced herself that by finding an answer to what had happened twenty years ago, she could fix everything. And she'd chosen me to go with her.

Until the TV hype she must have been thinking about this all those years, mulling it over internally without any feedback. It would be tricky to direct her through memories, expanded and contracted with time, in order to uncover specific facts detailed enough for a court of law. I sighed. I was the only attorney she knew and she had convinced herself we were friends.

"Okay, okay, tell me what happened after the shot."

She drew her feet up into a pretzel, a shape only a small person could have managed on the narrow wooden chair. Closing her eyes, she appeared to drift away mentally. In the late afternoon of that chilly spring day the sun had dropped behind the rear of the building. The long shadows from earlier had melted into the houses opposite. Everything glowed a little wickedly, black edges and blurred colors, disguised with the last shreds of daylight. The world outside my window—trees and roofs and cars—looked stretched and elongated like a Georgia O'Keeffe landscape. That distortion made it seem safer inside.

Here in the bold artificial light things held their usual shape. Rectangular desk on square carpet, firmly aligned with the walls and floor. Fluorescent lights eliminated shadows. It was my office after all, the place I spent countless ten-hour days, poring over paperwork and listening to pitiful stories, hammering out compromises. The front office was silent. Jillian had gone home.

For Lacy it hardly mattered where she was. The day she was being forced to remember must have replayed in her head a thousand times. Watching her twist her fingers and sink into the past, I forgot the custody trial scheduled for nine the next morning. I forgot the parents' meeting for my daughter that evening. There was no way to know then how Daniel Boyd Kellam—Lacy's secret for two decades—would change my life. She leaned forward, her face flush with emotion, eager to finally tell her story.

Three hours later, when I called home, Peter answered the phone. "Where are you? We were worried."

"I'm still at the office."

"We tried to call. You didn't answer."

"Sorry, Jillian must have routed calls to the answering machine. I got tied up with a client and forgot all about dinner."

"And the parent-teacher conferences."

"I know. I just remembered. I'm really sorry."

"I hope it's a big retainer."

"I'm not sure yet if there's a case."

It took me another hour to plow through the letters on my desk, and even then, I carried home the witness notes for the next day's hearing.

Our farmhouse was built in 1910. From the front porch we have a passable view of the mountains, better when the leaves fall. Outside of the pretentious columned portico, it is a simple farmhouse; Greek revival and a very American statement connecting where we'd been as a young ambitious country to where we were headed. Generous rooms with big windows and two staircases, perfect for entertaining and for raising a family. It suited us.

After my long evening with Lacy, driving up the gravel lane to the house, I searched the night sky. The world was a sad and disheartening place. I needed some inspiration. Orion, an old friend, hung above our rooftop, hidden partly by walnut and sycamore branches. His shoulders and sword, right where they ought to be, commanded the eastern heavens. That reassured me a little.

In spite of the court schedule I kept I loved being home more than I admitted. In our yard the trees rose, old and grand, like clusters of dowagers at a Southern wedding. Their branches swept down in elegant condescension. The wide porch invited you to sit and watch nature's waltz across the horizon. And Peter and the children were there.

Unable to put Lacy from my mind though, I didn't rush inside. The kids would be busy studying. Peter would be reading, dozing more likely, on his prized leather sofa. I leaned against the car and watched the stars.

My mind buzzed with phrases from fuzzy memories of law school classes on tort law, one person's wrong against another, or one company's against a person. I was an old lawyer. With one specialty. For the last two decades I had done nothing except try to impose some order on dissolving marriages. I'd been through enough trials to know that emotion had no place in the courtroom. When wives wept, I handed them tissues and told them they were only helping their husbands if they let him manipulate their emotions. When husbands ranted, I calmed them down with diagrams of dollars and warnings that courts rarely let fault issues affect the division of assets.

Legal training was just that. A repetitive, regulated, explication of facts in a certain order to lead to one result, the one the statute dictated. Like a cold, efficient accountant I advocated for one set of figures, correlated to the factual basis for each asset. Even non-financial contributions were touted in the same mechanical format. Dividing people's assets was one thing. Proving the value of a healthy child was another.

Peter's shadow crossed back and forth across the porch light as he moved trash to the outside can. "Jean?"

"Uh-huh."

"Coming in?"

"In a minute."

The wooden steps creaked. Easing himself next to me, he put one arm around my shoulders. His body was warm. "Who's running around on his wife now?" he asked.

"It's not a divorce."

"As long as it's not our divorce."

"Forgetting dinner might be grounds," I joked.

"It must be important if you forgot your own children."

I bristled. I'd hardly forgotten the children simply because I was at the office doing my job; a job Peter was forever reminding me was a valuable and important contribution. But as I was the one who hadn't called, I kept my temper.

"D'you remember Lacy Stonington?"

"Give me a clue?"

"Small. Black hair. Bounces."

"Little Miss Sunshine who drives the handicapped school bus?"

"Used to, but that's the one. Now I know why she did that."

"Did what?"

"Drove the bus. She had a baby in 1969, he's twenty-one now."

"Under that theory most of us would be driving buses for a living."

"Ah, but this baby is still a baby. After his first vaccination he suffered brain damage. He never grew up."

At first Peter didn't say anything, thinking, I was sure, how it would be to have a son who never talked or walked.

"She's taken care of him all this time?"

"She did for a long time, but eventually she had to put him in a state hospital. To save herself."

"Why bring all that up now?"

"She wants me to help prove the vaccination caused his injuries."

"Based on what?"

"He was healthy before the shot." I kept my eyes skyward, still hoping for that streak of magic. "I'll probably refer it to someone."

"You certainly can't do it yourself."

"Thanks for the vote of confidence."

"You might as well give her the house and your car and your 401K."

"Lawyers can learn new things. I'm not stupid."

"I never said that, but medical malpractice is pretty tricky."

"It looks like it might be product liability."

"The vaccine injured him?"

"According to the doctor on the television show she watched this morning."

"Jean."

"I know. It sounds absurd. I only promised to help her find the right lawyer. Still . . ."

He sighed, loudly enough for me to hear.

"What amazes me," I continued, "is that all these years she never mentioned this son."

"Why did she wait so long?"

"She thought it was her fault. They never told her it might be the shot."

"They, who?"

"God, Peter, I sound like her already."

Two weeks later I saw Lacy's daughter Diana at a high school baseball game. Even from a distance, she was quite a bit taller than her mother. Her long dark hair fell across her face; striking, not pretty exactly. In a farming community Friday nights mean high spirits. In the fall it's football. Winter, basketball. Farmers' sons make great ball players and every cousin and uncle comes to watch. Our kids loved to go. In large groups they wandered amoeba-like around the stands while Peter and I sat with friends.

In the chilly spring air of an early baseball game Elly snuggled between Peter and me. Stephen and Andrew, who were together when they left us, were nowhere to be seen. I was mildly irritated at Stephen, who at sixteen, was supposed to be keeping his younger brother away from unlit corners where fights were more likely. Scanning the crowd, I tried to remember what color jackets the boys had been wearing.

"Want something to drink, sweetie?" Peter asked.

"Uh-huh." Elly and I both answered at the same time.

By the time he came back the seventh inning stretch had been announced. I spotted Andrew in the midst of a group of friends, most of whom I recognized as his soccer teammates. His sweatshirt was tied around his waist; his baseball cap shoved down, which made his hair stick out in odd directions. Stephen had disappeared.

"I saw your friend the fruit loop," Peter said when he returned with hot chocolate.

"The what?" I asked while Elly giggled.

"The little woman who talks so fast."

I was stumped.

"The one with the malpractice case against her son's doctors."

"Oh, Lacy Stonington. Was she mad at me? I haven't called her back."

"I'm glad you didn't get suckered into that one. Just what you don't need."

"She's had a rough time."

"That gives her the right to hug perfect strangers and shriek across parking lots?"

"She's just being friendly."

Although Elly was sipping madly, I could tell her twelve year-old ears were perked and listening hard. I lowered my voice.

"Did Lacy say anything?"

"She loves you." Peter was smiling in spite of himself.

"I mean about the lawsuit."

"No, and you ought to leave that alone. Taking on those big

drug companies is a job for a mega-firm with two floors of lawyers who do nothing but. Their corporate lawyers would eat you alive."

"She'll never go to a lawyer she doesn't know."

"Great, then that's the end of it."

On the field the players took their positions again. Diana Stonington had left her friends and was standing in the scoreboard's shadow with a boy in a brown sweater. I wondered if it was her brother, Carson. But when the boy turned toward the light, I was surprised to recognize Stephen.

She was a senior, active in the drama productions. Speaking to a junior boy in public would be risky. Maybe that explained their distance from the crowd. While I watched, Lacy bent down from above them, across the railing in a bright red windbreaker. The black ten-gallon hat on the man next to her told me it was Moss. In pantomime she waved to the kids, but she must have called to them also because Diana's head jerked up. She took three or four quick steps away from Stephen into the light and waved hesitantly. He swung his backpack onto his shoulder and started back toward the stands, but in a sudden shift, ducked into the public bathroom.

I was so busy trying to see who or what he'd been avoiding that I almost missed what happened next. Moss stepped forward and drew Lacy to him with an arm around her shoulders. After their heads touched, he pointed in our direction. I wondered what he was saying to his wife about me.

Monday morning before Jillian arrived Lacy was back at the office.

"Happy Easter," she said after the door handle clicked and she peered around the doorframe.

"It's not Easter."

"Almost. Do you have a second?"

"For my favorite bus driver, sure." I sat on the arm of the sofa, cupping the coffee mug in my hands for warmth. "Want some?"

"I don't drink that poison. It's bad for you."

I sipped and waited, still irritated with Peter for painting her as a kook. I knew him better, and I knew he cared as deeply for his children as Lacy did for hers. What made it so hard for men to acknowledge that attachment?

Lacy drew some papers from behind her back. "I found these."

She handed me six or seven yellowed pages. They were letters, dated in the late seventies, from the training center administrator. The author thanked Lacy for her telephone inquiries about Danny and thanked another woman named Anna Kellam—Scott's mother or sister?—for sending twenty dollars for birthday money. The oldest letter was headed, "Fairfax County Social Services," and it was dated November 1970. In it the social worker recited a home visit with both of Danny's parents. Scott and Lacy were described in complete detail, including his hairstyle and her bathrobe, as was the one-bedroom apartment. Their comments and actions were summarized.

'Mrs. Kellam is an appealing young woman whose whole life seems to be taken up with this severely retarded child.' Dead plants were mentioned twice. And about Scott: 'He sat patiently during his wife's monologue.'

'She talked as if her husband were not in the room and sat looking at the wall almost completely away from him . . . She has said from time to time that it would be easier if Danny would die.'

Chapter Six
LACY

I talk too much. It's gotten me into a ton of trouble. Mosste tells me shush sometimes, but I can't help myself. I have to say what I feel.

Back when Danny first got sick, the doctors didn't tell me anything. They probably figured I wouldn't understand, no matter what they said. And by the time Danny had been in and out of the hospital three times, I was struggling too hard to keep things going to hear much of anything. But Jean could sort through all the complicated medical stuff. If my hotshot lawyer asked them something, they'd tell her.

One day at the office not long after our marathon first appointment, her son Andrew called just as we sat down. He'd forgotten his soccer uniform and they had a game. When she told him to wear his practice shirt inside out, he yelled into the phone loudly enough that I could hear him. The way she explained it to me afterwards — I didn't tell her I'd overheard — he thought it was no big deal for her to run the shirt over to him. I agreed. I would have waited.

But not Jean. Andrew needed to take responsibility for his own schedule and stop relying on his parents to rescue him. At the other end the phone crashed into the cradle. Obviously Andrew didn't like her answer. Kids.

My daughter, Diana, was trouble back then too. Out of the blue she had a long lost brother. So much talk about Danny this and Danny that was hard on her. She'd always been first until this long lost brother showed up. With the possibility of court and all the fuss about him, she was mad. Mad at me for giving up on him and for giving him away. I tried to make her understand. Think how it would be if every time you had to go to work or to the grocery store, the people you hired to watch your baby quit before you're finished. You have to pay people; none of your friends want to keep him because he can't do anything for himself. He can't tell you what he wants. He can't control his hands so he hits when he doesn't mean to. He drools and he wears diapers, but he's as big as a first grader. So it's messy. When he's scared, he yells. He's not like a regular baby, Di, that's what I told her.

Jean said Diana was just arguing because she was a teenager. She didn't want to be me, but she had to find fault with me in order to be herself.

"That's good, Doctor Jean," I said. It's amazing how easy it is to see the truth when it's someone else's kid.

Why is it things are so muddy when they're happening and crystal clear later when it's all over. After the emergency room nurse took Danny away from me, I could hardly think straight. For hours I sat there in the waiting room, just sitting, doing nothing, all by myself. Every once in a while someone would come and ask me questions and then disappear again. After four or five nurses a young girl with a ponytail and bright pink fingernail polish called my name. She'd been huddling with the nurses, talking behind her hand as if I couldn't figure out they were talking about me. With this disgustingly sweet little smile, she said the doctor was over on the Maternity ward and just hadn't made it to Pediatrics yet.

When she asked what medications Danny took, I blanked out. I never thought of the shot Dr. Stith had given him on Monday. Later, when I remembered it, I asked her, but she didn't even look up from her typewriter. Those pink fingernails just went right on typing. 'Three months old? Probably a DPT.' Like everyone in the whole world knew what that was.

After I signed all her forms, she finally told me I could go upstairs, fourth floor. There were all these closed doors with high little windows and no Danny. I looked through each window until I found him, sealed inside some kind of plastic hood. He lay face up with tubes that ran from a metal canister parked over by the wall.

It was a hundred degrees. Two huge fans, like in the post office mailroom, spun from the ceiling. His bed was smaller than a regular hospital bed, more like a cage with metal bars. Still he barely made a dent. On his chest they'd attached some kind of flat silver pieces like coins. More on his forehead. All those gray lines fed into machines. It felt like I was standing shoulder to shoulder with all the babies who'd ever died in that room.

I wanted to pick him up so badly I sat on my hands in the only chair, across the room against the far wall. There was a tube coming straight up out of a bandage on his throat. The other end was clamped to the crib railing. From a bag on a pole a clear tube drained into his arm. I had no idea what all that stuff was. Everything chugged along. And no one was there to explain. When the needles on the machines wavered, I had no clue what it meant. Every few seconds his eyes twitched and I'd get a glimpse of blue. I thought that was a good sign, but later another mother told me the machines were making that happen.

Doctor McIntosh, the hospital's baby doctor, finally came that night. I heard him, through the closed door over that piped-in background music, whistling and kidding the nurses. Until he read the chart he didn't even know Danny's name. But when he came out of Danny's room, he looked exactly like a helium balloon the day after the parade. Dragging his little ole chin along the ground.

He wanted to know what had Danny choked on. When he didn't get the answer he wanted, he demanded to know what Danny'd spit up. Only he used a whole string of medical words, gobbledy-gook. The only one I remember was coma.

Things stayed the same until the fourth morning. When I came out of the elevator a group of doctors was clumped around Danny's door. More came, like reporters hurrying toward bad news. There were too many of them to remember their names. Every day there were new ones.

As soon as they saw me, the whole conversation changed. It was obvious something was up. One patted my arm and said Danny had had a rough night. Another one said something about his nervous system. Most of the terms they traded back and forth, I didn't understand. What I knew was that I hadn't been there to rock him.

Someone said he probably wouldn't last the day. Through the glass window all I could see was his tiny motionless body on those white sheets. He could've been dead already. I didn't even notice the nurse when she came. Or the priest at first.

In a weasely little voice, with some kind of accent, he explained the whole procedure without ever once looking at me. How prayers serve to cleanse a sinner's soul. And how Danny would be allowed to join his Father in heaven only after he'd received the last rites.

Otherwise, the priest insisted, Danny was going to Hell. I told him right out that was ridiculous. Danny was only a baby. He hadn't lived long enough to sin.

The priest tried to explain how the Lord prepared a place for each sinner in His home, and that Danny was one of those sinners.

The time had come for him to join the Lord in heaven. He talked like it was a great celebration. When he flipped open the prayer book to the red ribbon, I slapped my hand over the writing. I didn't believe any of it. God wouldn't willfully take a child.

I called Scott on the payphone, but he was out, supposedly on a jobsite. 'Tell him his son is dying.' I didn't wait to hear what they said.

Then I walked down four flights of stairs out into that July sun. The pavement had separated from itself and where it floated in the air, a long strip of silver and black stretched into forever. Like the world had been split in two by an earthquake and I was standing at the edge.

With my hand on the building I followed the wall. Down the hospital sidewalk. Past the corner. Past the cars zipping by. I kept right on walking. I crossed the street. Someone blew a horn. A bus screeched. I never turned my head. Sweat dripped down my face. Right through my shirt. I didn't stop. I didn't wipe it off. At each store window I stopped. Then moved on to the next one. The first shop with baby things, I went inside. The saleslady rushed up to me like I might keel over right there. Teetering on the threshold, sweating and blinking in the sun, I must've looked like something from somebody's ragbag.

All the baby clothes were pink and blue. When I told her I needed something more formal, she wanted to know how old the baby was. She held up a teeny white suit with a miniature polka dot bow tie.

Darker, I said. From the sale table I picked out a navy blue outfit with tiny buttons shaped like stars. Too hot for this time of year, she said. And I told her, where he's going it doesn't matter.

After she wrapped it up in teddy bear tissue and decorated it with rainbow ribbon, I carried it back to the hospital. I stood in the hallway, holding that ridiculous package, waiting for someone to come out and tell me Danny was dead.

Chapter Seven
JEAN

I'm not from Virginia, but when people ask how I came to live here, my standard line is 'I married well.' Southerners love that, especially from a Yankee. I met Peter when he was at the business school, a year closer to his degree than I was. He was born and raised in the south, though not in the country. Long ago, after he drove an obviously tipsy me home from a grad school party one night, he would pass me on campus and tell me he had a tennis court reserved for midnight. His confidence that I'd say yes set him apart from the other myopic grad students. We became tennis partners. Once my New England buddies met him, they understood my fondness for Virginia.

After Peter and I married, we moved to the country and I opened my own office. Because legal books were one of the pricey things—and I had to watch my expenses—whenever possible I used the law library at the University. It's a state facility. Encyclopedias, journals, Code books, are all available to any eager researcher with a Bar card or a driver's license. By 1990 the forty-five minute trip from Parry's Crossing was old hat.

Lacy's vaccination claim was definitely not in my area of experience, Peter was right about that. None of the books in my office was on point. At the University though, it didn't take me long to rack up a pile of them. Four trips later I'd plowed through them all and found the regulations that inspired Lacy's television script.

Federal court, but better. In 1986 after two years of hearings Congress had set up a special court within the Federal Court of Claims to hear vaccine-related injury cases, to take effect in 1988. The National Childhood Vaccine Injury Act was a remedy law students dream of: precise, limited, and promising speedy relief. After photocopying pages of medical definitions and the entire legislative history, I carried everything back to the office and called the court in Washington, D.C. My head pounded with procedural questions. The numbered lines on the pad ran to nineteen.

Graduation from law school doesn't mean you know everything, it only means you're supposed to know how to find out. In Virginia Procedure — always taught by a sitting judge — I'd learned the most significant lesson of my entire law school career. Treat the Clerk of the Court well and he or she will be your guardian angel.

When I admitted my unfamiliarity with the Special Court of Claims to the Deputy Clerk over the phone, she explained there was a printed pamphlet of local rules. "If you're not admitted to practice before the Court, you'll have to find a sponsor."

"An attorney who practices regularly in any federal court or before the Court of Claims?"

"This court, of course."

"You don't have a list by any chance?"

"If you send a self-addressed stamped envelope, we can mail it to you. Along with the local rules."

"I'm worried about missing a deadline while I'm dealing with peripheral issues. Could you trust me to send the postage and mail me the names today?"

"We're not supposed to do that."

"It's for a good cause. This baby was vaccinated twenty years ago. Until a few weeks ago the mother never knew what caused his seizures." I could hear the Clerk holding her breath. I pressed, "All this time he's been in a state hospital and she thought it was her fault."

There was another extended silence before the Clerk spoke. "If you have a fax machine, I can send it now."

Of the six dozen cases pending before the Special Masters, temporary judges assigned to hear vaccine injury cases, the same two firms from D.C. were listed several times. Obviously they'd made a business of this kind of lawsuit.

As a novice I started at the beginning. If I was reading the Act correctly, recovery was supposed to be simple to ease the strain on families caring for injured children. The Act set out a table of injuries and a formal procedure for itemized exhibits. Because of the technical jargon, which required a medical school linguist, I didn't have any idea whether the listed injuries mirrored Danny's, though Lacy's description of the day she took Danny to the hospital sounded like an impressionistic version of the statute.

If a child's injuries were among those listed and their appearance occurred within 72 hours of the vaccination, the law 'presumed' the vaccine caused the injuries. Voila, a short-circuited path to proof that would help families get the help the statute promised.

It wasn't clear why the cases were taking more than a year to conclude. 1989 was the first year of filings. Two years later only one of those cases was ended. Over two thousand had been filed so far in 1990. That phenomenon didn't fit the plain statutory language. Laws, though, are written by politicians and regulations by bureaucrats; two different kinds of people with two different kinds of motivations.

As part of the legislative history I read dribbles from individual Congressmen's speeches on the House and Senate floor. At the instigation of two vaccine manufacturers Congress created the fund to protect the drug companies who were, at that point, defending more than 250 lawsuits. They couched the legislation in terms of helping families whose children had suffered injuries as a result of the government's mandatory vaccination program. Awards were to be made "quickly, easily and with certainty and generosity."[1]

Because the manufacturers had suggested the special remedy, they had contributed some of the initial funds. The pertussis portion of the vaccine figured in the majority of the pending claims. This was logical. The pool was huge. For every American child the government mandated five diptheria-pertussis-tuberculosis shots before admission to public school.

One senator quoted studies from London. The risk of permanent damage had been underestimated by four times. I found a small footnote that said U.S. research for a purified, acellular version of the whooping cough portion had been abandoned in 1972 because of the expense, an extra $12 per shot. Several legislators argued that was too great a burden for taxpayers. With government programs paying for a large number of low-income families' vaccinations, I understood the real economics. Not surprising that the government had not required the safe shot, part of their deal with the drug companies. Still, they were playing roulette with other people's children.

The statute seemed straightforward. Senators and Representatives had argued for a system that would be user friendly. They instructed the regulators to standardize the evidentiary process to speed payments to suffering families. Legal fees were paid in addition, not out of the award: generosity unknown in most legal remedies. From a lawyer's point of view it sounded easy, too easy.

Plunk in your two cents and win the prize. No wonder city firms who could walk across the street to the federal courthouse had enlisted repeatedly.

A child who died from vaccine complications received a flat award of $250,000. Under the 'cap' theory families who lost a child required less assistance than those who had to care for an injured child over a lifetime. Likewise the burden of proof in a death case was significantly lower than that in a case of less serious injury.

It smacked a little of the philosophy I'd run into when I was a novice lawyer handling criminal cases in the hollows of the Blue Ridge Mountains. If you killed a low-life, you received a lighter sentence than if you wounded him and he lived to wreak more havoc later.

Beyond the statute itself, the printed rules passed by the legislative branch, there's another part of legal research; court interpretation of the statute and regulations. Magazines, Bar journals, and case reporters all list court rulings that change or clarify the meaning of statutes. These rulings form the other half of the law, the half that lawyers call precedent; how different judges have interpreted the same issues, with slight variations.

This judicial fine-tuning is supposed to make the law flexible enough to move and change with the human condition. At this stage I didn't pay that much attention to the cases. That part of the research would be someone else's job, whichever expert tort litigator I found to take on Lacy's case.

I re-read the attorney list, hoping to recognize a name. Given Lacy's state of mind, what I wanted was another sole practitioner, someone who was used to dealing with fragile clients. I didn't think she could handle a big city toughie who would railroad her into a settlement just to get his contingency fee. Even without a complete picture of how bad Danny's injuries were, twenty-odd years of silence suggested Lacy wouldn't talk to just anyone.

Circling the names of three lawyers who weren't followed by big name firms, I scanned the legal opinions over the next few weeks for their names. Specialists invariably have their cases reported because they are involved with cutting edge legal issues. It's like learning how to fly as opposed to riding a bike. Any person, even another kid, can teach you how to ride a bike, but only an expert can teach you how to fly a plane. Lacy needed a trainer of jet pilots, preferably supersonic. And she was relying on me to find the right one.

In mid-June Peter and I stuffed our three kids, beach chairs, and boogie boards into the van and went off to the annual lawyers' conference at Virginia Beach. Family vacations were popular with my crew. Because my children were strong swimmers and good friends, we did a lot of reading at the beach. Peter took his turn being the designated spouse while I zipped off to sessions. If I were religious, in those three days I could complete my required continuing legal education.

And we socialized. Many of our friends from graduate school brought their families. My kids played with their once-a-year buddies and trailed along behind us to endless receptions.

I forgot Lacy until the second evening. When I mentioned the DPT issue to Cliff Marbury, one of my law school colleagues, he scrambled to find one of his cards. My stomach churned. Personal injury claims make monsters out of perfectly reasonable attorneys. Talking the entire time about a suit he'd just tried and won to the tune of two million dollars, he wrote furiously on the back of the card. He surprised me though, because it was some other lawyer's name.

"Call this guy. He's a bear. Rude, opinionated, downright mean sometimes. But he just won a big award in that special court they set up. The Bar journal reported it two or three months ago. He's a real pro."

Two months ago I hadn't known Danny Kellam existed, but a pro was just what we needed. I put the card in my pocket.

Saturday night the lawyers always had a band that played in the open-air pavilion next to the beach. In between sets to the ocean's percussion everyone's kids bombarded the hors-d'oeuvre table. Stephen had wanted to skip the dance this year. Baiting Peter and me, he used every opportunity to remind us by being sullen and uncomplimentary.

"Who likes this stupid music anyway?"

Peter shot him the evil eye.

Elly sidled up to Peter, swishing her sundress to make it swirl to the music. "Can we climb over the rail and walk on the beach?"

"I thought you guys wanted to go out to dinner with us?"

Stephen pulled Andrew aside before he could answer. They whispered to each other about ten feet away.

Peter handed me another drink. "I don't like the looks of that."

"Is this normal hormonal stuff for teenage boys?" I asked.

"He's mad about something."

"I don't know why he wouldn't go with the other high school kids to the teen night. Plenty of cute girls."

"Yeah, but they're related to his parents' friends."

Peter repeated the rules—stay with your sister, don't go in the water, leave a note in the room if you go anywhere else in the hotel—and I watched Andrew and Elly nod. Stephen stood apart and stared at the ocean. There was a bend in his shoulders, a weight that seemed to follow him, tying him to a place he didn't want to be. At least it seemed that way to me. I didn't like the distance between us.

"You okay, buddy?" I asked him at the rail. The surf broke ahead of us in the darkness, enough distance between the pavilion and the water to make it invisible, a roar without the lion's head.

"Yeah."

"That's it? Yeah?"

"Thanks for asking."

I ignored the sarcasm. "We like having you with us, more when you're happy, but there never seems to be enough time lately."

The waves pounded the beach. Faint fingers of spray fell on my arms and the rail. When he didn't answer, I tried again. "Were you pleased with your grades?"

"What did you want?"

"I didn't mean that. B's are fine, if you're doing your best."

He didn't answer.

"There's always next year." I was trying to sound less critical.

"That your motto, Mom?"

"Hey, I'm trying to make peace."

"I didn't know we were at war."

"It's not much fun to be around you lately, Stephen. You can't really expect us to guess what the problem is. If you can't talk to Dad or me, maybe Father Messimer or the school counselor could help."

"Things aren't that bad."

"That's a relief. So we might see some smiles?"

Without answering, he helped Elly over the rail, not two feet from where I watched. With an over-exaggerated grin, I waited until he looked back. His forehead was furrowed and he didn't meet my gaze, though I had the feeling he'd been checking to see if I was still there.

When we returned from the beach trip, the mail spilled over the bin on my desk. I had hearings in court the next morning and couldn't remember the names of the witnesses. Under strict instructions not to interrupt me, Jillian was fielding calls. About eleven she buzzed on the intercom. Lacy was out front.

"Schedule her for next week," I said.

"Well, I'm not sure that'll work. Ah . . . maybe you ought to come up here."

An enormous cardboard box sat in the center of the front room and Lacy sat beside it. On the floor.

"I found the pictures," she said.

"That whole box is full of photographs?" I asked.

Behind me Jillian laughed right out loud. Lacy smiled. She'd surprised us, and I was learning how much she liked to do that. Reaching into the box, she pulled out a coffeemaker and a handful of plastic dishes, scarred with silverware marks.

"Oh, not just pictures. His clothes and the other junk from the apartment. Janice packed it all up and mailed it back to me when I disappeared."

"I must have missed that. When exactly did you disappear, Lacy?"

"It's not important. But you need to see this sweet little baby. Look. Danny Boy."

She held up an eight by ten photo. The corners curled inwards like a paper croissant. While Lacy held the top on Jillian's desk, I rolled out the bottom. Daniel Boyd Kellam, three months old, lay propped against one of those fuzzy studio rugs. The photographer had caught him on the cusp of a smile. Reflected in his eyes, the studio lights twinkled.

His mother had combed his dark wavy hair off his face and the camera detail showed every comb line. He was a miniature version of Carson, the half-brother he'd never known. In the angle of Danny's head you could see his mother's good humor. *So, world, what marvelous thing is going to happen today?*

Lacy was grinning. "That's the blue suit Scott's mother sent when Danny was born. The suit makes his eyes bluer, don't you think?"

Jillian, her back to Lacy, shot a quick glance at me. I shook my head to signal her silence. The photo was black and white.

Chapter Eight
LACY

Scott worked all the time. Or at least he told me that's where he was. *He had bills to pay.* He came in late, showered while I reheated his dinner, then went to bed. After Danny and I had been home a week after the seizures, Scott moved the crib to the living room. *He couldn't work without eight hours.* After that, I slept most nights on the sofa or in the rocker with the baby in my arms.

Danny and I went back and forth to the doctors. Once a week at least, sometimes two or three times. They acted like everything was temporary. When Dr. Stith, Danny's pediatrician, came back from vacation, he explained it was like a stroke. Hearing and muscle use should come back after a while. He told me to let Danny sleep as much as he wanted.

The first night home from the hospital Danny was so droopy, but he was too fussy to sleep. The nurses had told me to feed him on the regular schedule, but there was no baby food. When Scott finally came home, I told him there was nothing to eat. He volunteered to get take out. Take out. As if Danny didn't exist. Scott said I needed to eat, that I looked like a bird, all scrawny, my hair every which way. What did he expect? I'd been almost living at the hospital for a month.

In the fall Danny had another coughing bout. Pneumonia, they said but I heard them in the hallway talking about seizures.

They upped his medicine. Whenever anyone clucked him under the chin, I washed his face. Germs were the enemy.

Scott was convinced they were using Danny for a guinea pig. He wanted me to stop taking him over there, probably because he didn't want to pay the bills. After I snuck a peek at the medical chart, I asked Snowden what 'shock' meant next to some long word starting with an 'e.'

I did everything exactly like the way they told me. But when Dr. Stith said Danny was blind, I knew that wasn't true. He was still smiling at me. To prove it, at Christmas time I bought all red toys and wrapped them for Christmas morning at Scott's parents' house. I couldn't wait for Danny to pick them out of a pile and show the doctors how wrong they were.

As a present for Scott's family I'd decided to make Gram's pound cake. When I couldn't find the recipe, I thought it might have gotten mixed up in Scott's receipts from paying bills. He kept a cardboard box of paperwork under the bed, including my pay stubs from the post office job. All that summer and fall while I was home nursing Danny he'd complained about how we had no money. No money for medicine, no money for special food, no money for an apartment closer to the hospital. Who did he think would take care of Danny if I went back to work?

It turned out Scott's bank paperwork was in the box and there was more than a thousand dollars in a bank account in his name. While I was looking at the statements, he came home. But when I asked him why my name as his wife wasn't on the accounts, he slapped me. I fell back over the box and hit my head. Bled all over the clean laundry while he screamed at me.

'Wife? You haven't been a wife in months. You can hardly tally up a grocery list; much less keep track of that kind of money. I'm the only one who's working in this family. You're just playing house with a rag doll.'

That's when he left. Took his stupid bank statements and left. But the next morning just like a rubber ball he's pounding on the door, begging me to let him in. He sounded really sorry and he looked miserable, like a kid in detention. When he asked so politely if he could take a shower, what could I say? Every day that week he came home for dinner. On Saturday as if nothing had happened he woke up early and packed the car with the playpen and the Christmas presents for the trip to his parents' house.

But Danny didn't pick out any of the toys. Although Scott's sister's baby was a month younger, he was all grabby and smiley, standing at the crib rail and waving Danny's red toys.

On the drive home Scott started in about how embarrassing it was. I thought he meant me. But then he said he couldn't pretend anymore that we were a happy little family. It was making him crazy. He said he just didn't want to be married.

Once Snowden found out that Scott was gone for good, he sent me to a lawyer who forced Scott to pay the rent. It helped, but I still couldn't work. Danny and I were forever trekking to the hospital for tests and check-ups. And that whole time with all the stuff they were doing I was thinking he would get better.

The next winter when he was still the same the hospital doctors scheduled this big meeting. Snowden even made me call Scott to come too. It was the first time they ever told us Danny wasn't going to grow up.

Even though Scott hadn't had a thing to do with us for a year, he took charge. 'Okay, sure, stick him in the state hospital. Lacy can go back to work. Things'll be normal again. Maybe I'll move back in.' Just like that.

It made me so mad I ran out, Danny and all. Snow was billowing everywhere and his snowsuit wouldn't go on. I was sliding on the sidewalk and bawling and trying to yank that suit up his legs. I went straight to Snowden. He was in his office without any patients, almost like he knew I was coming. By that time I was hysterical.

He telephoned back over to the other doctors and ordered Scott to come and take Danny home. So he could talk to me privately.

Snowden made things very clear. Scott wasn't going to pay the rent forever. How would I keep going? He spelled it out. As it was, doing everything for Danny, I couldn't take a shower. I couldn't leave him. I fed him. Rocked him. Slept with him.

Fine, I said, I'll give him an overdose of Phenobarbital and then take some myself. With your luck, Snowden said, you won't die and they'll try you for murder. We both knew it was an impossible situation.

When I got home, Danny was lying by himself on the rug. No quilt. There was Scott, sitting on the sofa—cool as you please—reading the newspaper. He couldn't even hold his own son for one lousy hour. I should have killed Scott right there, but I'd have gone to jail for sure and then who would have taken care of Danny?

Afterwards, after I'd kicked Scott out and shoveled baby goop into Danny and he'd spit it all out and I'd given him his medicine and bathed him and rocked him to sleep in the rocking chair, I stayed awake until I figured it out. Money. I just needed more money. With money I could hire some help. Then Danny wouldn't have to go away.

The next week when Scott called to drop off the rent check, I timed the visit so Danny would be asleep. I put motion sickness medicine in his bottle. When Scott knocked, I met him at the door with nothing on. For Scott it was always about sex.

That fixed things all right. Two weeks later I got this horrible pain in my gut. By the time Snowden put me in the hospital, Scott's gonorrhea infection had spread to my appendix. Snowden told me later that when Scott showed up after surgery, he grabbed him by the collar and screamed, 'Go away. She doesn't need your help. If she dies, I'll be here to hold her hand.'

Chapter Nine
JEAN

Even a person with no legal experience knows that if you want to hold someone accountable, you have to prove he's the only one who could have done it. A lawyer has to eliminate the possibility of other causes for a claimant's injury. After the television revelation, Lacy, in her eagerness to have some explanation after all those years, was convinced it was the DPT shot. The Special Court of Claims wouldn't be so accepting. She and I met several times over that summer to clarify my understanding of the facts.

I pushed her for details. "Before the vaccination Danny's records will show that he didn't have any 'conditions' that made him susceptible to seizures?"

"Suss-what?"

"Did any doctor or nurse tell you that he might have seizures if he ate a particular kind of food or something like that?"

"He was only three months old."

"Any specific tests that you recall?"

She pondered for a bit. "Stith did that scoring thing they do with new babies. I remember because the day Danny was born, Scott wasn't there while they did the test. When he finally arrived, I made Snowden explain it to him."

"The APGAR?" I asked.

"Yeah, that's it. Danny's score was 8. Snowden said he was as healthy as a horse.'"

Both Lacy and I sat perfectly still in the little square room. The phone had stopped. The fax machine was silent. The word healthy echoed in my head. It must have been ringing in Lacy's.

She talked for another hour. Early on I'd realized talking about this for her was therapeutic so I tried hard not to interrupt. Who else would listen? When Peter telephoned to find out if I was coming home for dinner, she hadn't been gone five minutes and I was still scribbling notes.

"If you're going to eat before Stephen's concert," he reminded me, "you have to come now."

"Where are the other kids?"

"Andrew's at soccer practice. The McLain's are keeping him. For dinner and until we pick him up afterwards. Swim team practice was cancelled so Elly's here. She can ride with us."

"I just need fifteen minutes to finish up the notes from my conference with Lacy."

"We can go without you."

"No, I'll be there."

"You missed the last concert." It was meant as a reminder, but it sounded like a dig.

Although I'd written down a few dates and names as Lacy talked, I wasn't sure my chronology was right. In her recollections she skipped around. A childhood memory from Twyman's Mill oftentimes came after a reference to an incident at the state hospital where Danny went just before his second birthday. Where he still resided. There were seven or eight doctors' names, and I was just beginning to sort out which doctor went with which medical facility.

With Peter waiting though, I flipped off the lights and tucked the pad into my briefcase.

I bee-lined for my car. But when it wasn't in its regular space, I remembered that I'd walked that morning. Once in a while I had a day without court and the luxury of it, rare as it was, justified celebration. From our house to downtown was an easy hike, less than a mile, even in business clothes.

Standing in the street, with the kids' schedule on my mind and Peter's impatience with me, I debated going back to the office and calling him to pick me up on the way. The choice of fifteen minutes behind my desk and fifteen minutes of fresh air didn't take much thought though. Like a little girl with her first pocketbook, I swung the briefcase as I crossed Main to cut through the drugstore parking lot.

My childhood had been spent biking everywhere. The suburb where I'd lived in Massachusetts was about four miles square and fairly flat. The high school was halfway across town and one car between three teenagers is almost like no car. Here in our Virginia farming community the roads were too narrow and hilly for easy biking or public buses. Walking became an evening pastime.

When the children were little, they'd run ahead and hide behind bushes, popping out to 'scare' us. Once the boys grew too cool to be seen with their parents Elly was our only walking companion. If she didn't have dance or swim practice or gymnastics.

The drugstore parking lot was empty except for their delivery van. In small towns after seven nothing's open and nothing happens. As I followed the sidewalk past the funeral home, someone darted out through the shadows and around the back of the old supply warehouse. Curious, I stopped and waited for a minute. Hearing angry voices, I stepped closer. Someone might need help.

"Then give us our money back, you dweeb." The voice was familiar.

"Brian?" I called. Stephen's best friend had moved here with his mother and sister when his parents divorced. Puzzled by their seemingly random choice of Parry's Crossing—they knew no one—neither Peter nor I had warmed to Brian, but we hadn't interfered either. A bright, shy boy, he was interested in the same kinds of music and books that Stephen liked. Their friendship had lasted almost eight years.

More than I, Peter had suffered through Brian's fluorescent orange hair, two earrings, random episodes of disrespectful language, and a major rock band break-up. I tried to be more patient—Stephen didn't exhibit any of that kind of counter-culture behavior—but then I was at the office a lot of the weekends when the two boys jammed with other friends.

"Brian?" I called again, but he didn't answer. When he came around the corner of the building, he was stuffing something in his backpack and clearly didn't expect to see me. On the far side of the empty building, running footsteps went in the opposite direction. I moved back under the streetlamp to get a better look. His new beard, barely a shadow on his cheeks, made a statement so typical of high school boys trying to be men. The orange hair had grown out and left a fringe of color at his collar.

"Friends of yours?" I asked. He flinched, then tried to cover it up with a nonchalance that never would have won an Oscar.

"Not really." He moved away from me in the direction of home, but not before the odor of cigarettes filtered between us.

"That sounded like trouble."

He shrugged. The implied dishonesty didn't make me angry exactly. It was more unsettling that I'd expected it. Perspective's easier when it's not your child.

"Smoking cigarettes can get you sent to jail."

"We're not," he spoke quickly, rearranging the backpack on his shoulder and taking another step to separate us further.

"If it's drugs, you can't come back to our house."

He didn't answer.

"I mean it. Don't get Stephen started on that stuff. They may think it's cool where you come from, but it's not here."

He ran then, calling back his good-bye, an afterthought of civility to normalize what had been a very weird encounter. I could hear Peter telling me how naïve I was to assume someone else could 'start' you using drugs. If there were anything Peter stood for, it was taking responsibility for your own actions, an idea sprung in whole cloth from his Roman Catholic upbringing.

By not threatening to telephone Brian's mother, I thought I'd behaved very maturely. I hadn't jumped to conclusions. I'd stayed calm and made my point. With all our talk, I couldn't imagine any of my kids being the least interested in drugs or cigarettes.

All the way home, though, I worried that I should call Mrs. Paleri anyway, to save Brian from something worse. If someone caught my son in a similar situation, I hoped they'd tell me. It wasn't until I was lying in bed next to a snoring Peter that the echo of Brian's denial came back to me. "We're not," he'd said about the smoking, but he hadn't said a thing about drugs.

On Thursday morning when Lacy telephoned, I was mad at the world. Jillian's doctor had diagnosed carpal tunnel syndrome. He'd written her a prescription for a wrist brace, a special keyboard support that cost $100, and five days away from the computer. Verbally I'd sympathized, but it would send my one person-office into a tizzy I could ill afford. Lacy didn't know any of this when she telephoned.

"Lacy," I answered her cheery hello with my sternest 'I'm busy' tone.

"Gosh," she said, "The famous attorney knows the voice of her least important client. That's impressive."

"Very funny."

"You didn't read the Richmond paper this morning?"

"Hah. The newspapers at my house are stacked knee deep, still in the wrappers. Don't leave me in suspense."

"You sound busy. I'll clip the article and drop it off."

"Wait a minute, after that lead-in, you can't expect me to work. Tell me now."

"Your divorce trial last week made the front page of the local section."

I groaned.

"No, it's good news."

"It can't be good. We lost."

"Yeah, but you shouldn't have, right? The guy's a creep."

The sudden pit in my stomach felt bottomless. If Lacy knew that from the newspaper article, it was bad. All that work and he must have gotten to his wife after court.

At trial, applying the hearsay rule, the Judge had refused to let my client testify about her husband's abuse of their two boys while she was at work. After she took the children and moved into a women's shelter, her husband had burned her photographs of their injuries along with her clothes and anything else in which she'd ever expressed an interest. With the support of the shelter volunteers, she had found a job. Hours of counseling from the social worker and the therapist and me had finally convinced her she should go forward with the divorce.

The trial, though, had thrown her back to the beginning. In a business suit her husband had disguised the bully and had snowed the court.

"Aren't you curious about what happened?" Lacy asked.

"I know what happened. He beat her senseless. Did he kill her?"

"No way. I told you this was good news. Before he could really hurt her, she shot him. Dead." Lacy announced, as proud as if she'd personally counseled my client to shoot.

"Damn."

"Why isn't that good? He hit her first. It's self-defense. She doesn't have to worry about him hurting the kids anymore."

"She won't have to worry about the kids, period. They'll send her to jail and place the kids in foster homes."

"But the police have to believe her." Lacy's voice rose a notch, the squeak a surprise to us both. "In the picture the kids look terrified. It's obvious they're scared of him. They'll tell the Judge."

"The Judge can't talk with the kids unless both parents agree."

"That's not fair. How can he know what the father did when they were alone unless he talks to the kids?"

"Fairness is not a concept the courts recognize."

She didn't have an answer to that. In the pause, over her short, uneven breaths, I thought about my own frustration with judges who didn't listen and lawyers who took advantage of the system.

"Do you think the court will listen to me?" she asked in a whisper.

I don't know what I expected, but I was relieved. This concern I could allay easily. "Different court, different kind of case altogether. The Vaccine Injury Act lists the injuries presumed to be caused by the vaccination. Once we prove a listed injury occurred within three days of the shot, the court doesn't have to choose whom to believe. The dominos fall automatically. That's why the medical records and the expert are so important."

Hesitating for a minute, she finally said, "Oh, I know dominoes," but she didn't sound convinced. I didn't have the heart to remind her that twenty-one year old medical records weren't going to be easy to locate.

When I checked pockets at the dry cleaner's, I found Cliff Marbury's business card from the beach conference. *Hamilton Fine* was scrawled on the back along with a telephone number. He sounded like a character from Charles Dickens. Recalling Marbury's transformation at the mention of Danny's injuries, his wagging finger and glistening forehead, it took all my self-control not to throw his card in the trash.

All day long each time I put my hand into my suit pocket to retrieve a pen or my glasses, I felt the card there. C. Clifford Marbury's televised advertisement for helping injured persons had earned him a reputation as pushy, particularly among lawyers who believed lawyers who advertised to be the worst kind of ambulance chasers. With a recommendation from Marbury, Fine might not be what we wanted after all, but his credentials were impressive.

Toe to heel, I struggled with my shoes by the back door, eventually working them free. My bare feet on the cool linoleum felt wonderful. The first of May I give up stockings, but even so, summertime in Virginia makes the layers of a lawyer's uniform unbearable. After peeling off my suit jacket, I fanned myself with the newspaper from the kitchen table. The fan whirled overhead.

Peter, a bottle of wine in hand, pointed to the newsprint I was waving. "I thought that might interest you."

Spreading the paper open on the table, I bent to read. Hamilton Fine was quoted three times, and one of the women lawyers from the Clerk's list made the final paragraph. The article reported that the time from filing to final order averaged eighteen months. With a child in a wheelchair who needed constant nursing, a year and a half would seem like forever.

Adorned with his red barbecue apron, Peter was grilling chicken for dinner, one of the kids' favorites, a recipe of mine from law school that had fooled him into thinking I was a good cook. He swept his lips by my cheek as he dug in the drawer for the corkscrew. After raising my face to the ceiling fan for a moment, I turned to page five for the rest of the article.

"It's the same lawyer Cliff Marbury mentioned at the beach," I mumbled, "He's supposed to be THE expert."

"Any friend of Cliff's is bound to be obnoxious."

"Thanks, thanks a lot. That makes me eager to talk to him."

"Since when have you ever been eager to associate co-counsel?"

"Who said anything about co-counsel? I told Lacy I'd find her the right lawyer."

"Oh, really? Judging from the time you two spend together, I'd say she thinks she already has the right lawyer."

He was right and I knew it. The more I heard about Lacy and Danny, the harder it would be to throw her to a lion like Fine. Even if his reputation were legit. I took the offered glass of wine and continued to read.

One at a time Peter plucked the pieces of chicken out of the package and swathed them in barbecue sauce. "You know what they say about old dogs."

"Thanks a lot." I took a sip. Nice. Dry and oaky. "The government regulations for the fund are amazingly clear. Fine will be trial counsel. I'll only be helping with preparation of witnesses, that kind of thing."

"And the emotional involvement, that won't hurt your perspective?"

"She's just a client."

"Right, and I'm just a friend."

"You haven't caught me weeping and gnashing my teeth, have you? I go to the office, I file motions, I try cases. What's different?"

"Ask your children. They're getting away with murder." He elbowed me away from the counter. "Here," he said, thrusting silverware at me, "Set the table while you're denying reality."

"What do you mean?"

"Sweetie, yesterday you let Stephen drive your car without going through the standard litany of no-no's or the projected insurance increase if he got a ticket. You baked me a chocolate cake three days before my birthday. Every night this week Elly's had a friend over."

I looked up from the newspaper. "That's ridiculous." Although he was smiling, it was hard to tell how serious he was.

"Mom," Andrew called from the other room, "Riley wants me to go to the skateboard competition with him next Saturday. Can you drive us? His mother has a garden club thing."

"Sure, just write it on the calendar or I'll forget."

Peter was laughing.

"He hardly ever asks for anything," I said.

"Maybe, but for all you know the competition could be in Alaska."

"Better than northern Virginia." I went upstairs to change and took the article with me.

In the morning I called Hamilton Fine's office, the first of three telephone numbers for him listed in the Bar Association's directory of lawyers. Personal injury lawyers use skeleton offices, sometimes five or six of them, because visibility brings in clients. The receptionist said he wasn't in yet. She referred me to his secretary. The secretary said he'd just left for court. I told her it was a new case, left my name and number, and took his fax number to send him a summary of the facts if he was going to play hard to get.

After brief interviews with two new clients, both anxious for no-fault divorces before September when their children would return to school, I started drafting the Kellam summary. Lacy had made her own list of the doctors, including the ones at the state facility. I gave that list to Jillian to type. Only Snowden's address included a telephone number. I wondered if Lacy knew it by heart. I wondered if it were still in service.

Working steadily through notes of scattered interviews with her since April, I could feel her frustration building. I tried to imagine myself all alone in a one-room basement apartment lugging around an almost two-year old who didn't walk or talk. Exacerbated by no guarantee of the next support check and no earthly idea why the baby wasn't doing what other babies did, Lacy's level of anxiety must have been inexpressible.

Had she been depressed? In not one conversation or explanation had she ever asked, why me? Her memories were often humorous, and except for Scott, she rarely criticized the people she mentioned. It made Danny's inability to respond to her even more tragic. By four-thirty I had five pages ready to fax, probably more information than Hamilton Fine needed to know at this stage.

"Can I read it?" Jillian asked when I handed it to her.

"After you send it."

I traipsed back to my office to dictate instructions on the new divorces. "Don't forget," I called through the doorway of the conference room, "it's confidential." The fax beep-beeped in reply.

At quarter after five I was still dictating. Jillian knocked on my door even though it stood ajar. Her eyes were red.

"Jillian. What's the matter?"

"I've been reading . . ." she managed to say, "about Mrs. Stonington's baby."

I grabbed the tissue box and handed it to her. "So you like what I wrote?"

"She's amazing. How could those doctors lie to her?"

"Well, uh . . . I don't know that they knew for sure what caused his seizures. We're looking at it now with a whole lot of hindsight."

"But the CDC article in the file says the manufacturers asked for the fund because they were being sued by so many families. They had to know. Lots of children were having the same reactions."

"That was 1986. Danny had the shot in 1969."

"How can the doctors' testimony help then?"

"I'm not sure. We don't even know yet if they will testify. There are a whole lot of issues still hanging."

"Is Mr. Fine going to help Lacy?"

"Don't know that yet either. He's never met her. But he won another case, a big one, in the same court so we're hoping he's interested."

"Greedy, you mean."

"That too."

She sniffled, but remained in the room.

"Was there something else?"

Her eyes shifted away from mine. "How does Danny look now? I mean, if his development stopped at three months, wouldn't he still look like a baby?"

"I don't know. But it's probably about time I met him."

I was just leaving the office when Fine returned my call. Jillian was long gone. I'd already plunked my briefcase on the sidewalk and was fumbling with the door key. As I stood in the open doorway, the message machine inside clicked. Fine's voice, deep and thick, without any resonance at all, made me think of steel bars and triple locked doors. It was the voice you imagine the hooded executioner would have. If he talked.

"Ah, Ms., ah . . . Driscoll, I received your message and this, this, ah . . . summary of the, ah . . .(rustling of papers) Kellam case. I'm not sure where you found my name." There was a long pause as if he were still wondering about my invasion of his space.

Further down the sidewalk from where I stood a group of teenagers huddled together. Periodically a shaggy head popped out and swiveled around, on the lookout for something or someone. I looked closer for Brian's unmistakable orange ruff of hair while I waited, keys in hand, for Hamilton Fine to decide if the history of Daniel Boyd Kellam interested him or not.

"It's not unlike the Carling case we won last winter," he announced through the answering machine.

The 'we' stumped me. The news article hadn't referenced co-counsel in its summary of the Carling case and, according to the State Bar directory, Fine had no law partners. After I met him in person two months later, I would realize it was the royal 'we.'

His pause caused me to wonder if he suspected I was listening without picking up. I'd done it before to avoid unpleasant conversations or disagreeable clients. The possibility that he knew that about me without having met me was unsettling though. Peter always says that if someone accuses you of disreputable behavior, it's because they've done the same thing themselves. From Fine's reputation and his tone of voice, I didn't think I wanted to be like him in any regard.

He talked rapidly, clearly used to giving orders. "Your woman sounds a little flaky. She's not faking this, is she?" I could hear phones ringing in the background. "I'm not interested in fronting costs. The medical doctor I use is damn expensive and these cases are highly technical. So don't think you can slide into court on my pocketbook."

I bristled. The guy had no manners, to say nothing of basic collegial courtesy. Many divorce lawyers displayed that kind of combativeness, but I wasn't expecting it from an unknown attorney over a personal injury referral. The bearer of gifts shouldn't be treated as an enemy.

After I put aside my own irritation, I realized Fine and Lacy would be a disaster. As tough and funny as she acted, the revelations I'd heard over the last few months made her particularly vulnerable. A bully wouldn't make this any easier, even if he were a bully with a reputation for winning.

The message tape whined a little as his voice bellowed into it. "I'm on the way to Arkansas. Damn automobile manufacturers scheduled three days of discovery in a slam-dunk products liability case, trying to scare us off. Call me Friday if you're still looking for a litigator. Or just send the medical records and a thousand bucks for my expert to review them. I never commit until I hear what the doctor says."

I could hear him, in no uncertain terms, telling someone he was busy, take a message, goddammit. I shut the office door. I hoped it was just that he'd had a bad day.

Chapter Ten
LACY

My mother had her own demons; something I didn't understand until I was grown. She never meant to have three children. In the fifties though, that's what women did. My older sister Miriam was born when my mother was nineteen, not long enough after she married my father. I'll save that story for later.

Gram named her only daughter Rae Ann for the sun. After five boys, she was supposed to be a ray of sunshine. More like a bolt of lightning. She moved fast, talked fast, and ran with a fast crowd. When she got pregnant the second time—me—my father disappeared. I only know this because my uncles teased her about it whenever they came home, though it made her furious when they did.

My little brother JT came six years later. He was John Thompson's baby, insurance that her new sugar daddy would stick around, not that anyone except Rae Ann wanted him to stay.

My earliest memory of my mother floats in the back of my mind, constantly shifting and very far away. Her image is a blur. High-pitched drawl and sun glinting off a tin roof. Kind of like how I think of the beach, though I've never been to the ocean. But the way it looks in the movies and on television, that same glistening haze that blinds you. Not so different from the way you feel after apricot brandy in the back seat of a boy's car.

In my memory I'm not connected to the shimmering woman in the scene. She's beautiful and just out of reach. Miriam and I are little. We splash and shriek as the hose snakes across the tiny square of grass that was the front yard at the Tyler Street house. Gram's ramshackle house, where my mother grew up—and after her, Mim, JT and I—but Gram isn't in this memory at all. Carrie, the girl who lived next door, holds the hose. If I'm five in that memory, then Miriam is almost nine and easily able to outrun me.

Rae Ann is lying on a wooden lounge chair that Uncle Jarrell rescued from the trash truck. It was one of those rare days when she wasn't working or out touring with John Thompson. A white sheet drapes the chair to keep her skin from sticking to the hot wood. Her red toenails line up like pickets on a fence, a clear line between her and us children.

No one told me that Uncle Jarrell had stolen the lounge chair. That came out much later. He confessed to the theft as a moment of weakness. But when I was old enough to hear the whole story, I could see that he enjoyed telling how he hauled the chair with its four or five broken slats over the fence behind the fancy country club on the other side of town. The Johnson kids are the only reason he got away with it. They distracted the gatekeeper by pretending to crash the dance. Uncle Jarrell bragged about putting the chair back together with Reverend Cottle's tools. Also *borrowed.*

How it irritated poor Gram, up to her elbows in biscuit dough, that Rae Ann used it to sit like the Queen of Sheba on that chair that didn't belong to her, mimicking the country club girls and pretending she was watching her children.

The way I remember that day she yells at us to stop spraying. "When John Thompson gets back, he's not going to be happy if I'm soaking wet." Then she raises the tall glass to her shiny red lips and sips. Ice clinks against glass. In the glare those twinkly tones distract me and her image won't quite come into focus. Lipstick scars on glasses stick in my childhood memories more clearly than almost anything else about my mother.

You have to understand, before Rae Ann went anywhere she put on her make-up. Even before she came out of the bedroom to see if we kids had made a mess at breakfast, she poufed up her chestnut hair, dusted her cheeks with rouge, and painted her lips. By the time I could count I knew why. She didn't want John Thompson to see her plain and pale. Once I was older, I understood she was afraid he'd leave her like my father had.

On that summer afternoon Miriam ignores Rae Ann's warning. "My turn," she says with a war cry and lunges for the hose.

While Carrie waves it overhead, Mim hops up and down trying to reach it. In the maple tree's shadow I'm standing in my undershirt and big girl panties when Mim begins to scream.

"I didn't touch her," Carrie yells.

Miriam holds her foot in both hands. "A bee. A bee. Ooowwww."

The abandoned hose makes a lovely rainbow arc of water. It paints the sidewalk and the street. Rae Ann never even opens her eyes. And then the big blue car pulls up to the curb. I start to shiver. John Thompson is home.

"Shut up," he orders, the first thing he says while he scuffs the dirt like one of those Spanish bulls getting ready to charge, smoke shooting out of their ears.

I inch back, but I can only go so far. When my cold back hits the warm tree trunk, I remember wishing I could melt right into that tree. Carrie's already gone over the porch railing.

Rae Ann calls to him in a soft voice like a movie star. "Sweetheart, you're off early."

Before she can rise, he's right there. He bends forward and I can't see, but I guess he kisses her because their faces are so close and she moans. When he finally stands up, he glares at the muddy lawn.

"Why do you let them carry on like this?" he says. "Inside, both of you."

Between hiccups Miriam hefts herself up from the grass and limps over to me. I follow her up the steps, but I can't help myself. I look back into a golden blur of oiled skin and sparkling jewelry and those red nails, all moving in slow motion. Rae Ann rises and stretches her arms into the air until her hands are clasped behind his neck. When she leans into him and kisses him full on the mouth, the length of her body fits perfectly with his. I can't look away.

More than that vision of the two of them as one, the grit of his voice comes back to me, hard and uncomfortable as a stone in your shoe. It's so clear in my head I shrink back, as if he were close enough to touch me again.

"They're brats," he announces.

And she doesn't say anything.

It's been fifty-five years, but I still hold my breath as I did then for my mother's answer. It was a personal rejection. I held that grudge for a long time. It's why I had to escape. As long as John Thompson was in Twyman's Mill, I couldn't stay. I hated all the John Thompsons of this world who crushed people, wiped out their personalities and their desires until they were paper dolls with ruby lips and scarlet fingernails like my mother, unable to stand on their own. No one was ever going to do that to me.

Except . . . once I had Danny, I let Scott do the exact same thing.

Chapter Eleven
JEAN

In September I wrote the second batch of letters to Doctors MacIntosh, Stith, and the hospital. In the interim I concentrated on other cases. Lacy waited patiently for the answers or at least she didn't worry me to death for updates. While she continued to stop by and tell me bits and pieces about Danny, she didn't talk about the medical records or the legal paperwork. She rarely commented on my progress reports. Or lack of progress reports.

In the meantime I learned all about her life as a newlywed. Before Danny was born she'd worked in mail delivery for the northern Virginia Post Office. Her boss Juice Washington had advanced money for her to ride the bus back to Tywman's Mill for her grandmother's funeral. Scott refused to pay or to go. She joked about her friend Janet Lonnick who also worked at the mail facility. Janet had, according to Lacy, a bust like Fort Knox and no fanny.

"Shaved off flat—have you ever seen that? Slacks always made her look skinny, but only from the back. She wore those stretch top thingies that reveal every little, ah . . . muscle."

Lacy's description made it easy to see Janet Lonnick in three dimensions. I laughed at the innuendo in Lacy's choice of words. With Janet's questionable business after hours, she'd tried to convince Lacy that selling her body would be an easy way to supplement her income. For Lacy sex was not something she could have sold. Not that she said it outright, but I gleaned it from her veiled references to John Thompson and her own absent father. In the jokes and the stories though, she found a way to put that part of her past behind her. She continued to amaze me.

In these less formal conferences she told me about her surrogate daughter, the neighbor's little girl, Lorelei, from the fourth floor, and how Lorelei's mother, Ginger, and Scott had carried on an affair for months before Lacy discovered them. Poking fun at her own lack of awareness despite one neighbor's warning, Lacy described her pregnant self.

"After all Ginger was beautiful and I looked like a dead spider; this big basketball for my belly and all these dangling appendages and dark shadows under my eyes. The idea of Ginger seducing my husband sure took my mind off the contractions."

In all the stories Lacy avoided the months that followed Danny's seizures. Anyone could see she blamed herself for his failure to recover. I speculated as to possible explanations. Because his illness had been shrouded in secrecy and because the doctors had never volunteered a medical explanation, she didn't actually know much about what had really happened. All her memories centered around her shock and grief over the change in her perfect baby.

Very little of what she told me could be presented to a court. While my collection of articles and notes about the Court of Claims and vaccination issues grew larger, my understanding of Danny's condition did not. The medical records were key. Snowden, as Lacy's obstetrician, was the only sympathetic doctor with nothing to hide. We needed him, but mail to his office address came back, *forwarding time expired*. In a disloyal moment I congratulated myself that at least he had existed at one point.

Despite my assurances to Peter that I would let Fine handle the court proceedings, Lacy's declaration in April that she wouldn't go to court if I weren't her lawyer rattled behind every conversation like distant African drums. Every time I talked to Fine I grew more sure that, if I left her to deal with him, there would be no case at all. And every time I talked to Lacy about Fine, she pretended it was irrelevant.

At home we were treading water. Stephen spent lots of time in his room or out with his friends. He insisted on doing his own laundry and refused to let anyone clean his room. Although the secretiveness bothered me, I told myself he was simply growing up and accepting responsibility for his own chores. Once Brian was banished officially from our house, Stephen stopped raising the point. Peter, thinking this was progress, seemed to have lost the energy to argue about the curfew or Stephen's mediocre grades. I was preoccupied with work, but the silence when we were all in the same room was dreadful. If I'd had a Saturday to duke it out, I'd have broached the subject, but it seemed as if my time at home operated on quarter-hours as well.

On the way back from a dentist appointment with Stephen I mentioned a college friend of mine who'd lost the opportunity to apply to medical school because of drug convictions. Halfway through the story Stephen began to run the zipper on his book bag, back and forth.

"Hey," I said, "I'm trying to tell you something important."

"I don't want to go to medical school."

"I know that. I'm worried about your buddy, Brian. I think maybe he's experimenting. He strikes me as that kind of kid."

Stephen kept up the background noise with the zipper.

"I don't know how much he and his mother talk. And his Dad's not around. If you told him how dangerous it is, he might listen to you."

Silence.

"Friends," the tension in my voice was obvious, "are supposed to help each other. Stephen?"

"Yeah, okay, okay. Just don't yell at me."

"I wasn't yelling."

But his look said otherwise.

Over those weeks while I was waiting for Danny's medical records and researching other vaccine injury cases, Lacy's need to talk and her fear of talking to a strange attorney grew in proportion. With Fine's frosty attitude and his refusal to consider the case before the expert's review, I started to worry we'd miss a crucial deadline.

On the first cool day in September Lacy's truck was outside my office when I arrived back from the courthouse. At first I didn't notice it because I was mumbling to myself about parents in general. In my afternoon court hearing my client had been found guilty of violating the court's order. Fined and not jailed, she would have more trouble than usual paying my fee.

She had refused to notify the father of their children's doctor's appointments. One of those overly protective mothers, she was convinced her ex-husband would appear at the doctor's office and make a scene. Never mind that he was Mr. Mild-Mannered Milk Toast, an airplane pilot who practically stuttered when he met a live person face to face. More than anything I was weary from trying to change her mind.

"Busy?" Lacy asked, bouncing out from behind the truck as I came down the sidewalk. It was impossible not to smile.

"How are you?" I asked.

"Better than you look. You're working too hard."

"No, just butting my head against a granite mountain."

"On Danny's case?"

"That too."

"Oh-oh. Can you tell me?"

"I applied for admission to the Court of Claims."

"You have to have a ticket?"

"Not exactly, but they want to know that you have the basic credentials."

"I hope they let you in."

We stood there, smiling at each other. I'd missed her good humor.

"What have you been doing?" I asked, not sure how I was going to explain that, to avoid the deadline, she was going to have to file the initial pleading in her name alone without either attorney.

"Canning and stuff. Mosste can't let a single tomato go to waste. He's one of those emergency preparedness nuts from the Fifties."

"Does he think we're in imminent danger from aliens?"

"He's not crazy." She pouted a little. Bending into the truck cab, she pulled out three grocery store bags filled with a rainbow of vegetables. "I brought you a few leftovers."

"That puts me in my place."

"With all the research and late nights, Moss is worried you're not eating right."

"What makes him think that?"

"He saw you at MacDonald's reading some kind of medical book. As big as a suitcase."

I couldn't recall when that would have been, but I knew the book he meant. The DSM was three inches thick and invaluable for cross-examining psychologists in custody cases.

"He can relax. That book deals with psychology, not biology."

"Oh, you think I'm a nut case, huh?"

"It's not for Danny's suit. I haven't even begun to collect the books for that yet."

"But you called and said you needed me to come in before the paperwork was filed."

"I'm worried about the timing. I don't want to miss any deadlines."

She sat on the sofa, the paper bags lumped on her lap. "So it is true?"

A client normally wants to know if he or she has a good case. Lacy was dealing with a bigger issue; one I'd lost sight of lately in my analysis of the statute and the legal footwork that preceded any lawsuit. She was still searching for confirmation that Danny's injuries were not her fault. A lawsuit wouldn't necessarily give her that.

Even if I already had a medical expert who could state unequivocally that the DPT shot in 1969 had caused Danny's seizures and his subsequent retardation, there were a dozen reasons why we might lose a court case, not even allowing for my inexperience with the peculiarities of the Court of Claims. For all I knew we might be out of court already on a technicality. I needed Hamilton Fine. And he needed medical records before he would commit.

I struggled with a way to tell her without disappointing her that we might not ever know for sure what had happened. We were dealing with educated guesses, trying to match them with very specific language in the compensation fund statute to win a monetary award. None of that would restore Danny to good health. I didn't know yet what she really wanted, but I suspected brutal honesty would send her running and we would never slay this dragon.

"There's a huge hole in my file about Danny after the seizures. About how he ended up in the state facility."

She followed me back to the kitchenette. After rinsing the vegetables in the sink, she set them in the dish drainer to dry, moving in her deliberate, competent way. "Scott drove us there."

"He came back to help?"

"You don't get it. Scott was glad to dump Danny. He never wanted a baby, period. Back when I first told him about the pregnancy, he told me to get rid of it."

Chapter Twelve
JEAN

"Bad news," Jillian announced after the long Veteran's Day weekend, plunking a pile of opened mail in front of me.

"More bills?" I asked.

She shook her head.

"Mr. Moriarty filed an appeal?"

She giggled. The Moriarty divorce should have died a quiet death two years ago, but, despite a three year-old official divorce decree, the Moriartys couldn't seem to live without each other. Multiple show causes had been issued, one spouse against the other, for visitation violations, failure to pay support on time, you name it. Assorted criminal charges had been filed over trespass, curse and abuse, and larceny. The Moriartys were amazingly well suited.

Lawyers often joke that only their own client is on the side of truth and justice. With Mrs. Moriarty I couldn't do it. She was my least favorite client.

Jillian shook her head, "No, ma'am. It's not the warrior Moriartys. The Narden Training Center wrote back. They won't let you review those records without permission from both parents." She pointed to the letter on top.

"Ugh."

"I knew you'd say that. Should I send Lacy a copy?"

I thought for a moment, trying to remember my schedule for the next few days. Lacy and I hadn't talked since mid-September. When she told me about leaving Danny at the state residential hospital I had taken pages and pages of notes. We'd both ended up in tears.

Since then Fine had written me two nasty faxed messages about the medical expert's vacation schedule and his own plans to spend a month on the Riviera. Having walked those trashy beaches myself where the world's millionaires supposedly trod, I was glad for him to go there. If he drowned ogling the bare-chested European women, I wouldn't mourn him.

Periodically Lacy asked me about 'the other attorney.' "He sounds like a real lulu," she said, sensing more from my cryptic reports than I'd meant to convey.

Later when she asked if she would need to repeat everything to him, I hinted that his personality didn't lend itself to non-legal summaries. She didn't ask that question again.

The fall school schedule didn't help. Suddenly we swapped the pool and yard work for endless soccer games and PTA meetings. Stephen had made new friends and I didn't like them either. Peter wanted to ban them, along with Brian whom he still blamed as the ringleader. When Stephen defended them for their individuality, if I was home, I played referee. The office was the most peaceful place I knew, and I used it to escape.

"I'll call Lacy myself," I said to Jillian. "Make her a copy of the training center requirements, but hold off on sending it until I decide how exactly to handle the elusive Mr. Kellam."

Although I picked up the phone and dialed, the minute it rang, I put it back down. Peter was right. I was 'conflicted' about the case. I had dialed Lacy's number by heart.

He'd brought it up one night when I couldn't sleep. "You're not used to liking your clients. They aren't usually your friends."

"That's an understatement."

"Seriously, Jean. This woman means something to you. That's dangerous. You've lost your perspective. You know what they say; only a fool has himself for a client. Well, it's the same with a friend."

I looked around for something to heave. When he was right AND pompous, I wished I'd married a proper Bostonian who would've been too busy playing squash to care whether his wife had grown too chummy with a client. I chuckled to myself though; a truly proper Bostonian's wife wouldn't have worked at all.

He rolled over and peered at me in the unlit bedroom. "I know you. You're purposely not listening."

"You're the one who said, if I wasn't happy, I should find something different, replace the divorce work with something else."

"I never meant for you to take on this particular case. You're emotionally committed to this woman. God knows what you've promised her. The next thing you're going to tell me is that, to truly understand the issues, you have to visit her son at the state hospital."

I went in the bathroom and shut the door. Peter groaned. His voice, muffled but strident, came through the door. "Tell me you're not going to see him? Jean?"

I ran the water and flushed the toilet at the same time. Luckily there was a stack of catalogues in the trash. I read every last one of them. Even with the overhead fan running on high, I could hear him fuming.

That same night I dreamed of Lacy and Danny and Scott. In the dream Snowden was a huge black doctor with a marked resemblance to Mohammed Ali. Like a Greek chorus they floated above me from a courtroom balcony, humming softly as I laid out the case to an invisible judge. Lacy wheeled a full-grown Danny, dressed in a dark suit, into the courtroom where he gestured in unison with the gallery and waved like a politician.

At the end of my speechifying everyone in the dream applauded and cried at the same time. Their tears fell like a waterfall on the courtroom, soaking the spectators and the jury and puddling in the corners. Suddenly my parents and Peter and the children and my old law professors were there too, clapping and hooting.

Stephen was the only one who sat stone-faced. I tried to move through the crowd, but I couldn't reach him. I woke up as the entire assembly broke into America The Beautiful. My cheeks were wet. Peter felt my forehead for fever and suggested PeptoBismal.

After his warning I knew I had to get someone else's perceptions of the events in 1969, someone who wouldn't sugarcoat it. Scott was the logical choice. I had to contact him anyway for permission to view the state facility's medical records. To ask Lacy for his address though would spark a tirade about his disinterest and bias. Worried over her reaction, I put it off. Instead I wrote the hospital again, adding a patient number from an old invoice she'd found in the photograph box. In still more urgent tones I recited our critical need for billing records as well as the medical notes. The statute required a minimum $1,000 in medical expenses for a family to qualify for compensation from the fund.

The yellowed hospital invoice listed four different dates next to four different doctors and a second three-night stay in early October, three months after the initial seizures. The whole bill came to $192. Even a novice could guess from the limited terminology that six-month old Danny had had the second DPT shot right on schedule.

When I heard Lacy's voice in the waiting room, I knew I was running out of time. Despite Peter's warning, a visit to the State facility was crucial to at least review their records. If Fine weren't interested in using his valuable time, I'd have to do it. And I could hardly go to Narden without seeing the patient. Not and look Lacy in the face when I returned.

"Moss wants to meet you," Lacy said, after Jillian had cleared her to come back to my office.

"We've met before. On the street."

"He means talk, face to face. He's like an old Indian chief. He wants to smoke the peace pipe with you. With Peter too. Seal the treaty, you know."

I realized I'd been avoiding her because I had no good news. Even I could see my reaction was not professional, but personal.

"So," she said, tapping her foot, "Check right now, with Peter and your calendar, and tell me if Sunday night's a good night."

"It'll just be Peter and me. The kids are at their cousins' on Sunday."

"That's okay. Check the calendar."

"You're going to wait?"

"Yup. Moss said, don't come home without an answer."

Sunday it thundered and spit hot hard pellets of raindrops in little bursts like gunshot. Peter and I worked separately at either side of the dining room table, talking sporadically and getting each other more iced tea or nibbles. Several times when the sudden shift in the rain's direction or volume surprised me, I looked up and caught him watching me. By mid-afternoon my eyes were blurry.

"You okay?" he asked.

I nodded.

"You keep rubbing your eyes like you're falling asleep."

"Doctors must purposely write this stuff in obtuse language so they're the only ones who can understand it."

"Everyone says that about lawyers too."

"But legal jargon comes from history. Most of these medical terms were coined in the last two centuries."

"Uh-huh, mostly from Latin."

I didn't laugh, though he wanted me to. After re-reading for the fourth time the definition of encephalopathic shock, I used the highlighter to mark the phrases that sounded significant.

"It's time to go anyway," he said.

I dawdled, straightening the papers and arranging my notes before sticking them in my briefcase.

"Jean, we'll be late."

"Why are you in such a rush to get there?" I regretted the tone of voice.

"Hey, she's your client. I'm only trying to be polite."

"That's not true. You can hardly wait to get there so you can figure out their angle and tell me another hundred reasons why I should drop the case."

He paused, one arm in the raincoat, and stared at me.

"Or better yet," I continued, "Why there's no case at all."

"What are you so uptight about? I thought you liked this woman."

"I do."

"Well, something's bugging you."

"Let's just go and eat the stupid dinner."

Before he started the engine he put my favorite adagio tape in the radio. I could feel him watching me and wondering, but I concentrated on the avalanche of rain gushing over the gutters. After the third deep breath, he turned the key and headed down the driveway. As he drove us through the slashing rain, I read haltingly from scribbled directions.

A dozen apologies ran through my head. I liked Lacy. From everything I'd heard about Moss, I would like him too. So what was my problem with this dinner? Because I realized, as I watched the car devour the black roadway, the dinner had been a problem from the beginning.

When we arrived, we sat for a minute in the car, hoping for a break in the deluge.

"I'm sorry I lost my temper," I said.

"Me, too. It'll be okay."

"I hope so, but I shouldn't blow my cool with you just because you're safe and you can take it."

"What makes you so sure I'm not going to fall apart?"

"Not Peter Driscoll. You wouldn't do that to me. You know how much I rely on you."

"I might be able to help," Peter spoke quietly without his usual assuredness.

"If I knew what it was exactly that was bugging me. . . You know me. I've never been one to obsess about clients. Sure, some I like, some I don't. Every lawyer feels that way. And some cases are easier than others."

The written checklist I'd made from the Vaccine Injury statutes floated in front of my eyes like the phantom blackboard during an exam. Fine had made his reputation on this kind of unusual litigation. We needed him, even though he was a jerk. I'd worked divorce cases with opposing counsel worse than anything Fine had shown us so far.

Lacy, though, like most clients, was nervous. In any lawsuit a client has more at stake than the lawyer. *Heck*, I told them, as part of my standard spiel, *this is your day in court*. I'd spell it out in black and white. *You know the facts. You know who'll make the best witnesses. If you can't persuade me, you certainly can't expect me to persuade the judge.* I'd end with, *When we're done here, I go home to my dinner and my family. You're the one who has to live with the ruling.* That speech created an incentive for clients to do more of their own legwork.

The answer to Lacy's mess, I was convinced, was in my notes, in the material I'd already compiled, but I didn't know what I was looking for because this whole area of law was new to me. I wouldn't recognize it. The truth was I needed Fine. It would be malpractice for me to try this case by myself. The panic I'd felt as a new attorney returned. Because of my growing conviction that the lies went beyond Lacy's case, I didn't dare give her the standard speech until I knew more. I was afraid she would expect me to take on the entire industry. Yet every day I was more convinced that the legal remedy would not fix the problem.

As adamant as Lacy was that I could make things right, it grew harder and harder to look her in the eye. With my hand on the door handle I braced myself for a complicated evening.

"Not so fast." Peter leaned over and kissed me. "If it's meant to be, it'll work out. Have a little faith."

"I just wish I had some medical evidence to go with the faith." Neither of us laughed.

Lacy stood in the doorway, holding the screen door open in one hand. "You found it." She stretched out both arms, pulled me in from the rain, and gave me a hug, then Peter. "Yuck, you're all wet."

"It's what the kids have been telling him for years," I said.

The house was a standard brick ranch. From the driveway you went in the back door to the kitchen. The table took up most of the room. Knotty pine cabinets dated the house; early Fifties, before the onset of avocado green. Bar stools with black vinyl seats stood at the counter. I knew from Lacy's stories it had been Moss' house before they married.

"Hi," Lacy's daughter glided into the kitchen, flinging her long black hair over her shoulders dramatically. She gave her mom a friendly shoulder-to-shoulder bump and fixed on me.

"Diana," Lacy said, "This is Mrs. Driscoll. And Mr. Driscoll."

While Peter waved from the far side of the room where Moss was showing off ancestral portraits—sepia photographs in stiff poses—I stretched to shake Diana's hand. Up close, the color of her hair matched her mother's perfectly. And Danny's. I wondered how much she knew about her older brother. Lacy hadn't said whether she'd taken Diana or her brother to meet Danny. From the wall of school photos, glossy color eight by tens in dime store frames, I could see that Danny was not an integral part of the family history.

Diana stepped back to avoid the handshake and looked put out, though it could have been an act for her mother.

"Mrs. Driscoll's an old friend," Lacy explained.

"I thought she was Danny's lawyer," Diana said.

Lacy laughed nervously. It made me wonder what she'd told them about the lawsuit.

Peter rescued us. "Lawyers can be friends. And we are definitely old."

From Diana's expression I didn't think she bought his explanation for our presence in her house.

"Aren't you a little late?" she said before disappearing down the hallway. In my mind she didn't mean for dinner.

Lacy bustled back and forth, putting out a sample of everything she'd canned that summer. "You sit," she said to Peter as she delivered dish after dish from counter to table. She motioned to another chair for me.

"Aren't the kids eating with us?" I asked.

"They ate already." Moss said with his eyes on Lacy. I wondered if he'd talked her out of having them there or if they'd been glad to be excused.

She took my hand and Moss's on the other side. "Grace."

He spoke so quietly I had to strain to hear. "Patient and generous God, bless these people together here tonight to share your bounty. We thank you for the rain and the clearing, the plentiful table and the seeds of friendship you sow for us. Keep each one of your children safe from harm and disappointment and teach them to accept this imperfect world and their place in it. Amen."

Before Peter let go of my hand, he squeezed it. I was glad he was here. It might help close the gap between my increasingly bifurcated life as lawyer versus wife and mother. At last he would see how needy Lacy was and why I had been unable to abandon her.

We ate until it hurt. Diana drifted in and out, whispering little snippets in her mother's ear and glaring at me. When I tried to ask about her activities at school, she pretended not to hear, exiting quickly, her head down.

"Please ignore her." Lacy said. "She's mad about something that has nothing to do with y'all."

"Listen," Peter raised his glass of iced tea, "Teenagers are experts at knowing how to get attention. We have two, you know, and one in training."

"Stephen and Andrew." From the hallway Diana's voice curved around the doorframe.

"Missy, come in here." Moss's voice had lost the soft edge of its southern drawl. "If you want to be part of a conversation, sit down and look a man in the eye."

She dragged a stool from the counter and perched there, her head swiveling between the adults like an owl waiting for a mouse. She ended up face to face with me.

"So you know our boys?" Peter began, raising an eyebrow to silence me.

"Everyone at school knows Stephen Driscoll. He's the man with the weed."

Before I could speak, Moss had Diana's arm in his and they were marching out of the room. Lacy's face, flushed from cooking, had gone white.

"I'm so sorry. She's been like this for weeks. The system, she thinks, has robbed her of a brother. She's just trying to fight back and she sees you as part of the problem."

Peter's hand held mine, trapping me at the table. Flustered at the scrap of information, the urge to follow her and demand a retraction was so strong I had to grit my teeth.

Chapter Thirteen
JEAN

After dinner Lacy asked Moss to show us the garden, but Peter volunteered to help with the dishes and shooed me outside. The sky had cleared completely in the east. Beyond the neat row of white pines that edged their yard, lingering storm clouds to the west made broad bands of deep crimson and purple striations like canyon ledges.

While we toured the yard, the sheepdog stuck to Moss's heels. "Snowball," he said after a bit of roughhousing with her.

"She a good guard dog for Lacy when you're on the road?"

"Well," he drawled, "Not particular fierce if you talk nice to her, but she'll bark you into the next county. She recognizes a stranger, all right." He tossed her a ball. "I'm supposed to tell you about the garden."

"Is it yours or Lacy's?" It was a struggle to keep my mind away from Stephen. Were there other deceits he had perpetrated on his well-intentioned but stupid parents? How deep was he into the very things I'd spent hours convincing myself he was too smart to ever try?

When Moss spoke, I had to force myself to pay attention. Stephen wasn't his problem, and, until Peter and I got home, we couldn't do anything about it anyway.

"You could say it was her garden, but she don't work it."

I looked puzzled.

"She likes sweet potatoes so there's two rows of them and one of everything else. The kids aren't much on vegetables." He shrugged, digging the toe of his cowboy boot into an edge of plowed earth where a clump of chicory clung.

"How's she holding up?" I asked.

"She's never stopped thinkin' about Danny, but the other kids had to be dealt with." He lowered his voice. "Now that they're older, more independent, he's on her mind more. Although she'd never up and say it out like that."

I nodded, knowing exactly what he meant. I'd seen it in the single-minded conversations and the sudden silences. "Is she discouraged about the doctors' records?"

"She wouldn't say if she were."

"Do you think she's upset?"

"Not upset. More frustrated-like."

"Good for her, it's taken me fifteen years to admit that about legal things."

"It won't last."

"What won't?"

"The hold-up. Something's bound to break."

"What makes you so sure?"

"When Lacy wants something, she'll worry you with it until she gets it."

"Tenacious."

"Ay-yuh," he said, squinting into the sun that hovered beyond the pine border.

"I've tried to tell her the court may not connect Danny's injuries to the vaccine."

"She hears you."

"I'm not so sure. There are certain things she won't talk about. It makes me think she's expecting miracles."

"She'll be okay, no matter which way it turns out."

I tried to imagine sitting inside a strange courtroom, Lacy at my elbow, and watching that determination drain away as a stern judge told her the evidence was insufficient or there was no causal connection. I hoped Moss was right. He knew her better than I did.

"Sometimes," I was trying to explain my own doubts, "When she talks about back then, it almost feels like she's there. And not here. She remembers so many details."

He strolled to the other side of the furrowed square and picked a small pumpkin from the dirt. "Has she ever told you how we met?"

I shook my head, anxious not to cut him off just when he'd decided to be forthcoming. And I was curious.

"We were introduced before Danny was born. Back when I drove long-distance runs."

"At the post office?"

"Yeah, but she was married. From the way she talked, even before Danny, Scott was not always the perfect husband. Then she was gone for a year, longer actually when we got to counting later. I wondered what happened to her, but the post office folks didn't say much."

"Not even her friend Janet?"

"Janet and I never got along. She was too . . . free and easy." A lesser man would have winked.

After a suitably pregnant pause he continued. "All of a sudden Lacy was back, throwing mail again."

"She was glad to see you?"

"I didn't think she remembered our one conversation. A couple of trips later I heard her blasting some kid who'd smart-mouthed her. When she noticed me listening, I asked her if she always talked like that." His eyes closed as if he were savoring a particularly juicy piece of steak.

"Like how?"

"Like a truck driver."

I couldn't help laughing. The vision of Lacy at twenty-one whipping an underling into line didn't surprise me. That vein of hidden iron was beginning to reveal itself.

"She said no, but she kept staring at me. I thought maybe she was mad at me for putting in my two cents worth. Juice—that was her boss—he called her down for slacking on the job, but she talked right back, told him she was busy. Busy looking, that's what she said." He grinned. "She didn't say anything else for a while, but before she went on break, she asked me . . ."

Rapping on the kitchen window made us both look up. Lacy made a funny face and tilted her head in a question. "Dessert," she said through the screen.

Moss and I groaned in unison.

"He's telling me a story," I said.

"That's what I was afraid of," she called through the screen.

"Hush up, woman. I'm just getting to the good part."

"Oh, Lordy. Come in here so I can set her straight."

Once we were all reassembled with blueberry pie and ice cream in front of us, Moss spoke, his fork poised above the plate. "I was telling her 'bout the time you asked after my mustache."

Lacy interrupted. "He was leaning against the wall—those long legs and the boots and the cowboy hat—just waiting for me to make a fool of myself. When I asked him if he could kiss with that wooly thing on his face, he didn't even gulp. Plain and simple, no smile, he says, 'I ain't had no problem.'"

Everyone chuckled. Moss's face turned a little pink in the warm kitchen.

Lacy wasn't finished though. "I bet you ain't, that's what I told him."

They were both grinning. In the doorway Diana stood, trying hard to keep from smiling. Peter had taken my hand under the table.

"I wasn't going to tell that part," Moss said.

"That's not the end?" Peter asked.

Neither of them answered. Looks went back and forth across the table. Diana disappeared again.

Finally Lacy nodded at Moss. "Go ahead. You tell."

"After they loaded up my truck that night, I found her in the cab, asleep." He looked sheepish.

I could easily imagine him in that ten gallon, full of secrets, just waiting for the world to figure it all out. "The suspense is killing me. What'd you do?"

"She rode with me."

"On the mail run?"

"All the way to Missoura and back. Told me the whole story. John Thompson hitting on her, Scott's cheating, the coma, and them taking the baby to Narden. Boy, did she need a friend."

"A friend, eh?" Lacy held his gaze. "I wanted him to know what he was getting."

"You knew he was the one?" I asked.

A grinning Moss passed his plate for seconds.

"I knew," Lacy announced.

"And you've been together ever since?"

"Yup."

"Mom," Diana called from somewhere else.

"Later, sweetie."

"Mom."

"Let her wait." Moss's voice was low but steady.

She appeared, her pocketbook hanging from her shoulder, her hair twisted into a freefall knot, leaving wisps in all directions. She had put on dark purple lipstick. With the eye shadow and the sixties' print sundress, she was making a clear statement. "Carson needs to be picked up from work. We may stop and see some of his friends."

"Midnight," Moss said. Although she winced, she pecked his cheek and Lacy's before leaving.

After the screen door slammed, Lacy brought coffee in mugs to the table. "I was a troublemaker when I was that age."

"No?" I laughed. "Who would have guessed?"

Peter drove home. The clouds had blown off and left the stars like beach glass on the sand. His hair—what he let the barber save—ruffled in the breeze from the open window. It had been a long time since we'd been out to dinner without the kids. He was clearly savoring the peacefulness.

Hovering in the periphery of my churning thoughts was a vision of Stephen and Brian out behind the garage divvying up baggies of marijuana into their backpacks. I couldn't believe my son would risk it.

During the summer the kids managed their own laundry and lunch since Peter and I were both at work. The boys cut the grass in between their restaurant jobs. I was proud of how well they handled those responsibilities. Once school started again, we all struggled in September to get back to a schedule.

This year the transition had been smooth. Or maybe I just hadn't been here to notice the snags. It was impossible to imagine how and when Stephen could manage to buy and sell drugs without our noticing. He would know how apocalyptic breaking the law would be for a lawyer's family. Weird friends didn't mean you sold drugs. It was much more credible that it was simply a stab by Diana to make me squirm for putting Danny in the spotlight. Poor Lacy.

"I like them," Peter said after a bit.

"Funny couple, but you can tell how right they are for each other. Think people say that about us?"

"No," he laughed lightly. "They say you're damn lucky I put up with you."

"Ouch."

At home the music blasted from Stephen's closed door. I found Andrew working on a report for history.

"Uncle Charles brought you home?"

He hummed a yes, but the pencil kept on scratching across the pad.

"Andrew, is Stephen okay?"

"He said he was tired."

"No, I mean, at school, with his friends, in general. Do you think he's happy . . . with himself?"

"Anyone would be depressed hanging around his friends. They never go outside."

This wasn't working. I'd have to confront Stephen directly. But when he didn't answer my knock, I tried the handle. It was locked.

I couldn't keep myself from yelling. "Peter."

His footsteps raced up the stairs. By that time I was pounding on the door. My imagination was tearing through scenes of the rescue squad carrying an inert Stephen down to flashing lights. After rattling the knob with no success, Peter didn't stay, but came back within seconds it seemed with his toolbox and took the door off the hinges. Elly was squeezing my waist, her face buried, and

Andrew stood at his door, his lips set in a look of disbelief that this was really happening in our house.

With the door still in Peter's hands, I pushed Elly loose and rushed to Stephen's bed where he was rising, squinting at the light and shaking his head as if to clear the tumble of voices.

Without thinking I hoisted him to standing and pulled him to me. He let me hold him close like that for a few seconds, then wiggled as if he didn't want to be rude to an elderly relative who was hugging him too long.

Peter tugged my shoulder back so he could see Stephen's face. "Why did you lock the door, son?"

"Which door?" He was rubbing his eyes and blinking while the rest of us stood mesmerized.

"God damn it, Stephen," I said. "We don't lock doors. If you're doing something you're not supposed to be doing, don't do it here."

Stuttering, he went out into the hallway and bent to the door handle. As he fumbled with the lock, my heartbeat steadied. The door had locked accidentally. He had nothing to hide.

It was Diana Stonington who had the agenda: a new brother usurping her position in the family, upsetting her mother, diverting attention from her own penchant for drama and center stage. Her accusation was a ploy, a way to strike back at the unfairness of the change in her own life. Lacy had warned us about her daughter's anger.

I shuddered with a sharp pang of guilt. Poor Stephen. Here I was, preoccupied with my law work, leaving the children on their own all summer and after school, and then, at the first wild accusation from a stranger, I'd leapt to the conclusion that they were dishonest when they never had been before.

"I'm sorry. I thought . . . Diana said . . . Never mind."

"No more locked doors." Peter said, hefting the door to its hinges.

Tuesday Jillian interrupted me in conference with Mrs. Moriarty.

"Excuse me," I took the phone off speaker. "It better be good," I said.

"It's Lacy. Long distance."

She hadn't mentioned a trip out of town. I punched line one. "Where are you?"

"I found Doctor Stith."

"What?"

"Danny's doctor."

"I know who Stith is. Where are you?"

"At the Springfield bus station. I came up to get the medical records."

"They already told me no. And the hospital. Three times. I was going to see if Narden had copies."

"But we still need the doctors too, don't we?"

"So you talked to Stith?"

"He retired years ago, but his partner's still here. In the same office. Dr. McIntosh."

"Stith's associate from Danny's first admission?"

"Bingo."

I could practically hear her grin through the phone line. "He talked to you at his office?"

"The nurse wouldn't let me. I even tried to make an appointment. I had to wait for him in the hall after they closed the office."

"But you talked to him in person?"

"You betcha."

She was loving this. Fancy Jean with all her diplomas and thick law books had failed miserably, but Lacy, like the cartoon dynamite that keeps showing up, solves the problem.

"Okay, okay. The suspense is excruciating."

"Forget ex-crew-whatever. Guess what?"

"What?"

"When I asked him if he remembered Danny Kellam, the first thing he said was, 'Sure, the DPT baby.'"

Chapter Fourteen
LACY

Even after Doc Snowden convinced me that Danny would be better off in the state hospital, I kept putting it off. Gram hadn't raised me to give up. With her voice in my head, I convinced myself if I loved him hard enough, he'd get better. To keep up my spirits I used to have these imaginary conversations with her. I'd pretend we were sitting on the front porch at the Tyler Street house again.

Gram had this way of accepting everything that happened as if it were meant to be. When it rained and we kids couldn't play ball, she'd say. 'This here's a cleaning house day, that's all. Your room's been waiting and waiting for some rain so it could breathe in some of that fresh cool air.' She'd throw open windows and make us cart the blankets out to the porch. When we were little, she'd let us make forts with them using the chairs from the kitchen. And she'd let us draw with chalk on the bedroom walls before we washed 'em down.

If one of us were sick with the up-chucks, she'd thank the Lord. 'That a'girl. Flush out that evil. God's just making sure you're clean on the inside too.'

Once when I was about twelve, before we knew John Thompson was messing with Miriam—we only knew she was sassy one minute and crying the next—I asked Gram what possible reason the Lord could've had for sending us trouble like John Thompson.

"Lace, honey, where would we be without JT? Your little brother's a gift from heaven if ever there was one."

I did love JT. He was like my own baby, really. Rae Ann didn't pay him much attention, except to show off when John Thompson was home. I bathed him, I read to him at bedtime, I sat with him during thunderstorms. Rae Ann didn't like his gooey fingers on her clothes or his constant questions.

"But why doesn't God flush out John Thompson?" I asked Gram, sure that God had overlooked us.

After she thought about that for a while, the answer came to her. "He's our test, our hair shirt. Long time ago, when they had castles and priests who lived together in little walled towns all to themselves, some of the monks wore prickly shirts called hair shirts."

"Like the horsehair sofa that Cameron's mother has?"

"Itchy like that and rough. To remind them every minute how lucky they were to have been saved by Jesus dying on the cross."

"John Thompson's like a mosquito then."

She laughed, but whispered, "Best not say that where he can hear, child. And best not try and swat him either."

"How do we get rid of him?"

"It's like anything else, dear child. You have to trust in the power of love."

A dozen times I'd heard her tell Rae Ann and Miriam the same thing. "I don't know what that is, Gram."

"Sure you do. You're living proof of it."

She stopped knitting or shelling peas or whatever her hands had been doing and took my hands in hers. "When your mama was laying in my big bed, ready for the birthing, so ready she was telling the Lord to move along. You know how your mama does when she's in a hurry. We were trying to get her to slow down. Cameron's mother was there, but the doctor hadn't come yet. Athanea helped with everyone's babies."

Even as a child, I knew Missus Coleman knew things, secret things, and she had a special way with plants. She could cure most anyone. That next spring when Danny still couldn't hold his head up straight, I called long distance to ask her what to do, but she'd passed away. Only Rae Ann hadn't bothered to tell me.

Gram was forever moving her hands as she talked, drawing shapes in the air to match her words, the way deaf people talk. That day on the porch she made a huge round circle and I could see my mother bloated and slow with JT. She must have wanted to tie up John Thompson real bad to let herself get like that a third time.

"Rae was awful big though," Gram continued, "and you were so late we worried you were maybe too big a baby for her. Your mama was narrow-hipped—ever so particular about staying thin—and not very strong. Something was wrong. Your head weren't coming like it should've been. Athanea told Rae to be patient, but she weren't listening to anyone. She pushed anyway.

"When the baby come out, she was all blue. Strangled in the cord, poor thing. Already dead. Athanea laid her up on the dresser in a shoebox. So we could bury her later. Athanea was working to calm Rae down, talking low to get her to stop screaming and cursing. I was sponging up all the mess. Rae was so loud we was afraid she'd frighten Miriam all the way down on the front steps, where we'd sent her to watch for the doctor. She weren't but four.

"And then all of a sudden there was another head and more shoulders and feet sliding out and Rae Ann shrieking, what is it, what's happening? Twins, Athanea says, just as surprised as the rest of us was. You were that tiny. I guess she figured you'd been crushed by your sister. And Rae was bleeding so much that Athanea just stuck you up on the dresser next to the first dead baby and didn't pay no attention.

"The doctor came then and everyone was talking at once, trying to explain. I just snuck out with you. Wrapped your teeny little body in one of my old nightgowns and rocked away on that front porch. Poor Rae, she wouldn't have anything to do with you. So I fed you boiled milk with an eyedropper and took you to bed with me. It was the power of love that brought you back, child."

All this talk about Gram makes me think of her hands, those tough, dry shallow places on her thumb and her fingers. She was the workingest woman. When I was a little girl, I used to touch those hard places. 'Ouchies,' I called them, but she'd say, 'No, girl, those are God's marks. They don't hurt. When the flood comes, he's got to be able to find the poor ones. To raise them up.'

She never saw my Danny. When she died, late May, early June, I think, Danny was brand new. I was still on leave from the post office and Scott wouldn't pay for the bus to the funeral. But Juice did. He gave me an advance on my pay 'cause I was supposed to start back in July. Later, when I didn't come back to work for so long, he used to tease me about that $67. 'You're a mighty brave little gal to steal from the United States government and think you could sweet talk them into getting away with it.' It was years later I found out he paid it himself, never even put in the paperwork for an advance.

Not long after that Scott took off and left Danny and me alone together. We moved downstairs to the basement apartment, a studio, cheaper. No one visited because they didn't understand a one year-old baby who didn't sit up or walk. Snowden kept after me though. When he caught us in the hospital, he'd turn me sideways. 'You look like a zipper,' he'd say, 'You're not eating.'

That winter he sent me to a doctor who worked for the county. A doctor for crazy people. Mark Vanterhoff. The first time I went to his office he put out his arms to take Danny. I wouldn't let him.

"Stingy, eh?" he joked.

"I don't know you. And I don't like doctors."

"Doctor Snowden didn't say anything about that."

"He's a friend."

Every time after that Mark asked for Danny right off the bat and every time when I refused, Mark would just shrug and start talking. Lots of times with Danny in my lap I would fall asleep in Mark's office. He had a big old leather sofa. It wasn't hard as tired as I was. At home I could only sleep when Danny slept. I had to rest my hand on his back so I'd wake up if he were having trouble breathing.

Later Mark and I got to be good friends. That spring he found a woman to come to the apartment every morning and cook breakfast and clean a little. Eventually the grant money that paid her ran out and she had to stop coming. But for a while I had a nap every morning in my own bed. I even stopped losing weight. For those four weeks.

Sitting there in Mark's waiting room with Danny in my lap, I could see in the faces of all the other mothers that they knew something wasn't right. Even other children could sense it. Danny wasn't getting better.

One night after we'd been in the apartment without a break during a three-day snowstorm, I was so lonely I called Rae Ann. "How's JT?" I asked.

"He's at Fort LeJeune. Training."

"Big army man, huh?" I could hear the radio blaring in the background. "Aren't you going to ask about the baby?" I said.

"Is there any change?"

"Why don't you come and see for yourself? There's room enough."

"Aren't you working all day?"

"I'm still on leave."

"Geez, Lacy."

"If you came, I could get my re-certification done. Then when Danny goes to the training center, I'd be ready to work."

"I'm not babysitting."

"You watch Miriam's kids."

"They're not retarded."

I hung up. After I finished gluing the phone back together, I called Janet. She could always make me laugh.

"I'm coming right over," she said. I never could figure out how she managed to get there in the snow. She spent the night and we made stew with a bunch of canned stuff in my cupboard and macaroni noodles. Danny liked macaroni and cheese.

"I know what let's do," she said the next morning. "Let's get Danny all dolled up and take him over to the Sears & Roebuck picture studio and have his picture taken." She disappeared into the bedroom. "Where is that cute little suit the girls from work gave him last Christmas? That one probably still fits."

We did it. Although the line wasn't too long, it hardly moved. Most of the kids were fussing and whiney. Not my Danny. I was so proud of him. He gurgled and slurped in the stroller while Janet kept me in stitches pretending to know the secrets of everyone that passed. She made up some wild tales. She had to go buy a new pair of undies because we laughed so hard she peed in her pants.

When one of the babies wouldn't cooperate with the photographer, the mother behind us began to complain, "Any old five month old can sit up and smile."

She was really getting on my nerves. Everyone was tired of waiting, but kids are kids. They operate on a different wavelength.

"How old is your son?" she asked, trying to be chatty, I guess, so we wouldn't think she was such a witch.

"He'll be two in April," I said.

Finally it was our turn. They had this platform covered in white shag carpet, and they'd been sitting the little babies up against it. Some did better than others, but I knew Danny couldn't stay upright without help. I laid him down on his stomach and wiped off his chin where he'd been drooling.

That woman in back of us started in again. "Will you look at that? That boy's almost two years old and he can't even lift up his head."

Janet whispered to me, "Ignore her." But the woman kept on and on.

When I couldn't stand it anymore, I whipped around. "If your child had been in and out of the hospital for practically his whole life, he wouldn't be able to pick up his head either."

Do you know, that woman turned around and walked out, after waiting all that time? Janet copied her little behind wiggling away and everyone in the studio laughed. And she wet her pants again.

I never talked to Rae Ann after that. She died the next year. Oh, sure, I went to the funeral. Miriam needed help. She had four kids of her own by then and my Danny was gone. The day after the burial, while I was sorting through some things at Gram's house for Miriam, John Thompson pulled up in a shiny new Cadillac. This one was white. Gram had left the house to Miriam, not Rae Ann, I suppose to keep him from getting his hands on it. He had a beer bottle in his back pocket. I could smell it before he opened the screen door. Some flophouse girl hung on his arm, but when he saw me he sent her to wait in the car.

I continued to empty the drawers. "What do you want?"

"So you're your Mama's girl after all, come to take what you can."

"You don't know what you're talking about."

He inched closer and ran his fingers along my arm. "You're looking so fine, Lace. Thin. No, sheik. You got Rae's bones after all. Can't we be friends?"

"Don't you touch me. I'm grown up now and I know how to call the Sheriff."

"Feisty. I always liked that about you. You were the only one who could give me a hard-on just being in the same room. Come on. One dance. For your Mama's sake."

I kicked him in the gut—or close to it—and left. Never did go back to Twyman's Mill.

Finally just before Danny's second birthday Mark and Snowden ganged up and convinced me I had to let Danny go to the state hospital. They called it a training center. Before I could change my mind the State people wrote to say they had a place for him. That must've been Mark's doing because up until then Snowden had been saying they had a waiting list.

Scott drove us to Narden. He didn't want to, but his mother or Snowden must have shamed him into it. He never asked me what would be convenient, just called to say he'd be at the apartment to pick us up at a certain time on the day the hospital designated.

The whole way there Danny slept. Scott didn't say a word. I thought I would cry, but I didn't. I tried to think of Gram. *What will be, will be.* When we got there, they made me fill out a mess of papers. Then they said we had to take him to Building Ten. Scott insisted on driving over there. I walked though, carrying Danny. I suppose I was delaying again, but I didn't cry.

We waited forever there too. Danny was as good as gold, never fussed. The nurse kept coming out from the office to check on us like maybe we were going to hurt him or run off. The fourth or fifth time she came out she asked me why was his face so chapped? I told her what did she expect when he drooled all the time and couldn't wipe it off himself.

She disappeared into that office so fast it made a coyote look slow. But when she came out the next time, she took him right out of my arms. Although she held him the right way, she never looked at him or swayed at all like mothers do.

"You can go home now," she said.

"Where are you taking him?"

"All entrants have to be examined and quarantined."

"Quarantined from what?"

"From anyone who might catch his germs."

"He's not sick."

"All the babies here are sick."

"I've changed my mind."

Scott threw a fit. "You're crazy." He threw the door wide open and pointed at me. "She's crazy," he said to the nurse. "I'll be outside when you're through arguing, but I'm not waiting forever."

The nurse disappeared with Danny. I didn't cry then either. But through the wall I could hear him fussing. When she came out, I asked her why was he crying. She said it wasn't Danny. But I knew what I knew. Finally after two hours, when I refused to leave, they let me feed him. I rocked him and rocked him. After a while he went to sleep and I just kept on rocking. When another nurse came in, she took him to the quarantine room. They insisted he had to be alone for ten days. No contact with other patients or outsiders.

Once he was gone, really gone where I couldn't hear him, I walked outside. Next to the car Scott was smoking. Two ladies were coming in, and just as I opened the door, this wail came out of me, out of nowhere. Sobbing, I crumpled on the sidewalk. Scared those ladies to death.

After those first ten days when I knew the training center people wouldn't talk to me, I called every week or so. I'd ask them to put Danny next to the phone so I could hear him breathing. They never would. They'd say he was fine or he was sleeping. I wanted to go and see him so bad, but I had no way to get there and no one to give me a ride. Anyway you weren't allowed to visit for the first two months. I went back to work at the post office. To try to forget.

But every day when I came home his crib and his toys were sitting there. 'Damn,' I told Snowden when he called to check on me, 'I should have taken that Phenobarbital. It would all be over.'

That wasn't a good time for me. After two years living for Danny, I had to relearn how to live for me. I was going crazy. I read every book I could get my hands on. I worked and worked. That helped some.

After a bit the girls at work started to invite me places. A couple times Janet invited me to dinner. The first time two guys showed up halfway through the salads. They pulled chairs up to our table without asking and made kissy face with her. When one of them put his arm around my shoulder, I dragged Janet into the bathroom and asked her what was with them. Relax, she said, they'll pay you.

Pay me for what?

She explained this was how she made her car payment. She said it was easy, quick money. You didn't have to spend the night with them or anything. We went back out and I told them, thanks, but no thanks, I came for dinner, I'm hungry, and I'm nobody's dessert.

For months it went along like that, some days better than others. Then Moss showed up. It's not that he made me forget, he just gave me something else to think about, something bigger than my crumby little life.

Sometimes I used to think my second family was a lie. I felt like I was play-acting at being a mother because it didn't seem real without Danny. After a while though, it turned into my life. With Moss it was different. He wanted the babies too. And he understood that I didn't love Danny any less just because I loved another baby.

Moss and two kids and a house with a riding mower. It was a perfect life. The American dream. Just as if I'd never had that first baby.

Chapter Fifteen
JEAN

When Stephen arrived with Andrew and Elly from a church fellowship pizza party, I'd been home from the office for an hour. Claiming exhaustion after a marathon faculty meeting, Peter had gone right to bed. From the living room where I'd set up a card table and spread out my legal work, I heard the kids' voices in the driveway. They'd been arguing about something from the car to the kitchen, but stopped instantly when they saw me.

"Fun time?" I asked.

The murmurs were universal, but not revealing. Elly came in, gave me a hug, and curled up on the sofa.

Whispers filtered in from the kitchen. "Getting a drink," Andrew called above the whispers. "Where's Dad?"

"He crashed."

Elly opened one eye. "Stephen let Andrew drive part of the way home."

"On the driveway?"

"Down Main Street and up the driveway."

Another act of rebellion and the fear I'd felt at Diana's chilling revelation returned in spades. I was mad. "Stephen, I need to see you."

He popped into the doorframe, a huge grin on his face, and instantly disappeared. Elly giggled. Andrew was laughing too.

Holding my breath, I kept my voice low. "I mean in here, kiddo."

Without the least sheepishness he walked in and stood directly in front of me. "I have try-outs in the morning."

"For orchestra?"

"Uh-huh." He moved to the stairs. "Chip Petersen's gonna be first chair if I don't get my beauty sleep."

"Wait a sec. What's this about Andrew driving on Main Street?"

"Big-mouth," he shot at Elly. "It was after nine, Mom. No one's out around here after nine."

"We didn't pass a single car," Andrew said.

"Not even the town police car." Elly piped in.

"You kids go up now. Stephen and I need to talk."

The boys exchanged glances, but Andrew went without any more argument.

Although Stephen lounged in the wing chair—normally worth a reminder about its mended leg—I was preoccupied with more important issues. He beat me to the punch.

"Did you wreck another home in court today?"

I waited until Andrew's bedroom door shut upstairs, hoping the delay might signal to Stephen the seriousness of the conference. "That was rude. And inaccurate. Actually I've been having a difficult time concentrating since Sunday night." At his confusion I felt a frisson of satisfaction. Something juvenile in me wanted him to feel the shock I had. "That's when we heard you were dealing drugs at the high school."

He'd been in the middle of a drink and sprayed water in a wide arc, sprinkling me and the sofa and the wall. Rushing off, he returned with one of the kitchen towels. "Sorry, Mom. Sorry." Manic mopping, but no outright denial.

"Well?"

"How can you believe that kind of garbage?" He stood back and rocked on his heels, swallowing the beginnings of a smile.

My anger erupted. "What in God's name is funny about this? If the general public thinks you're a drug dealer, it doesn't seem terribly funny to me."

"The general public? Who told you this?"

"Never mind who. You're obviously hanging around with the wrong crowd if that's what people think. Reputations in a small town are built over many years. Can you imagine what this kind of thing could do to my reputation as a lawyer? Or your father's at the university?"

"It's just a rumor."

"Rumors don't start from nothing."

"This is really just more grief about my friends, isn't it? You've never liked any of them. Even though you don't take the time to get to know them. Just because Brian's mother smokes cigarettes, you think he's a cocaine addict."

"Brian has nothing to do with me. You do. You're my son, and I won't have you ruining all our hard work. Your father and I like being part of this town. "

"Why? It's ridiculous. County fairs and Firemen's parades. It's a fairy tale."

"When you're on your own, you can choose where you want to live, but as long as you're living here with us you'll follow our rules."

"You live here?" He ran up the stairs and slammed his door.

I hardly minded the last accusation I was so relieved that he'd categorized Diana's charge as a rumor. It was a denial of sorts.

The week after our dinner with Lacy and Moss, Peter walked down to the office one brilliant fall evening to meet me. Everything dripped gold. The streets were littered with leaves. People and cars still bustled about, which was unusual for Parry's Crossing after the shops closed. I heard his voice down the sidewalk before he reached my open door.

"Knock, knock," he said after good-byes to the unseen friend.

"Hi," I said, "I'm just finishing up."

"That sounds familiar."

"Sorry, I'm not feeling terribly creative lately."

"Poor Jean. Something I can do to help?" He kissed the back of my neck.

"Yeah, rout out Danny Kellam's medical records and make those doctors cooperate."

"Whoa. Tall order. I thought Lacy found a doc who admitted it was the DPT."

"She did, but since then he's talked to his lawyer."

"Damn lawyers screw up everything." Peter laughed and grabbed my briefcase. "Can a boy carry your books, miss? Would that make you feel better?"

I cut off the lights and locked the door. Slipping my arm into his, we started up the street. "What I don't understand is why there's so much willingness on the part of the doctors to protect the manufacturers. Everyone admits the vaccine has a percentage rate of side effects that includes seizures. Seizures cause brain damage. They've codified it into the compensation fund, for God's sake. Why don't they want to help Lacy? How can it hurt them?"

"They can't be proud of what they did. Admitting a mistake isn't easy."

"They didn't really make a mistake. The vaccine has saved lives. They just covered up what happened, which makes it look like they were lying."

Several people we passed looked up from their conversations. Peter whispered, "Lower your voice. They'll think we're headed for divorce."

"They probably already think that since I'm never home."

"If you wanted to be home, you would be."

I pulled my arm free. "Is that what you think?"

"What else can I think? When you are home, you're still working. You've missed a zillion events in the last twelve months. The kids say you never return their messages."

"That's not fair. I'm in court when they call."

"Jean."

We walked along without talking. At the bottom of the drive I stopped and caught my breath. "I'm really sorry. This isn't the life I would've chosen."

"Us, you mean?"

"No, working this way. I never expected to work like this. I'd much rather be doing things with the kids, but there's always a new crisis, a client with an emergency. It's one long emergency." I wiped at the tears. The gravel on the lane made walking in the dark tricky.

"Shut the office down. Give the cases away. We don't need the money."

"There's no one in town who'll take the time to do it right. Lawyers hate doing divorces. And what do I tell Lacy? She's counting on me. Everyone in her whole life has let her down. Except Moss. She can't do this by herself. Fine's an ogre. He eats people."

"Whatever," he said and marched ahead.

Because lack of medical records continued to plague us, I knew I would have to move forward on the training center angle. On one of the new client data sheets I'd made Lacy complete back in the spring, I found Scott Kellam's telephone number. Jillian was at lunch. On the front door she'd hung the 'Closed Until Two' sign. I dialed and held my breath.

"Hello?" A woman answered. Her voice sounded old and worn. "I'm on the phone," she said to someone close by.

After I introduced myself and asked for Scott Kellam, she interrupted me. "He's not here. Give me the number and he'll call you back."

I didn't hold out much hope. Lacy had warned me that he wouldn't be forthcoming. When she had refused to call him herself, she'd tried to make me promise I wouldn't.

Early on in the fact-gathering stage, she made her case. "He won't remember any of it. He was hardly there. Except for driving me to Narden that one time to deliver Danny, I don't think he's ever been back to the state hospital." If half of what Lacy'd told me about Scott's behavior after the seizures were true, her resentment was deserved.

The problem was he knew too much. And from his disappearance back then, it was guaranteed he didn't have the emotional bias Lacy did. Although I understood her feelings, I hoped to be able to flatter him into talking about his work, clearly the only steady thing in his life, and from there to the two years he had in common with Danny.

For the lawsuit I needed a signed release from Scott as the other natural parent. I had prepared the papers to appoint Lacy as Danny's legal guardian over his person and his property. They were ready to file except that Scott had to consent to her appointment and waive his legal interest in possible recovery. I'd been delaying that chore, but the training center protocol forced the issue.

"When do you expect him?" I asked. The voice in the background, male, talked rapidly and increasingly loudly. The woman said something I didn't catch and then the male voice spoke into the phone.

"This is Scott Kellam."

"Jean Driscoll. You actually know me, Mr. Kellam. I'm the lawyer who handled the no-fault divorce between you and Lacy about ten years ago." I waited for him to make the connection.

"Don't tell me we're not divorced?"

"Oh, no. This has nothing to do with that. Lacy's trying to get Danny's legal situation straight and she needs to be the official guardian of his person and his property."

"He doesn't have any property."

"Not now, but that may change."

"Her family win the lottery or something?"

"Actually I'm handling a lawsuit to pay for his medical care. It involves a medication he was given that may have caused the injuries he suffered in 1969."

"God, she's still trying to save him."

"That's not it exactly."

"She could sue the whole United States government and he'd still be retarded. What's the point?"

"I'd like to send you some papers that say you have no objection to her acting as his guardian in legal matters. It would also give us permission to look at the state's files. Could you do that?"

"Hell, he's always been her baby. Send away."

"I need a current address."

He gave me the address. "This isn't a trick to stick me for child support, is it?"

"No, no trick. But because you're his natural father, you'll also have to waive any interest in anything we recover for Danny."

"I don't want anything from Lacy. She knows that. Is that all?"

"Actually, no. I wondered if you might have any of the letters or medical records from back then."

"What in the hell would I've saved those for? She dealt with all those people. I was working. Someone had to work. Sick kid, crazy wife. No, I didn't save that stuff."

The woman's voice asked him a question. "Hang on," he said. They talked heatedly. I could hear him cutting her off more than once. Finally she was silent. He retrieved the receiver. "I have to go to work."

"Sorry to keep you. Just one more question." I took his grunt for a yes. "If we get to court, it'll be in Washington. You remember how wrapped up Lacy was back then in caring for your son."

"That's a more polite way to say it than I would."

"I might need you to testify about that." I didn't give him a chance to say no. I just thanked him and hung up. Fair warning, I thought.

Not only had Lacy brought about the first major breakthrough by confronting Doctor McIntosh, but she returned from Northern Virginia with a present for me—a boxful of ancient medical records from his pediatric practice. When Stith retired, the younger doctors stored the old files in the basement on pine boards separated with cinder blocks. Unfortunately they'd had two floods in the intervening years. Lacy said the room was a mess, but she talked one of the nurses into letting her scrounge around. She didn't tell me how.

After a few mildew-choked hours, she located a warped box labeled 1969-70. Inside she found Danny's footprint from the hospital among a handful of pages with his name typed in the corner. The handwritten notes about him were initialed by A.D.S., M.D. Birth records showed a routine delivery, healthy baby. The date of the first DPT shot was recorded on the last page: June 30, 1969. The last entry read, "Referred."

"They're still practicing in the same little house with the blue shutters," Lacy said, dumping the box on my desk. "Except Doctor McIntosh is semi-retired and Stith is dead."

"That's not good," I said.

"I knew you'd say that. Why do we need him if we have these?"

I tried to think how to explain trial procedure without spoiling her sense of accomplishment. "They're a great start, Lacy."

"But?"

"But you know the old proverb, a picture is worth a thousand words?"

"Sure."

"A live witness is like a picture. Stith's notes can be introduced as long as someone in his office identifies them as records kept in the ordinary course of their business, but it would be much more powerful to have the doctor himself who stood by you while Danny was attached to those monitors."

"But I can tell all about the time in the hospital."

I ignored her comment. "A live doctor would give us the ability to defend against claims by the government."

"What kind of claims?"

"That there are other explanations for what happened."

"That's ridiculous. You said yourself the shot within 72 hours is enough all by itself."

"No, what I said was, 'From the way the statute reads, it sounds like that's what you have to prove.'"

"So what other claims can they make?"

"Pre-existing condition, intervening event, improper treatment."

"Is that all?" She laughed, but she didn't look like she thought it was funny.

"That's what comes to mind quickly. All things Dr. Stith could refute if he were alive and able to testify."

"There were other doctors."

"I know. But first we have to convince them to talk."

At five I took the box home, part of my new resolution to be more accessible to my family. Stephen was scrambling eggs in the kitchen.

"Little late for breakfast," I said, stashing the box around the corner in the dining room. A recollection of stoned college friends eating everything in sight flashed into my mind. I felt sick to my stomach.

Stephen slathered the toast with apple butter. "I felt like eggs."

"Funny," I said, "You don't look like—"

"Don't do that, Mom. That's Dad's line."

As I poured myself a glass of tonic and squeezed a lime into it, I noticed my hand shaking. The distance between us loomed larger. The stakes too high for this kind of hit or miss contact.

"Homework done?"

"I'm glad to see you too."

"I was just trying to get a feel for tonight's schedule."

"I'm seventeen, Mom. I don't need you to remind me about my homework."

Scooping the eggs onto the spatula, he pivoted on one foot. Before the spatula reached the empty plate yellow goop dribbled along the floor and the counter.

"Stephen."

"It's food, not paint."

I left the room, my temper barely under control. The book I'd found at the library about teenagers and drugs said we were supposed to let him make as many of the lesser decisions as possible. Eating should have been safe.

Elly was curled up on her bed, reading.

"Hi," I said.

She nodded and kept on reading. When I didn't move on, she spoke, her head still buried, "Hi, Mom."

From behind Andrew's door vibrations emanated that rattled the doorknob and the hinges. He insisted that he worked better with music, that it drowned out the other noises. Exactly what other noises, I wasn't sure. Before I even opened the door I felt pulverized.

"Turn it down, bud. You'll be deaf before you're twenty."

From the far side of his bed he popped up off the floor and frowned. "You're home early."

"Doing something you shouldn't be?"

"You always do that to me."

"Do what?"

"You know."

"I was only asking what you were up to."

He snorted and turned back. When I walked in far enough to see where he was sitting, an open textbook was spread on top of a notebook.

When Peter arrived, I was in our bedroom sorting papers furiously from Lacy's box: birth, pre-DPT shot, doctor's visits post-July 1969, and correspondence. Pediatrician Stith had written and received a lot of letters about Danny from a lot of people. The box was almost emptied.

"Tornado?" Peter asked.

"I thought I'd make everyone happy and come home early," I said through gritted teeth.

"Oh," he said in a small voice. He disappeared into the closet and reappeared without his shirt. Eyeing the bed covered with paper piles, he walked to the armchair and sat and removed his shoes one at a time. After I finished dividing, I bundled the categories together with metal spring loaded clips and dropped them back into the box.

With the post-July 1969 pile in hand, I sat down and started to read.

"What do you want to do for dinner?" he asked.

"Stephen just fed himself and the other kids are busy. I thought I'd read a bit, then go throw a salad together."

"Just salad, Jean? They're growing."

"I can't think right now. I'm sure there's barbecue or chili in the freezer. I'll do that. Give me ten minutes."

Copies of Stith's records, such as they were, went to Hamilton Fine by overnight courier. Months before he'd sent us a terse letter outlining the services he'd provide for his fee. When I warned Lacy that one-third of the recovery was the usual fee, she said she didn't care about the money. Fine agreed to split that with me, two-thirds for him. I'd modified the written agreement to include the usual fee reduction if the claim was settled before trial, and to set out that costs came off the top before the fee was calculated.

Although Cliff Marbury confirmed on the phone that it was the industry standard, it surprised me when Fine returned the agreement without signing. He'd been out when I called to find out why and I couldn't sleep at all that night. When I finally reached him two days later, he was more brusque than usual.

"Miss Driscoll," he started as if I were the old maiden aunt who needed a lecture in real life skills, "You forgot to include the hospital admission records."

"I don't have them."

"You expect me to try a case that depends on the timing of the reaction without independent proof of the time it occurred?"

"Stith's records show the date of the vaccination. The letters between the doctors show the date of Danny's admission. Lacy can testify to everything else. She says they drove to the ER right after breakfast."

"What about the permanent diagnosis?"

"No one issued one as far as I can tell."

"Someone must have. Whoever authorized his placement with the State."

"Those records have been requested."

"Half-assed way to prepare for trial."

"I thought you needed the expert's opinion first before you decided whether you would try it?"

He paused long enough for me to know I'd gotten to him. "Send me the other records as soon as you have them."

I was listening to the dial tone.

When I saw Lacy next at the grocery store, I told her I was planning the trip to see Danny. "What days are you off?" I asked.

"Why?"

"I'd like you to go with me, show me around."

"I . . . they're short-handed here. I can't go."

"Oh, come on. One day. They'll understand." I headed for the manager's office.

"No," she said emphatically.

"Okay, you ask him when it suits you. I just thought one day might be better than another. Let me know. I have a couple of open days each week between now and Thanksgiving."

She looked relieved.

When a week passed without a call or visit, I tried her again on the phone.

"Thought I'd go to Narden next Thursday. The judge here is at a conference. No court."

"I'm substituting on the bus route that day."

"Is Friday better?"

"No, I can't do it that day."

"They said any day next week. You pick."

"I can't go. I mean, at all."

Normally she'd have talked a blue streak about why and how she'd come to her decision. The silence made a bigger impression.

"Never mind," I said, "The nurses can give me the tour. Probably better anyway for me to pump them for information so we see who knows what. Better for picking witnesses."

"I'm letting you down. I'm sorry."

"No, no, it's okay. Really." Avoidance was a parenting skill I understood.

After dinner the night before I was to meet Danny and his nurses at Narden I passed Elly's room. The top panel of her door was newly decorated with a collage of photographs and slogans cut out of magazine pages. The colors were great and the attitude—girls can do it all—had been a favorite of mine growing up. When I stopped to read more, she hopped up from her desk.

"It won't hurt anything. It's Elmer's Glue. I can wash it off."

"I wasn't going to tell you to take it down."

She shrugged as if she wasn't sure she believed me. I tried to remember the last time I'd been in to hug her goodnight. Twelve was too early to grow out of that stage. Peter was right. I'd missed a lot of evenings this year.

"So what's on your schedule for tomorrow, El?"

"Tennis practice and dance." Then she added, for the benefit of her absentee mother, "At seven-thirty."

I couldn't recall if it was ballet class or jazz but I wasn't going to ask and let her know I'd forgotten. I'd look it up on the bulletin board downstairs. An awkward pause hung in the air.

"What are you doing tomorrow?" she finally asked.

"I'm going to see the little boy I told you about with all the problems. What do you think I should take him?"

"He's like a baby?"

"Uh-huh—except big."

"A Disney movie?"

"That's a great idea. His mom says he likes music."

"Why does he need a lawyer?"

"He doesn't really, his mom does. When people aren't able to do things for themselves, their parents or people like parents called guardians have to take care of their business."

"How did he get like that?"

"He was hurt by some medicine he had as a baby and his mother wants the company that made the medicine to admit they caused his injury."

"Is she that goofy lady who always talks to you in the grocery store line?"

"Yup."

"Dad says she's crazy."

It took an effort not to raise my voice, but it wasn't Elly's fault, I told myself. "He's just teasing, sweetie. He hardly knows her."

"She loves everyone. That's crazy, isn't it?"

The day I scheduled the trip to the state facility Andrew had his soccer championships.

"Reschedule," Peter said while we lay in bed after the alarm rang, listening to the sounds of the kids in their usual bathroom to bedroom shuffle. "What if he loses in the first round and you miss his only game?"

"He won't lose. The team's too good. I have to go to Narden. The administrator made a special request to have the old records located and they're cluttering up his office."

"You could've checked the game schedule first."

"The championships are never listed ahead of time. They don't know which teams are where."

"When they bury you, do you think Lacy Stonington will be there?"

I gave him my most withering look. "The kids understand that sometimes work takes precedence. Andrew even said he's probably not starting."

"Oh, good, he's already under-confident and his mother's more concerned about someone else's child."

"It's my job."

"It's not your job. You're a divorce attorney. You're play-acting at being Lacy's savior. Don't ask me why."

"You're being irrational."

"I'm being irrational? That's a joke. You can't fix her son. Somehow she's convinced you to tilt at windmills with her. It's absurd. Those doctors aren't going to jeopardize their livelihood for a woman they barely remember. What happened to your legal training? The case is a loser."

Fumbling with the last few things for my briefcase, I struggled for a way to convince him that he was wrong, but I wasn't sure he was. "Tell Andrew I'll be there for the semi-finals."

The drive to the state training center where Danny lived wound through mostly open fields and timbered hillsides. Each little town sported a convenience store, a gas station, and an old schoolhouse with two main doors, one for boys and one for girls. Most of the white clapboard schoolhouses stood wide-eyed, abandoned, replaced by modern brick buildings with flashing pedestrian lights and 'State Softball Champ' signs. In my briefcase I had a copy of the 1971 introduction letter from the Fairfax Social Services worker.

As I drove in, remembering Lacy's recitation of the events of February 16, 1971, I tried to imagine myself fifteen years ago, giving up a two-year-old Stephen to strangers. To lose that evening hour rocking him to sleep, the midnight peek to see if he was covered, the morning squeaks and smiles; it must have been devastating for Lacy who had no idea what was wrong with her son.

While I could see Peter's point about my sympathy for her extending beyond my usual interest in clients, I couldn't understand why he was pushing so hard for me to withdraw at this point. We had no trial date. I hadn't committed anything to witnesses. Fine was in the mix and the expert had the medical records, such as they were.

Stephen was cooperating with our new house rules and his grades were no longer dropping. Although he admitted some of the kids he knew had tried marijuana, he swore he hadn't. I had wanted to know if there were other drugs around school, but he had shaken his head and walked away. After several long sessions, tears on all sides, he promised to work harder on his schoolwork. Peter and I, scurrying for cover from the bombshell, decided we'd give him the benefit of the doubt.

Thinking that was resolved and we were back on course, I was puzzled by Peter's refusal to even try to understand how I felt about Lacy. I wondered if there was something else bugging him, something he hadn't told me.

The State residential hospital perched on a plateau over the city. The trees were tall and full, the lawns green and wide, and the buildings adorned in nineteen-fifties' international style. No fancy landscaping and not many signs to direct me through the maze of cracked pavement and weedy sidewalks. There were no people outside. After I signed in with the receptionist, I was handed a visitor's pass to attach to my blazer. They gave me directions to drive to Building Thirty, but I walked instead, trying to form a more accurate picture of how it would have looked and felt in

1971. This would have been the way Lacy walked that February with two year-old Danny in her arms. I passed no one.

Inside the glass doors of Building Thirty I showed my pass and, when they asked, my driver's license. They buzzed me in. "Someone to see Danny Kellam," the PA crackled, showing its age.

The heavy double doors at my back, I stood in a room that felt empty, though it was scattered with wheelchairs. The linoleum floor, gray with random specs of a darker gray, stretched out like mudflats in the early morning rain. Without the windows the room would have been dark. Less than half of the fluorescent light fixtures worked. Some were shuddering in their final moments.

In each chair was a person, half child, half man, some stubbled, most drooling, all twisted in one way or another. They wore nondescript clothes, clean and hardly worn, but somehow ill fitting or awkward because of their crooked limbs. The windows began chest high so that the only view was the cloudless sky beyond the bars. It was the sky that saved me from immediate depression. This was a place where the passage of time was the sole accomplishment that mattered.

A low and constant babble continued, interspersed with clipped efficient tones from uniformed assistants.

"Time for your bath, Sam."

"Ms. Barclay wants to check your vitals, sweetheart."

"We need to start down to music therapy."

I tried to decide which patient looked like Lacy. Across the linoleum a stout woman with her hair under a kerchief strode toward me.

"Ms. Driscoll?" She was carrying an oversized terrycloth bib.

"You must be Jenny," I shook her hand. "Lacy's told me so much about you. The good mother, she calls you."

"I don' know 'bout that."

"She appreciates what good care you take of Danny. She says you've been with him since the beginning."

"Tha's right, tha's me. But she love him too. Best she can."

"She's told you about our project?"

Jenny looked over her shoulder at a wheelchair facing the north window. It had to be Danny, but his head was lower than the blue vinyl chair back so it looked empty.

Another uniformed woman rolled by with a patient, nudging Jenny's elbow as she passed. "Taking Danny down to music today?"

"Hey, Joann," Jenny answered quietly. Nodding, she leaned closer to Joann's patient. "Good morning, Jeremy, you got on my favorite shirt again. I like that blue."

A squeal pealed out of the boy in the chair. His hands whacked the padded arms repeatedly.

"All right, kiddo. Hold on, hold on," Joann said, "we're not in the music room yet."

Jenny was watching me fumble with my pen and pad. "They all like music. Danny especially."

"Is it time for him to go down too?" I asked.

She shrugged. "But I know you drove a long way to see him."

"Well, yes, but I want to talk to you also, so if this isn't a good time, I can come back in a little while. They have all kinds of papers for me to read over at the main building."

"The session's an hour. We be back here for lunch about 11:40."

"Great," I said, but she was already across the room, swinging the wheelchair by the window back toward the double doors. Her head was down by his and as they passed I heard her low murmurs and a series of guttural grunts in reply. The top of his head was all I saw. Thick black hair, just like Lacy's.

Over at the administrator's office, the files for Daniel Boyd Kellam filled four cardboard boxes. Jenny's name appeared often. In the earliest daily notes he was not quite two years old. He needed to be carried, fed, and bathed like an infant. He responded to his name and to music. Non-verbally.

The admitting physician had written in neat, tiny script:

"2/26/71 Diagnosis on admission: Severe mental retardation secondary to encephalopathy due to post-natal injury, microcephaly and convulsive disorder. Encephalopathy due to unknown cause."

I don't know why I had expected anything else.

Chapter Sixteen
JEAN

"What the hell is this?" Fine demanded early one morning on the phone the next week. Papers rustled through the receiver. With Jillian at my elbow I stood by her desk, wondering if the waiting client could hear him from the sofa.

"I don't know what you're talking about," I said as politely as I could. "I'm here and you're there. Are you referring to something in the mail?"

"You know damn well it came in the mail. They carbon copied you."

"They, who?"

"The Court of Claims."

"Do you want to tell me what it is or do you want to wait while I open my mail and look for it?"

"It's a goddamned dismissal for lack of medical evidence."

If I were a different kind of person, I might have been able to quip back, 'That sounds serious.' Instead I choked on some dust particle and ended up giving the phone to Jillian to take a message. From my office I could hear her trying to calm him down.

With the unopened mail in hand I shut my office door and searched for the one with the Court of Claims on the return address. My stomach was churning. Dismissal is a word that sends shivers up the spine of the most capable trial attorneys. To be out of court before you started, that was the most ignominious error you could make.

The envelope contained a single page. The heading for the case, 'In Re: Daniel Boyd Kellam' was printed very officially at the top. It was headed simply 'Order,' not Final Order or Order of Dismissal.

"Thank God," I said to the walls, praying the omitted language was significant. I forced myself to keep reading. Because I had been worried about the filing deadline for vaccinations administered before the Act's inception, in early October I had filed a simple Petition over Lacy's signature and attached Lacy's handwritten summary of the events. Fine hadn't been involved. And busy hunting down records for his expert, I had neglected to tell him.

When nothing else followed, the Court must have considered what they had—her summary with my letter—and dismissed it as not meeting the statutory requirements. I had planned to supplement when we found the doctors' records. I simply hadn't realized they would dismiss without giving us time to do that, particularly when I had filed a later notice, listing Fine as lead counsel.

Begging him now to work some magic would be bad enough since the initial filing wasn't done with his blessing. But if it were irreversible, explaining it to Lacy would be nearly impossible. I could almost hear her chipper little voice saying the money wasn't important now that she knew what had made Danny sick. I sat for a long time composing mental motions to reopen. The sick feeling lingered in my stomach.

In response to Jillian's two page message from Fine, I dictated a short letter, explaining the misunderstanding and asking the Clerk of the Court to let me know whether I needed to speak to the

Special Master in person about re-opening the case or setting aside the order. Although it was embarrassing to have the judge know I'd made a mistake, it was twice as bad that Fine knew. Gritting my teeth, I copied him as counsel of record. I would have to put my name on the pleadings or they wouldn't even consider my request. Later I'd figure out how to justify it to Peter.

All morning I expected another call from Fine or a scathing fax about the ineptitude of rural attorneys. When nothing came, at lunchtime I faxed the letter to the Clerk personally with a note that I'd follow up with a telephone call to see what should be done. Think positively, I told myself. I mailed the original and Fine's copy, assuming a few days for cooling down might help.

On the way to the coffee shop for a quick salad, I met Moss. He had a motorcycle helmet under his arm. In the bright October sunshine his shadow lay in a long stripe behind him like a cartoon Abraham Lincoln. The wind whipped between us and my jacket blew open.

"Winter's coming," he said.

"Surprises me every year. It's these Indian summers that Virginia dishes up like ice cream sundaes to tempt you. You think you're in paradise until that cold rain starts in November."

Behind the mustache I saw the edge of a smile. "Did Lacy tell you our news?" he said.

"News?" With dread I stopped walking. Lacy's Diana could be pregnant or her Carson could have been drafted. I realized it had been more than a week since I'd been to the Training Center, and I hadn't called to tell her how it had gone.

"We're moving."

"Away from Parry's Crossing?" I shifted the law journals I'd brought to read during lunch to my other hip.

"Henryville," he said, grinning as if he'd won the Lottery.

"That's in Virginia?"

"Ayah." Which didn't tell me anything.

"And why have you decided just now to move away?" I guessed from the grin that it wasn't Lacy's decision.

"It's more about moving there. I found a piece of land I like."

"You know people down there?"

Shaking his head, he put on the helmet. "I'm sure Lacy'll tell you all about it next time she sees you." He dropped the bike and eased it out of the parking space.

Maybe Lacy already knew they'd dismissed her case.

In the state hospital records there were nineteen certificates of recognition for Danny's successful completion of the goals recited in his annual IEP (Individual Education Plan), one for each year he'd spent in the state hospital. He could use his thumb in opposition for a palmar grasp of small objects: a rattle, a tennis ball, a crayon. He turned his head to a sound source. He recognized his name. He could sip from a straw. On May 4, 1977, after five years of 'training,' the social worker wrote, 'He now laughs.' He was eight.

Because the state rules prohibited photocopying records, I took notes, almost a pad full of medical scribbles describing Danny's days and their attempts to train him. Re-reading them weeks later, the entries still jarred me.

When Danny turned ten, they recommended toilet training. They gave it up four years later. Four years? There were a series of encouraging monthly entries from the music teacher, but in 1986 seventeen year-old Danny was downgraded from Music Education to Music Therapy, diagnosed as unteachable. In September 1989 they noted that his child-size wheelchair was too small and he needed an adult size. He was twenty years old and weighed 81 pounds.

Once Jillian typed my notes, we sent them to Fine, and he filed the official subpoena through the federal court for certified copies of the state records. It was the only way we would be allowed copies without both parents' signatures. Scott Kellam had not returned my paperwork, though I was still hoping. I had not yet told Lacy anything about my conversation with him.

In the meantime Fine filed papers regularly with the court. He filed affidavits explaining what had been done, without success, to obtain the birth records and the 1969 hospitalization records. He filed an amended petition, which, linked with my September 1990 filing under Lacy's name, saved the tolling of the statute and reopened the case for further evidence. He filed a brief in support of the motion to reopen, which he edited after I had written it at his insistence.

I could find no fault with his professional actions, but his bedside manner was outrageous. Even the worst divorce clients I'd handled had not been subjected to the kind of abrupt and continuous belittling he showered on me, and Lacy by inference. With Peter's attitude about the whole thing, I had no one to sound off to, and that feeling of being alone made me more than a little tense.

In Fine's spare time he lined up the doctor in Boston who would be Danny's medical expert. Dr. Gainesboro had testified in Fine's other vaccine injury cases. After the doctor read Lacy's handwritten summary of the events surrounding the first shot and the seizures, he sent a preliminary letter to Fine agreeing to review Danny's medical history. A separate page outlined his fees; separate entries for review of records, opinion, written report, court appearance. Fine made me sign it along with Lacy and Moss.

She called one day from Henryville to tell me she loved me. "What do you think about this new doctor?"

"He's Fine's first choice."

"What about you?"

"Doctor Gainesboro's one of the most sought after experts in this field. He knows what we need to win."

"Fine wouldn't use him if he didn't. I bet Finey baby hates to lose."

"Listen, you two need to meet. I know he's gruff, but he's tried several of these cases, won them all. Plus tons more personal injury cases. Everyone I've talked to says he's the guy."

"Whatever you tell me to do, I'll do."

"No, you have to do what Fine says. He's lead trial counsel. That's why it's time for you to talk with him."

"I'm right here waiting. He's got my address."

"He's not going to drive all the way down here."

"Good, I don't like him anyway."

"You're making this hard."

"He scares me. He's always angry."

I didn't know what to say.

"You go meet him first," she said. "Ooops, there's Moss and the rice water is boiling over. I love you."

In Lacy's file there were three letters from me suggesting Fine come to my office, promising to have our mutual client available for a conference. Without complete medical records he'd been putting off the meeting legitimately. Eventually, though, they would have to talk face to face. The fireworks would be something else.

Two months before trial all the medical records that existed had been received and forwarded. In early September, a year and five months after Lacy's first visit to my office, Fine called me before forwarding a copy of Dr. Gainesboro's report. I was out and he left a message.

"Doc wrote, sent exactly what we needed. I've filed for trial date. Get your client down here in the next two weeks."

No name, no request for my available dates to be sure a trial date didn't conflict with my schedule, no please and thank you. Typical Fine.

Once I'd arranged a time with his secretary I called Lacy.

"Guess what? The time has come. Can Moss bring you up here to my office on Friday? I'll drive you to Hampton."

"You'd do that for me?"

At three on Thursday I had a conference with a man whose son was threatening to run away if he couldn't go and live with his mother. My client believed the mother's boyfriend might be abusive to his son. It took me almost an hour to convince the dad, with no hard evidence of abuse, that he should compromise and let the fourteen-year old go for the summer. A trial period might change the boy's mind, and it would be better than filing a missing person's report.

With kids in crisis all choices are hard choices. No solution is ideal. I almost told him about Lacy, her decision to give up the son she loved because she couldn't give him what he needed. No one warns you about those hard choices.

When I emerged with the father of the teenager, Andrew was in the waiting room. His book bag sat on the floor, the straps curled around his feet like a policeman's ankle cuffs. He looked as miserable as a prisoner might. Along his forehead and collar, the hair clung to his skin, tan still from a summer of camp and mowing grass. He waited, buried in a magazine, while I shook hands with my client and traded good-byes.

Convinced Andrew must have blown a test at school and wanted to enlist my help with Peter, I sat next to him on the faded lumpy sofa, the first furniture purchase Peter and I had made as a couple. Andrew flipped the pages of *Newsweek*.

"He wouldn't let me interrupt you," Jillian said.

"That's okay, he was being polite. Did you want to run the mail up the street, Jill? I can lock up."

Andrew kept his eyes in the magazine until she had gone.

"So, bud, what can I do for you?" I asked.

He didn't answer right away. I glanced over at the page he was reading, his appearance here out of the ordinary.

"Are you gonna be late tonight?" he asked.

"No, I'm pretty much done now. Did you come to walk me home?"

"I can."

"Everything okay at school? The play rehearsal's going okay?"

"Yeah." He peered at the open magazine page.

"Is this for an assignment?"

"Nah, I was just looking. Dad says this magazine is liberal, but I don't see much difference from the other ones."

"I don't read all the magazines here. In fact I usually don't have time for any of them. They're for my clients. Part of the waiting room experience." I couldn't see where he was headed.

"Your clients read this political stuff?"

"Actually no, they're a pretty conservative bunch. This is the country, lots of farmers."

"So why did you pick these magazines?"

"It's kind of standard lawyer's office fare."

"To make people think you're smart." It was perceptive for a thirteen year-old.

I knocked my shoulder against his. “Can’t fool you. Adults are silly sometimes, aren’t they?”

He nodded, but without enthusiasm, as if it pained him too to admit it. “The sports pictures are good, though.” He closed the magazine and smoothed the cover the same way I did when I’d read something thought-provoking. A jolt of satisfaction shot through me. My son, my genes going into the future. In spite of his honest analysis I still felt he admired what I did for a living. Would he emulate me someday and go to law school, filled with dreams of righting old wrongs and saving people as I had when I sat in that first law school classroom, eager for my turn at the Socratic dialogue of student and professor?

Down the street I could see the same group of teenagers that passed by every night after five. They clumped together and moved slowly, talking a blue streak it appeared. Hopefully saving the world, probably denouncing some girl.

“Do you know where Stephen is?” Andrew blurted into what I had been considering a companionable silence.

“Sweetie, I have no idea. You didn’t come here and wait all this time to ask me that, did you? It should be marked on the calendar in the kitchen at home.”

Andrew’s eyebrows made a dark mark of frustration on his serious face.

I thought harder. “I guess he’s at orchestra practice.”

“No, I mean . . . you should know.” Deliberately he laid the magazine back on the coffee table.

“Did Dad put you up to this?”

“No. I . . . Don’t tell Dad.”

“Don’t tell Dad what?”

“Where Stephen is.”

“Is he somewhere he shouldn’t be?”

Andrew nodded, his face turned away from mine.

"This game isn't funny."

"No, Mom, really. He hangs around the old depot, and there are some kids there who are . . . they aren't . . . they're smoking."

"Cigarettes?"

He stood up and grabbed his book bag, telling me more than if he'd voiced an outright no. Reaching out, I took his arm, but he tugged it away.

"I'm going home," he mumbled.

The door swung shut behind him, clicking officially into place and separating us more distinctly still. Through the wide panes of the reception room window I watched him on the street. Hunched over, he bypassed the clump of teenagers and marched to the top of the hill and out of sight. I yanked the curtains shut, closing out the voices and the occasional car churning up the street. Poor kid, he'd been forced to commit the worst sin of childhood, to squeal on his brother. I hadn't meant to drag Andrew into the controversy, but he clearly felt some responsibility. Maybe because I'd asked him about Stephen earlier.

If I'd been braver, I would have streamed after him and reassured him. But I needed time to consider. That's what lawyers do, isn't it?

The next morning Moss brought Lacy early. They were in the waiting room, having traveled the night before and stayed with her sister, when the phone rang. I answered it in my office. It was early yet, no Jillian.

"Sorry to interrupt, Mrs. Driscoll," It was the Town Police Chief. "We have your son Stephen here at the station."

"The station? Is he hurt?"

"No, ma'am. He's under arrest. But since he's a juvenile, he can be released to a parent."

"Arrest?" I could hardly speak, but I managed to get up and shut the door.

"I'd rather explain it here than over the phone. Three boys, but the other two got away. All truant—"

"Can I speak with him?"

They put Stephen on the phone.

"They won't let me out unless you come down and sign for me."

"I'm inclined to let you sit there for a while. What the hell were you thinking skipping school?"

"They said I'd have to go to Juvenile Hall if you didn't come."

The police must be trying to scare him. I'd never heard of anyone being sent to Juvenile Hall for playing hooky. "Chief Hollowell says there were three of you. Who were the other kids?"

He mumbled. The names didn't include Brian.

"Smoking buddies?" I asked. I could hear the sharp inhalation at the other end.

His voice shrunk to almost inaudible. "Never mind then."

"You haven't left me much choice."

When I came out of my office, it must have been obvious I was upset. Lacy winked. "You don't want to go and see that snotty king of the hill either, do you?" she asked.

"Do I look that bad?"

"Pretty bad. But Mosste can drive us. Just like a chauffeur. We'll sit in the back and pretend we're famous. I brought homemade zucchini bread. That'll make you feel better."

Despite my horror of whatever waited for me with Stephen, the incongruity of Lacy's mood helped. I hugged her. "I'm sorry. I can't go after all. My oldest son is in some unexpected trouble."

Lacy kept her hand on my arm, but she didn't ask. I sped past the awkward moment. "Try to make Fine laugh. If you stick to the facts and don't go off on a tangent, you'll be fine."

"Fine, hah. I don't even know what a tangent is." She hugged me again, whispering in my ear. "Your son is more important."

At the tiny two room headquarters for the town police, Stephen sat in one of three folding chairs in the hallway. No deputy stood guard but a security camera whirred from one corner of the ceiling. I didn't greet him, but marched into the Chief's office and motioned for Stephen to follow me.

Although Peter and Chief Hollowell had played recreation league basketball together before we had children, he wasn't smiling. "I've been over the charges with your son. They're misdemeanor charges. No priors. He can be released into your custody. I'll get the bond paperwork ready while you two talk."

Without meeting my eyes, Stephen stood as close to the door as he could. How does it happen that the baby you rocked in your arms can grow so distant you don't dare reach out and touch him?

"More than just truancy?" I asked.

He handed me papers that had been balled up in his fist. I smoothed them out and read silently.

"God damn it, Stephen. You lied to us. No matter what you've heard from your West Coast friends, marijuana is dangerous. And illegal." I stepped closer and looked into his face, but he wasn't conceding anything. "As hard as your father and I work to give you the opportunities you have, and you have to act like some street punk. I left a waiting room full of clients."

"Go back to your stupid clients."

"Those clients pay our bills."

He moved along the wall, keeping his distance from me where I stalked back and forth in anger.

"This is a mess, I can't even think. We'll have to sort this out at home."

"I don't want to go home."

"You've changed your mind about detention?"

"I don't want to listen to you ranting and raving about how I'm always making mistakes, can't study right, have the wrong friends, don't help enough." He was crying but trying to hide it. All of a sudden he was a little boy again, struggling with a box twice his size.

Chief Hollowell knocked. "Safe to come in?" He touched Stephen's shoulder and spoke quietly. "Your mother's in shock. Don't forget you've known all along what you've been doing, but this is the first she's heard of it."

But he was wrong.

Chapter Seventeen
JEAN

I telephoned Peter from home. When I heard his voice though, I froze, unable to think where to begin.

"Hello?" he repeated, "Is someone there?"

"It's me," I barely managed to say.

"Jean. Are you okay? Where are you?"

"Home." I could imagine him twisting his wrist to expose the watch, registering that it was too early, unease creeping in when he realized something must be wrong.

"What's the matter?"

"Stephen was arrested this morning."

"That's not funny."

"It's not a joke."

"Where is he?"

"In his room."

"I'll be right there."

With a sandwich and chips on a tray, I went up to Stephen's room. He sat at his desk, a textbook open in front of him. The waiting must have been killing him.

"Did you want to tell me about it?"

"I wasn't ready for the history test."

"Pretty weak excuse. And it doesn't fit with the rest of the facts."

"Mom, don't talk like a lawyer."

"Your father is going to be so disappointed."

"What's new?"

"Stephen. He doesn't deserve that. I'm worried about these supposed friends. Do you think they care about you? They ran off. Didn't even stand by you when you got caught."

"I would've done the same thing."

"Well, that's another disappointment, but I'm not so sure that's true."

With his index finger he rubbed his eye, bending over as if there were something in it.

"We were just trying it."

"It's illegal. You don't get to make that decision."

"I don't get to make any decisions." His voice rose and he kicked the desk leg as he talked. "Anyway, what do you care? You care more about your clients than anything else. Dad says you're standing in for Don Quixote."

He might have taken my silence for agreement, but I didn't have an answer for him. The hardest thing about being a parent is letting your child make decisions that have dangerous consequences. And if he doubted me that much, we had bigger problems. I didn't know what to say.

"Dad and I will talk this over. In the meantime you need to study. Hard. Tomorrow morning we'll call the teacher. They may not let you take a make-up test, but you need to be ready. And no phone calls. That's the end of these guys."

"They're my friends."

"Time for new friends."

Worried about Stephen, I drove mentally with Peter down Route 15, across the river, past the elementary school where all three children had gone, over the railroad tracks, and through the cattle field. The blackened pine woods passed, as they do in a car, in a blur of perfume and mystery. Fence rails strung along in front of yellow and green fields like interference on a television screen. The familiar can so easily become something foreign.

While I waited, I called Fine's office to be sure Lacy had arrived.

"I can't disturb him right now," his receptionist said. "He's in with a client."

"I know. She's my client too. If you would just confirm that it's Mrs. Stonington and they aren't killing each other, I can go on about my business."

"That's confidential."

"Not if I'm part of the attorney-client relationship."

She spouted off some windy explanation that sounded like Fine had printed it and taped it to the desk.

"Look," I raised my voice. "If I say Mrs. Stonington is there, all you need to say is yes. Pretend I'm asking you if it's Monday."

She didn't refuse so I continued, "Is Mrs. Stonington there?"

After a long silence, " . . . it's Monday," she said glumly.

"I won't tell your boss," I promised, feeling more like him than I wanted to admit.

Standing in the kitchen with one ear cocked towards the driveway for Peter's car and the other towards Stephen's room, I made coffee even though I never drank it except at the office. I rifled through the stack of magazines, but found them offensive in their obvious manipulation, confusing need with want. I pitched them in the trash. The sugar dish was already on the table. I poured milk into the small crockery pitcher Peter had given me on my first Mother's Day, forgetting that he didn't use milk or sweetener in his coffee.

When Stephen was born, we were giddy with love for him. Our first baby. We took him everywhere, talked about him endlessly. Silly bores really. He was the manifestation of our love for each other, but he was more than that. He was the future. We wanted him to be happy, but we expected him to make a mark on the world, to be someone special or do something special because he was so special to us. I saw now what a heavy burden that was for a child.

Very quickly we realized he had his own personality, likes, dislikes. As he grew older, and we had the other two and juggled work and parenting, we also were forced to admit that each of them would exercise his or her own will in the process. Psychologists will tell you that a child who is not allowed to exercise that will cannot be successful, in his separation from his parents or otherwise. It's not an easy lesson for parents.

Among the hospital pages about Danny I'd noted a ten-line entry about their training him to feed himself. In detail they described the day he refused to use the spoon taped to his arm to deliver food he didn't like. It was an exercise of will that celebrated his individuality. Even paid caretakers had noticed it. One deliberate act in long weeks without any response. No wonder they were excited for him.

I thought briefly of Lacy, telling me my son was more important. More important than her son? More important than Andrew and Elly? More important than lawyering?

When I heard Peter's car on the gravel, I stood at the stairs and listened harder. In the living room the clock ticked loudly. Stephen would be waiting too, nervous and feeding his anger to protect his underbelly. For all Peter's criticism of my recent absences, I recognized he was not an easy parent to please.

He and Stephen maintained a distance that sprang from natural personality differences, I'd always told myself. Right brain, left brain. A leader and a thinker. When Stephen was little, I'd been the mediator: telling Peter to give Stephen space, defending his creativity as valuable in a world of traditionalists. But it came out sounding like criticism of one or the other, and the distance remained.

"Jean?" Peter called from the kitchen, his voice full of uncertainty, as if he doubted I would be there despite the unspoken promise. When I went to him, he held me, gently, lightly, as if I were fragile. "What happened?" he said after a bit.

"He skipped school."

"That's it?"

"No, they found marijuana in his backpack."

The next morning after an endless, sorrowful night without sleep, I suggested calling Chase Taggert. Peter stopped shaving in mid-stroke. "Won't they handle it all in the probation department since he's a minor?" he asked.

"He has to have an attorney of his own. I know next to nothing about criminal law."

"Ah, an epiphany."

"We're talking about Stephen." I snapped my watch into place and shoved my feet into my navy pumps. "A bad deal now and he'll never live it down."

"I just want him to live through it. The stories I've heard of juvenile facilities are horrifying. Despite Stephen's mien of sophistication, he's amazingly ignorant about the real world."

"He just wants to be treated like a grown-up."

"He needs to act like one then."

"Hey, you're talking to an ally here."

"Sorry." He took my hand and held it against his cheek distractedly. "It's just . . . I never expected to have a son who was a criminal. Or a drug user."

I didn't answer. Still in shock myself over Stephen's anger at us, I reminded myself there were worse things that could happen to a son.

As it happened, Chase Taggert came by the office the next day, wanting to chat. He pulled a chair closer to my desk and propped up his feet as if he were ordering a beer. Jillian shut the door to the outer office firmly.

"You're looking particularly beautiful today, Jean."

"You want something from me. What is it, Chase, my oldest and dearest friend?"

He grinned. "You are quick for someone your age."

"Same age as you."

"Give or take a decade." He was grinning, but I couldn't summon a smile.

"What is it?"

"I'm going to the islands for three weeks. Right after the holidays."

"Alone?"

"I asked a woman I met."

"Bully for you."

"Will you cover for me?"

"I won't be much good for your kind of clients."

Chase smiled. "Don't kid yourself. Every case in the world revolves around love. Love triangles, love of booze, love-hate. You know love from your cases. The great motivator. Heck, love inspires more murders than psychosis or greed."

I nodded. For all his sour sense of humor Chase understood humanity. How he kept at it when the guilty went free and the innocent were jailed, I didn't know.

Outside my window in the empty alley sunshine freckled the pavement. The scenery hadn't changed from the day before, but my world was very different.

"I've got a new client for you," I said.

"You don't sound very excited. Pro bono?"

"No. It's our son, Stephen."

"Now I'm really sorry I was flip. Traffic ticket?"

"I wish. He skipped school with some friends, and when they corralled the kids, Stephen had the marijuana."

Hopping up, Chase waved his arms earnestly as if he were winding himself up to a faster thinking speed. "No problem. First offense, good student. The court knows how kids get mixed up in stuff without criminal intent. We'll get him some community service. It'll be over before you know it."

"Thanks." I stared at the wall of diplomas that had so impressed Lacy. What good were those accomplishments if I couldn't get the right message across to my son?

"You don't sound convinced."

"No, I mean it, I appreciate your help, but I'm worried he's not going to stop using. Any ideas for curing that, Master Wizard?"

"I'm not a good one to talk to on that score, Jeannie. I've been breaking the rules my whole life." When he stopped pacing, he sat again, watching my face. "I can scare him a little. Tell him war stories about kids gone wrong, trapped in the system. I can even get him a weekend in Juvey, if you think that'll help."

"I don't know. For the first time in my whole life I don't have a clue. I'm scared. For him and for us."

"Parenting's harder than what it's cracked up to be."

"How wise of you, you non-parent, you."

"Sense of humor, Jeannie, that's what'll save you, get you through whatever life deals you. Because frankly—and I know this probably shocks the hell out of you, kiddo—but it's out of your control. The sooner you realize that, the better off you'll be."

I hated to think he might be right.

Chapter Eighteen
LACY

Jean said Stephen's friends were the problem, but I knew she was worried about him too. She had a lot of experience with the crazy way kids think when their parents split up. I couldn't believe she didn't see some of the same things in Stephen. When my Diana announced at dinner he was involved with pot at school, we all assumed she was lying, ticked at me or all of us because Danny was clearly the focus of our meeting that evening.

After the Driscolls went home, I asked her to apologize.

"For what? You keep telling me how important it is to tell the truth."

"Is it true?"

She smiled in a catty way and I didn't like it. But kids aren't perfect people either.

"You hurt Mrs. Driscoll on purpose."

"This whole lawsuit thing is a circus. They'll make fun of us. Of you."

"I'm the one who asked for this, not the other way around."

"I don't see her talking you out of it."

"She couldn't if she wanted to." I was starting to boil a little. "When you have your own babies, you'll understand better."

"That's what adults always do, just remind us that we're too young to understand. Instead of trying to explain it to us."

She had me there. I couldn't even explain it to myself. When I was a little girl, I used to climb the beech tree between Cameron's yard and mine and talk to the stars. They all had names. Not those fancy scientific names from books, but names I gave them, kid's names. They were my buddies when Miriam was too stuck up or I needed to forget John Thompson's threats or Rae Ann's lack of interest. I'd tell them stories about how life was going to be when I was in charge.

When John Thompson kicked Miriam out, because she wouldn't let him touch her anymore—fed up with him, she'd decided if she married someone else and left, she'd be safe—I knew it wouldn't be long until I had to go too. I couldn't talk about it with Rae Ann. She always took his side. Gram, forever generous, was away for long stretches tending to her sick brothers and sisters.

It was pure luck that Scott came along at the right time. The first night I met him I decided he was going places and I was going with him. I didn't know it then, but it was a big mistake. Not marrying for love.

That first year was my dream. Hard-working husband, nice apartment. I started eating right and sleeping all night. On Sundays when Scott didn't have to work, we'd drive down to the river with a picnic. He talked about all the different places he'd lived when his dad was in the army. About the skyscrapers and harbors in countries I only remembered vaguely from elementary school geography.

Silly me, when he started talking about those places, I thought someday we'd go there. Fly in a plane, I'd never done that. It wasn't so ridiculous. His engineering job had potential, even though he was a junior worker. He was all the time bragging about how big his company was and all the airports and convention centers they had contracted to build. Of course I didn't know then how he was with money.

By the time I found out, it didn't matter because something better happened. I got pregnant. Even though Scott complained before, during, and after, I ignored it. I had my baby. Since I was little and Rae Ann had sent me with John Thompson in his big blue car to the free clinic for my breathing shots, I'd loved babies. My Danny was going to have everything those clinic babies didn't; a smart father, a mother who paid attention to him, and an education.

I was going to be that perfect mother. Pouring through the parenting magazines at the doctor's office, I read about formula and baby food. I only fed him the recommended brands. I made his first doctor's appointment for the exact day he was three months old and I made sure they gave him all the shots.

But once he got sick, our life started to crack apart like an old willow from the weight of all those twisty branches. With my baby in the hospital, suddenly I was that girl from Twyman's Mill again, silly and scared. I didn't understand what the doctors were talking about. Scott didn't want to hear it. Once they released Danny to come home, his limitations became more obvious. None of the mothers at the playground wanted their children to play near him. They asked questions I couldn't answer. No one could.

The only thing I knew for sure was what Gram had taught me, the power of love. So I loved him. When he couldn't sleep, I didn't sleep. We'd rock for hours, staring at the wall with the magazine covers in dime store frames I'd thought were so sophisticated when Scott and I had first moved there. More and more Danny and I were alone. The neighbors stayed away. He had trouble swallowing. Sometimes it took me four hours to get three ounces of formula in him, and then it would be time for the next feeding. Fresh air, someone said, so I walked him for miles. Between Christmas and Fourth of July I replaced the stroller wheels twice. Someone else suggested moist air. I boiled water in an open pot all day and all night. But he didn't get better.

After I had my gallbladder surgery in November, we slept together on the floor on the quilt. If I needed to move him, I dragged him on the quilt because I wasn't strong enough to lift him. Diana's right. I gave up. I had no choice. Probably I shouldn't have listened to them, but they were smart official doctor people. And who was I? Some skinny little runt from the mountains who hardly understood how to scramble eggs. Everyone acted funny around me, like I'd done something that made Danny stop breathing. Scott agreed with them and I had no family to help me. If I hadn't let Danny go, we both would have died. I'll never make Diana understand. When Jean said I'd have to explain it to the court, I didn't know how I could.

Chapter Nineteen
JEAN

The invitation arrived in a red envelope. Without commenting on the return address, Jillian separated the family pile for me to take home. While I chopped vegetables for Rocky Mountain Chowder, Elly opened the mail.

"Hey. A party," she said once she'd split the red envelope and withdrawn the sheet of red paper.

"Oh, goodie. To all of us?"

"It's from a man named Henryville. No last name."

I glanced over her shoulder, holding the knife away from her and reading sideways. "Henryville's a place. Way down south of here. It's from my DPT client."

"Why is she having a party?"

I read further down the page. "It looks like her friends are giving the party to help her raise money for the court case."

"I thought she was going to court for money."

"Kind of, but the hearing is in Washington and that's pretty far from where she lives."

"Do they have blue grass in Henryville?"

At Elly's puzzled look, I had to think twice before I realized she was reading from the invitation.

"That's a kind of music. Like country but with different kinds of fiddles and guitars."

The boys came in, shoulder to shoulder, dragging book bags and arguing.

Stephen was loudest. "They're a fad. They won't have any lasting impact on real music."

"Mom," Andrew squeezed himself between the counter and me. "The Beatles are more than a fad, aren't they?"

I handed him a carrot. "There's music and there's music. I think Stephen's talking about classical music not being affected by any particular rock group. That's all."

Stephen jumped in, "They haven't changed the forms or the instrumentation. In fifty years no one will be able to distinguish them from any other rock and roll sound." He slung his bag over his shoulder and disappeared.

"Jerk," Andrew said, stealing another carrot from the cutting board.

"Differing opinions is not cause for name-calling."

"He's so obnoxious though. He always thinks he's right. And he won't consider anyone else's music as worthwhile."

Elly chirped. "We've been invited to a bluegrass party for Mama's crazy lady client."

"Elly," I said. "She's not crazy."

"Bluegrass," Andrew said, "That's not even real music."

By the time Peter came home from work, things had calmed down and the dinner table was set.

"Five minutes," I said.

"Time for a glass of wine on the front porch?" he asked.

After I turned down the soup, I joined him there. Shuffling out of my shoes, I flexed my toes in the cool air.

"It feels good to sit down," I said, but he didn't murmur the expected agreement.

"I balanced the checking account today." There was an ominous tinge to his words. "When were you going to tell me about the check to Hamilton Fine?"

I put down the wine glass. "You know how Fine is. He called and demanded upfront money for the medical expert. Everything's a rush with him."

Peter didn't answer.

"Lacy doesn't have that kind of money. It's like a loan. After the trial, we'll get it back."

"Jean. You're talking like a teenager. A lawyer can't have an interest in the outcome of a client's case. Besides this isn't a decision you ought to make without consulting me."

"I can't decide on my own to spend a thousand dollars? I've spent that much before without asking permission. We have plenty. She has nothing."

"What if you lose?"

"I'll give you the damn money from the office."

"It's not about the money. You're not going to withdraw, are you?"

In the twilight the words pealed forth like funeral bells. I struggled with an answer. He deserved one as hard as he worked to take up the slack with my court schedule. Through the second floor window I could hear Stephen's Beethoven battling Andrew's Abbey Road. At least my children weren't milktoasts. Even without me around all the time, they weren't afraid to voice their opinions.

I thought about the synergy between husband and wife, how wondrous it was that when one oar dipped the other dug deeper. Peter and I were a team. He was right though, he deserved better. I should have talked about it with him beforehand. If, so far, I hadn't made him see how needy Lacy was in spite of that cheerful, dare-the-world-to-talk-back exterior, could I convince a judge?

With the trial date set and less than four weeks away, Lacy's distrust of Fine grew exponentially. "He doesn't care too hoots for Danny. He likes money, that's all this is to him."

"I wish I could have seen you two the day of your conference. I hope you told him a thing or two."

"Not me. I did exactly what he said. When I started talking about stuff he didn't want to hear, he just told me to turn it off. *Answer the question. No background, no explanations, no feelings, just facts, short and sweet.* Lacy, girl, I said to myself, you've met your match. The man is smart and mean."

"I'm sorry. I'm the one who brought him into this."

"No, we need him. You're right, but I don't have to like him. The devil serves a purpose too."

Passing by the doorway, Jillian heard me laughing and mouthed silently, "Lacy?" Lately, Jillian knew, Lacy was the only one who could make me laugh.

"How about the party plans?" I asked Lacy. "Are you sure you've got room for the Driscolls?"

"I wish you were bringing your kids. Mine are being weird and yours might snap them out of it."

"Anything's possible, I suppose. Weird is normal for this stage. . . . I think."

She chuckled. "The guest room is all yours. You have your own bathroom, and if our hound doesn't keep you awake all night, you'll be comfy."

As it turned out, Andrew had rehearsals for the Christmas play and Elly had a sleepover too good to miss. We planned to leave them at separate friend's houses and Stephen at Peter's sister's in Waynesboro. As long as Stephen was still on probation, we'd been careful to keep him busy. A weekend away might present temptations for him. To head off any problems Peter volunteered to talk with him before we left. After ten minutes I could hear their voices from the kitchen. I went upstairs to mediate. Peter paced at the end of the bed.

Stephen was sitting at his desk, book open, his back to his dad. "I'm not stupid."

Peter turned a despairing face to me. "I didn't say you were. I just don't think you understand what another charge could mean. Because you're seventeen, they can bump you to adult court. Then it'll be on your record forever. And you could go to jail." He was losing the battle to keep his tone even and unemotional.

"We're not going to have a second charge, are we?" I asked quietly from the doorway.

Stephen's face was red. "This whole thing's just a good excuse for you guys to keep me locked up."

"We agreed Brian was off-limits until your probation was over," Peter said.

"You said that. I didn't agree to it."

"You're not in much of a position to disagree with anything we say."

"He's not dangerous. Lots of smart people smoke marijuana recreationally. He's the only one in this crumby town who talks about things I like to talk about." Stephen's voice spiraled out of control again.

Peter looked at me, but I had no idea what to say.

"To hell with the fact that it's against the law." Peter said, brushing past and out the door. "He's going to do what he damn well pleases."

Stephen buried his head in the book.

"Stephen?" I insisted.

"I'm trying to study."

The urge to yank him around to face me battled with my panic that we'd already lost him. Apparently he didn't care what either of us said. "We have to resolve this before Dad and I go. The Stonington case is a pretty important case for me. And it's the biggest thing in Mrs. Stonington's life. She's never been to court before and this is about her first baby, who's been sick for twenty years. You've heard me talk about it. Dad's mostly worried about you being unsupervised while we're gone."

"Dad's worried about not being in charge of the rest of my life."

"That's not true. But you have to earn certain freedoms." I could feel the tension in my shoulders from gripping the doorknob. I let go and flexed my fingers.

He grunted.

"And now unfortunately, because of what you did, you have to earn back some of the freedoms you had and lost."

He slammed the book down. "I might as well just do it Dad's way. It's easier."

"So, we're agreed. No giving Aunt Christy a hard time this weekend?"

When he mumbled back, I took it for a yes, but it didn't feel like a victory.

Most of the way to Lacy's I slept. I put the seat back and let Peter rip down Interstate 81. He was working out his anxiety. I was avoiding mine.

My own depression about Stephen sprang from fear, not shame. In the mad dash to understand teenage drug use, I'd spent several lunch hours at the library and an uncomfortable conference with an investigator from the Sheriff's department. Nothing I'd read or heard since the arrest changed my mind about marijuana being a threshold drug. Stephen had always been interested in things outside the mainstream. So bright, so creative, he thrived on conversations with adults: his teachers, our friends, faculty contacts from Peter's committees. They raved about his mental acuity.

But here was a negative side I hadn't anticipated. He craved the unusual and he'd gone looking for a new experience, which happened to be illegal and dangerous. With college less than a year away, soon, too soon, he wouldn't have to look at his parents after making a bad decision.

I'd been working extra hours with the usual divorces and staying up late studying the compensation fund cases so I wouldn't look like a novice when we got to court. Between Andrew's soccer and Elly's dance rehearsals, few opportunities arose for Stephen and me to talk about more than the disciplinary measures. I left him articles to read. On the way to and from the office, I wrote myself little notes about things I meant to say, but it never seemed quite the right time.

Peter had imposed restrictions on Stephen's after school activities. Because I agreed we needed to look united, I accepted them without discussion. Stephen didn't balk openly, but he disappeared into his room more often and made an even more pronounced effort to be late for family activities. A protest I didn't condone, but understood. I kept telling myself I was luckier than Lacy who'd never had the chance to talk with her son about anything.

Once Peter turned off the interstate, we stopped twice to ask directions. Downtown Henryville had sprung from a crossroads similar to Parry's Crossing, without the railroad tracks. With the courthouse on one corner and the community bank on the other, we could have been home.

I read Lacy's handwritten note on the back of the invitation out loud. "Turn right at the light."

"Can we assume there's only one light?" Peter asked, arching his neck to see ahead.

While we were sitting there, a shiny forest green Jaguar drew up behind us, honked once, and snapped out around us. It whizzed through the intersection, spinning out of town in a blur.

"He's in a hurry to get to his own funeral," Peter said, quoting his father. Even if it was an old joke, laughing together felt good.

"We're early. We could get out and walk around a little," I suggested.

He parked in the lot for a flower store, closed up tight, with a sunflower sign in the window that said, 'See you when the sun shines.' "Where is this party again?" he asked.

"The Baptist church. Lacy says it's the biggest building in the county except for the farmers' co-op."

"I'd hate to make a mistake and be eating fertilizer for dinner."

The sidewalks were raised above street level, but so were the buildings. Every store had its own set of granite steps and an iron railing. Painted on the glass storefronts, the name of each establishment appeared in colorful letters. Even the bank windows sported gold lettering in curly-cued Old English.

"Ah, ye old barber shop," Peter said, clowning like Fred Astaire in front of the candy striped pole. He trailed me down the block.

"This must be the grocery store where Lacy works," I said.

"I thought she was a nurse's aide at the old folks' home."

"She quit when they cut her hours. And her favorite old geezer died, so she wasn't having as much fun."

"Oh, that's relevant to the DPT lawsuit," Peter quipped.

I punched his arm.

"Seriously, Jean, I'm glad you insisted I come. I feel better already."

"It's proximity to Lacy."

"No, it's thinking about something other than Stephen."

"I hate to remind you, we have two more teenagers. They'll go through something else."

He stopped. With his hands stuck in his pockets, he reminded me of the boys. Not quite sure of themselves but damned if they'd let anyone see them nervous. "Do you care that little?"

"What the hell do you mean by that?" I stood ten paces away and glared. Didn't he realize what a terrible reflection Stephen's actions had on my reputation as a lawyer? How awkward it was for me to ask the police department for help with clients who lost control while my son was one of their cases?

He shrugged. "You sounded so cavalier."

"I've been reading the books the counselor gave us. It's what they say. Teenagers rebel to distinguish themselves from their parents. It's part of growing up." Taking his hand, I tugged him back in the direction of the car, wishing back the good feelings of the afternoon. "I'm sorry."

"I never broke the law," he said.

"Drinking beer in high school was legal in Virginia? It sure wasn't in Massachusetts."

"Beer was just for fun. No hidden psychological meaning to it."

"That's exactly what Stephen says about the marijuana."

After unlocking the car doors, Peter stood and surveyed the street behind us. The windows reflected the pink and gold of the sunset. Everything in Henryville was in that one-block square downtown. The security would appeal to Lacy.

"I always thought he was smart enough not to fall for that stuff," Peter said. "It was Andrew I worried about because he wanted to be part of the group so much. Stephen didn't seem like he needed that kind of acceptance."

"Life was so much easier when they were little."

"Doesn't part of you wish they could've stayed that way forever?"

"Don't ask Lacy that question. She never had a choice, but I'd bet money on her answer."

The Baptist Church was easy to spot. Lacy was right. They'd put Christmas lights on the fences around the parking lot and the sign was lit by two overlapping spotlights. Over the official brick sign they'd tacked a banner that read, 'DC or Bust: Bluegrass Lovers for Lacy.' Just inside the gate the green Jaguar was parked. 'P I ATTNY' the license plate said. Fine had beaten us there. I should have guessed.

If Lacy hadn't introduced us, I could have picked him out of the crowd even though I'd never met him. His sport coat was navy blue cashmere, and his pale blue button down shirt was starched Egyptian pinpoint. Someone, not Fine I'd bet, had polished his tasseled loafers to a brilliant shine. Not even a colored handkerchief as a concession to the occasion, the jerk.

"He's worse than I expected," I whispered in Peter's ear.

"Relax," he whispered back, "At least he came. From everything you told me, I would've thought he'd never show his face at a social function without silver candlesticks."

Lacy, subdued and polite in front of the big city lawyer, shook Peter's hand, and turned to the next guest while I asked Fine about his trip.

He ignored the generic travel question. "Have they combined this function with someone getting married?"

"Not that I know of."

"All these people came for Mrs. Stonington?"

"Yup." I watched the confusion on his face and loved it. Payback for all his rudeness. "It means a lot to Lacy that you came."

"She must have called ten times."

"A woman who knows what she wants."

"I had to cancel an entire table at Senator Shockwell's gala in Norfolk."

I wished I'd had the guts to ask him what that cancellation cost him, but I didn't want to scare off Lacy's star guest. The car alone would impress the local Baptists.

"That was generous of you," I said instead.

"Mrs. Stonington refused to leave a message. My secretary said the woman had the dingbat idea she needed to invite me personally."

"Mr. Fine, does your secretary have a name? I feel like she's my best friend."

He looked so blank I felt sorry for him. "Never mind," I said. "Have you met Moss yet?"

"Moss is . . . her dog?"

"Husband."

"The father of the DPT baby?" This guy never stopped.

"I think I'd say 'Danny' while you're around Lacy, sir. And no, Moss Stonington is hardly Scott Kellam." With the emphasized enunciation, I glared a little, ticked that Fine hadn't remembered, but then again maybe he hadn't even read the file yet. When Lacy grinned back at me from the middle of a group of women in calico clogging dresses, I dropped it. "Moss is the husband of her other two children, Mr. Fine."

"You can call me Fine."

He was all heart, though I didn't think I could have managed a chummy 'Hamilton.' I tried to concentrate on the band, wondering why Lacy had insisted on inviting him when she disliked him so. I could imagine him threading his way through the crowd, asking if anyone had been rear-ended and handing out cards. More and more, I admired her talent for character assessment.

At my elbow Fine stood fanning himself with a discarded church program. As the music wound into a steady thrumming, we talked over logistics; witness order, exhibits, and scheduling.

He must have been one of those babies who never bonded with his caregiver. When he was in charge, he shone neon, but he never smiled. I watched his teeth, perfectly even and brilliantly white, as he enumerated his agenda for trial. It chilled me to see how completely engrossed he became in the minutiae, even as I chided myself silently. This was what I had wanted, an expert.

He was pontificating. "Send the witness addresses when you get back to the office. You can talk to them later. I have filing deadlines, and that Greek bitch from Justice is breathing down my neck." Still giving orders, he pulled a leather calendar from his coat pocket and dashed off a few quick notes to himself. After studying two or three pages of the calendar in rapid succession, he turned back to me. "Kordoba, Adriana Kordoba, that's her name. She's handled a lot of Medicaid fraud for Justice. Headline stuff. Don't know who she ticked off, but DPT litigation must be like the doghouse for her."

His holier-than-thou attitude was beginning to wear on me.

"Excuse me, did you just call Ms. Kordoba a witch?" I said.

"Witch?" But he knew damn well what I meant.

I was seething. In the right circumstances he probably waxed eloquent on downhill trends in the legal profession since the first woman sat for the bar exam.

I talked through clenched teeth. "I generally prepare witnesses before they testify, but if you're going to examine them, maybe you'd like telephone numbers in addition to addresses."

"I don't need to talk to them."

"Some of them don't remember much. They need to review. It's twenty-two years ago."

"I know it's twenty-two years ago. I know we don't have a single doctor from back then, and I know we have very few medical records. This is your case, counselor; I'm just trying to get it over with."

Steeling myself not to do an about face and walk away, I managed to choke out, "Gainsboro's ready, though, right?"

Fine harrumphed and took a long swig from a very sophisticated stainless steel thermos. Water? Or something more energizing? For Lacy's sake, I hoped I hadn't made a mistake.

I pushed. "You said his reputation was unparalleled."

"It is, but we have to get over the first hurdle. Seventy-two hours. Did you read the statute?"

Even though it was insulting, I didn't want to create a scene. But he was just getting warmed up. "The issue is did the kid suffer within 72 hours? Suffer: meaning hypertonic response, anoxemia, cardiorespiratory arrest, encephalopathic shock. Without medical records, that's a big hump."

"But Lacy . . ."

"Do you think Special Master Walters, a federal judge with thirty years experience, is going to be swayed by a ninny like Lacy?"

I could only stare. I was damned if he was going to spoil this evening for Lacy, to say nothing of belittling a woman who'd managed to live through what would have destroyed most people. While we were talking, I inched towards the opening in the fence. "Don't you want to see what they serve for dinner in bluegrass country, sir?"

Across the fence long tables with bright red and yellow tablecloths dotted the field. Wildflowers in big jugs adorned the tables. A spicy barbecue smell rose from an open pit roaster twenty yards beyond the last table. In the triangular shade of a huge magnolia, also strung with Christmas lights, they'd built a plywood stage.

Two huge bearded men in overalls, in different stages of 'worn,' played guitars. Between them a little bald guy with wire-rimmed glasses plunked a mandolin. At the rear of the platform on a raised section the drummer could have made the cover of *Rolling Stone*. He wore alligator cowboy boots, a matching hat, and a leopard skin vest with the ubiquitous flannel shirt. In tight black leather pants, the fiddler was a she. Her flannel shirt was tied at her midriff. Playing Bluegrass must be good exercise.

"Come over and get some dinner," Lacy called back to us once Peter had drifted off toward the music.

"Coming," I said, but Fine didn't move. As new guests walked past us and out into the field, he was looking down.

"Is there a problem?" I asked.

He analyzed the ground. Although I couldn't see anything out of the ordinary, he hesitated, scanning the tufts of hay on the other side of the gate. Finally, he said, "My shoes."

"It's okay, the guys in the cowboy boots don't want to dance with you either."

"No, they're handmade. They cost seven hundred dollars." Small drops of perspiration had beaded across his upper lip. "How recently do you think there were cows in this field?"

"You'll have to ask Lacy." Before I burst out laughing at my esteemed co-counsel, I went off to find Peter. He'd enjoy the joke.

In spite of two barbecue sandwiches with coleslaw and an enormous piece of applesauce cake, I danced with Peter until the last band quit. He danced two with Lacy, but she was the most popular girl there. Moss never danced, I learned, but if you watched carefully, his toes tapped to the beat. If I hadn't known him, I would have taken him for shy, but the falling-in-love story made that an impossibility.

At one point Lacy was filling me in on local gossip—who'd sent their parent to the nursing home in order to move their boyfriend in and which church-fearing folk were making May wine in their basements—when I saw Fine being asked to dance by a lady in a flamingo pink jumpsuit.

Lacy shrieked over the music to me, "Betty Sue can really dance. Watch." Not surprisingly the man had no rhythm. It took him three dances to break it off, and Peter said Betty Sue accosted Fine again in the port-a-john line.

At midnight the lead guitar player coughed into the microphone. "Would Miss Lacy and her Moss man please step up front?"

Lacy hid her face in Moss's shirt. "Oh, gosh," she whispered, "They had to go and make a big deal of this."

"Go on, now. You asked for it, writing that big wig judge to make those drug companies pay for their mistake."

"They want you up there too," I said to Moss.

"Nope, ain't no way. Not my lawsuit."

"Please. She's a little nervous, don't you think?" I tugged at his sleeve.

"Lacy? Hah. Wouldn't hurt her to be nervous oncet in a while. Anyway she shoulda thought of that before she took on the federal government."

On the stage the bandleader held the microphone close to his beard, Lacy's hand in his. The crowd cheered and hooted. Lacy curtsied.

The loudspeakers erupted. "Everyone here knows Lacy and Moss. They come down here from up north, from the big metropolis of Parry's Crossing 'cause they liked our music."

"Go, Steamboat Ron," someone in the back yelled.

Peter raised his eyebrows, which made me giggle.

Steamboat Ron continued. “I could tell you a zillion stories about Miss Lacy. Half the residents at the Sunset Vista Nursing Home swear she’s the only thing that keeps them alive. I’d sure like some of whatever she feeds them old coots.”

The crowd laughed with him and so did Lacy, her high-pitched glee carrying above the crowd. From the edge of a knot of locals in plaid shirts Fine pretended to be stargazing, but he probably didn’t miss much. If he’d come to get to know his client, he was getting his money’s worth. Steamboat Ron, beaming, gestured towards Lacy.

“I heard tell she gives away Christmas trees to kids who don’t have one, and anyone who hasn’t tasted her blackberry tarts is a fool. She sets ’em out on the ledge to cool. Right, Moss?”

While Ron was enjoying himself as much as entertaining the rest of us, Peter had found Carson and Diana. The three of them were thick into some conversation that looked more serious. Illuminated by the colored Christmas lights, their faces moved in changing planes of color like a kaleidoscope. When Diana stopped talking, Peter began slowly, bending his head in his characteristic way as if he found the whole thing immensely fascinating. Both kids remained fixed in place, following his hands and head as he moved through the subject, whatever it was.

Ron trilled a note or two to get everyone’s attention again. “Tonight is our Henryville County send-off for Miss Lacy on her quest to slay those vaccine breeding dragons. And we have a little something to help her get there.”

In cowboy hats and bandanas two boys clumped up to the stage with a pickle barrel, the two-foot size from a real country store. When they took off the lid and raised it up, it was full of dollar bills. The crowd went wild. “Go, Lacy, go,” they chanted.

“Just so you know it’s for real. We got the President of the National Bank of Henryville to count it. One thousand eight hundred and forty-two dollars and change. That oughtta go some for those fancy lawyers."

When I looked over at Fine where he was leaning on the fence to wait out the speeches, his jaw hung slack. I edged closer.

"I didn't think there was that much money in this county," he said.

"People can surprise you," I answered.

Then I noticed he was barefoot and his feet were green.

Chapter Twenty
JEAN

Waking in the night to Snowball's distant barking, I rolled over to see if Peter was awake. He was gone.

Lacy's guest room opened into a bathroom and the kitchen. Peter was neither place, though both doors from our bedroom were wide open. A light breeze filled the curtains, filtering moonlight and the power company utility light at the garage, half a football field away. At the back of the house Snowball crackled through the woods.

"Peter?" I whispered as quietly as I could. Moss might easily wield a 30-06 for nighttime intruders. From the kitchen I caught the dark slash of a lean frame, sitting on the picnic table at the far edge of the yard. "Pete?"

He motioned with one hand, but didn't answer. Tiptoeing through the wet grass, I shivered. We'd never thought to bring jackets for this kind of mountain chill.

"You couldn't sleep?"

"Shhhh." With his free arm he pointed across the field of stubbled hay stalks. "There are four of them."

"Deer?"

As he nodded his head, he stretched out his arm and drew me close. He rubbed my bare arms.

"Sorry," I murmured in his ear.

"It's okay," he said quietly. "I've got lots on my mind."

"I'll drive home. You can sleep."

"Look."

Squinting at the far side of the meadow, I saw the first white tail. Then two, then three. A fawn followed slightly behind the doe, and another smaller female, all foraging with their heads down. To the far side, with Peter's direction, I found the buck. Except for his size, it would have been hard to see him because he held so still. His antlers were enmeshed in the washed out shadows of a waning moon. Peering into the ribbed darkness of the young forest, I could see how erect he kept his head. When his family moved downhill, he sidestepped just enough to keep them in view.

Here on Lacy's hillside they were safe. They must know that since it was their home. In spite of the buck's familiarity though, he kept watch. And when Snowball, returning from her trek to the north woods, caught our scent in the front yard, she bounded across the lawn joyfully barking. In a flurry of hooves and tails the deer flew across the expanse and disappeared over the ridge.

"What were you talking about with Diana and Carson?"

"He said something about his mom that came off kind of cold. They both feel like she's been dumping lots of stuff on them lately. Dredged up because of the case, I guess, but he and Diana hadn't heard much about their half-brother until this happened."

"Feeling left-out?"

"And a little jealous."

"Being related, Danny's problems must be a little terrifying to them."

"That's not what's bothering him. Lacy talks about what a sweet baby he was, carries his baby picture. Things she never mentioned before. Carson said they didn't know they had a brother. And she won't take them to see him."

"She's only gone thirteen or fourteen times herself in twenty-one years. But they have actually been. One of the state logs shows a visit with Moss and two children. They must have been too little to remember."

"She ought to consider a family trip now, so they understand why she's acting like she is."

"After all this time it's going to be pretty tough."

"The vaccination explanation ought to make it easier."

"She wouldn't go, even with me. Didn't come right out and say no, just made sure she was busy."

Peter squeezed my shoulder. "You know what she told me tonight? In the middle of a conversation about chocolate cake. She only weighed 80 pounds when she left Danny at the state hospital. Did you know that?"

I hadn't.

Although Dictator Fine had seen to the issuance of the witness subpoenas, I'd sent him the list without Scott and Doctor Snowden. Lacy and I had argued about their purposeful omission several times, but in the end I had done as she asked.

She tried to explain. "Snowden promised to come if I needed him. He's a phone call away, but he has good days and bad."

"All the more reason for an official court summons. If he's unexpectedly detained, we can ask for a continuance."

"I won't live through a continuance."

"Lace, it's no big deal. The court does it all the time. They have other cases to hear so they don't mind."

"There's only enough money for one trip. And Mr. Neiderman, my boss, says he can't keep juggling the schedule for me. This job is important. There aren't many jobs in Henryville for fruitcakes."

"If Moss isn't coming, Snowden's even more important. He's your moral support."

"You're my moral support."

I ignored that. "He's the only one besides you that was around back then. For heaven's sake, he was there at the hospital the day after the first seizure."

"He knows things about me that no one else knows."

"You little chicken."

The whole idea of Lacy relying on me made me uncomfortable, not just because of Peter's objections. With Lacy it was easy to enjoy the quick humor, the perky cock-eyed view of the world and easy to forget that Danny's disappearance into the land of green corridors and grunts and apparent blindness had wounded her irretrievably. I'd had glimpses into that nightmarish wasteland. Yet only Lacy knew what it was to stare into those eyes, trying to find the perfect boy she'd known for those three months in 1969. I didn't want to be responsible for sending her there permanently if the very real trauma of courtroom politics pushed that simmering guilt to the surface.

In spite of her smiles and pledges of love, I could see in her constant deprecation the impossible contradiction of being a mother who had not been able to save her child. For Lacy this case was not about the money. She wanted, needed forgiveness. And courtrooms did not dispense that kind of medicine.

The week before the trial Moss telephoned my office. Since I was in court with a recalcitrant father, Jillian took the call and the message. It was the first time Moss had initiated contact. During my hearing in Family Court, Jillian's head popped into the window in the door for just a second, then disappeared.

"What's up?" I asked her when we took a break and I had a chance to call the office.

"Mr. Stonington called."

"Moss called me?"

"He's worried about Lacy. Says you need to call right away."

"Is she home?"

"I wrote down all the numbers."

The Court agreed to an early lunch break and I practically ran to the office. Moss answered on the second ring. "I hate to bother you, but she's all twisted up about this. I seen it coming. She talks tough, but . . . the mailman brought this paper, something or other about the court. She just lost it, went crazy. She's calling Attorney Fine the worse kind of names, crying, carrying on. Maybe you can talk to her."

"Is she at work?"

"She doesn't go in today until three. I came home for lunch, but once she read the mail, she went down to the basement. Looking for evidence, she says. She's tearing through those old boxes, searching for God knows what. If it isn't too much trouble, I think you better talk to her."

Poor Jillian, she was sitting on the corner of my desk with creases in her forehead, her fingers fiddling with the file tabs on the folders she held in her lap.

"Is she sick?" she asked when I told her I was on hold.

"No, she's nervous. Fine sent her the witness list. Can't see why that would upset her, though. Did we get a copy in today's mail?"

"I'll check." Off she went.

"Jean." Lacy sounded shaky.

"Are you okay?"

"Just mad as a stuck beaver."

I stifled a laugh. That sounded like the Lacy I knew. As Jillian walked back in, she slit the envelope and handed me the folded letter. I spread it on my blotter.

Lacy blasted away, "Do you know what that son of a gun did?"

"I hope you mean Fine and not the Special Master. Or Moss."

"Of course God himself, Fine. He summoned Scott."

I saw the printed name at the same time and jabbed my finger at the paper on my desk for Jillian's benefit.

"And?" I was thinking hard, but legally it made sense to me. In that instantaneous recognition of smart trial strategy, I realized that Peter had been right from the beginning. I was too close to this whole thing. I should have turned over the whole case.

At least now we knew Fine had read the whole file. Arguably Scott could be a useful witness in spite of the lingering animosity he felt. Or, if Fine's reputation matched reality, he might have chosen Scott because of that bias. If Scott's testimony corroborated Lacy's but his mindset was uncooperative, his reliability could hardly be questioned. Fine hadn't told me everything he did. He was lead counsel after all.

Months earlier I'd sat through a long session with Lacy about Scott's desertion. She told me about living alone after he left, about talking to the neighbors through closed windows because she was afraid to let them in and expose Danny to the germs. She described an evening in the winter of 1970 when, at her wit's end, she'd called her high school friend Cameron in Twyman's Mill.

Nine hours later Cameron had showed up at the apartment with flowers and Chinese food. He bathed and fed the baby. Lacy remembered sitting on the bathroom floor with Cameron and laughing at his rendition of their childhood adventures. She talked in a slow voice about how easily Danny fell asleep when Cameron rocked him.

"Once Danny was asleep, Cam held me. As a friend. It had been a year since anyone had even hugged me. He said lovely things to make me feel better. That the loneliness wouldn't last forever, that good things were in my future. How could he have known about Moss? Or that six years later I'd have Diana and then Carson?"

This was not the kind of information I could pass on to Fine. Her argument against using Scott as a witness was emotional, but not totally off base. If Scott was so eager back then to wipe Danny out of his life, why should he be cooperative now?

Her tirade didn't stop with Fine. "Scott doesn't know diddly about Danny."

"Maybe Fine just wants him to establish that Danny was in the hospital on July 2nd."

"I don't give two hoots what Fine wants. Scott will come with his itsy bitsy new wife. He'll parade all around like he's the great daddy when he didn't do a damn thing. If they need someone to tell the Judge Danny was in the hospital, I can do that."

"They need corroboration."

She was quiet suddenly, the wind just gone from her sails. "Corroboration?" she repeated.

"When more than one person says the same thing, it's more believable."

I could hear her breathing on the other end, gulping in air and letting it out slowly. Moss said something in the background.

"Hey," I prompted, "You okay?"

"Are we gonna lose?"

It was an impossible question, but one most clients ask at some point. I wasn't ready for Lacy. "I wish I could predict."

"Danny needs a new wheelchair with an adjustable headrest, and Jenny says he should wear high tops 'cause his ankles get rubbed so raw on the metal edges. That's all I really want, enough to get him what he needs. You're my lawyer. Tell me the truth."

"I don't think we'll lose, but Fine's just doing what he does best. You don't need to talk to Scott. If you want, we can keep him in a separate room."

"His wife too?"

"His wife too."

"Did I ever tell you how he gave me the clap?"

Saturday morning before the trial, with the exhibits spread out on the office conference table, I reviewed my examination notes. Two days before, after no apparent deliberation, Fine had changed his mind. He would handle every witness. Lacy had hung up when I first called to alert her. When she called back, she explained that she didn't want to have to answer his questions. She asked me very politely if I would persuade him to let me ask her the questions we'd planned for her. Although he recited a dozen reservations and only agreed to think about it, I simply told her it was set. I didn't want her to worry about it while she was traveling.

The hotel Jillian had booked for us was three blocks from the federal court building near Pennsylvania Avenue. Even after the train ticket, one hundred and twenty-nine dollars a night for a hotel room had shocked Lacy. With Doctor Gainsboro's fee and transcripts from depositions he had taken of the witnesses two months ago, almost all of the money from her Henryville supporters was gone. Once she found out we would have connecting doors, she relaxed enough to promise me she would get on the train at least.

When Peter heard about the connecting doors, he shook his head. "Don't forget this is not a pajama party. You need eight hours of sleep to function."

"Yes, Dad."

He blew me a kiss on his way to the gym.

While her train traveled north from Roanoke, I checked my briefcase and stowed the gear in my car.

Moss telephoned. "She's on board."

"How's she holding up?" I asked.

"The conductor's from a little town near Twyman's Mill. He said he'd make sure she got off in Washington."

"Probably knew her grandmother."

"That's what he said."

"Did you remind her to pack for three days of hearings, just in case it spills over?"

"Ay-yuh."

"I'll pick her up at the station. Once she's in her room, I'll have her call you."

"Okay. I'm headed back to the store." He sounded lost.

The night before I had been ironing blouses, debating with myself whether to stay home and let Fine handle the whole thing. When Stephen had refused to eat dinner with us for the second night in a row, it had kept me awake worrying. Was he mad or not hungry? Weight loss and disinterest in food were two key signs of depression and drug use. Since the fundraiser for Lacy Peter had stopped trying to persuade me to withdraw, but this change in Stephen's behavior scared me enough to make me re-consider.

He came in to the laundry room with his English paper. "Will you read it? Just for sense. Don't worry about the grammar."

"When's it due?"

"Tuesday, but you'll be gone." His eyes looked red to me, and the way he brushed the hair off his face made me think of Peter when his back was hurting. I had explained the trial schedule to each of the kids several times, but, even with my long hours, they weren't used to my being away overnight. During the last few months with Stephen on probation and my preoccupation with trial preparation—they'd overheard Peter and I arguing—they had to be more aware of the tension between us.

"Dad could edit," I said, thinking what I really should be asking Stephen about was the latest meeting with his probation officer, but I didn't want an argument just before I left.

"It's not the same."

I winked. "He's a tough critic."

"He doesn't really get what I'm trying to say."

"You'd be surprised. He said your book review was . . . insightful. That was his word."

Stephen shrugged and handed me the pages, smiling shyly.

"I'm impressed you wrote it early."

"Brian's doing the same issue, and then we're going to talk." He was watching me. "On the phone. He's really in the dumps about everything."

"It can't be easy for him without his dad."

"He quit smoking."

"How did that happen?"

"I told him he ought to try to talk to his mom instead of avoiding her." He grinned and went downstairs.

This was a gift, unexpected and rare. The kind that every parent holds close to his or her heart. Every parent whose child grows up.

Chapter Twenty-One
LACY

Moss was different, different from most men I knew: quiet, but not a pushover. There was no moving him once he made up his mind, which he took his time doing. He always had an opinion; he just didn't offer it unless you asked. Not at all like John Thompson, who was loud and stupid, but big enough to make it happen his way no matter what. He never thought out anything ahead of time.

Peter Driscoll wasn't like either of them. Once I had a chance to talk to him, really talk, I understood Jean better. Independent and quick—I already knew—but what I didn't figure was how hard it was for her to rely on anyone. Peter knew her and he knew enough not to tell her how she ought to solve the issues with Stephen.

Most girls grow into understanding men by watching their own fathers. I used to think if mine had been around, maybe it would have helped me. Once I met him though, I wasn't so sure about that.

When I was five, I was scrounging around in one of Rae Ann's drawers, looking for make-up on a dare from Miriam and I found an old black and white photo shoved in the way back. In the bent photo a tall serious man in a bathing suit smiled. His eyes were twinkly, not squinty at all like John Thompson's. Because the man in the picture looked like Miriam I guessed it was our father. I'd never laid eyes on him, but he had the same curly black hair, same mushed-in nose.

If Rae Ann had hidden that photograph, it meant she didn't want John Thompson to see it, which I took to mean she still loved my father, which meant he might come back someday. And John Thompson would leave. Typical little kid thinking. Anyone would have been better than John Thompson.

One Friday night he and my mother went out dancing, a pretty standard thing for them. This particular night, though, Gram was gone, staying with her sister in West Virginia. She was always streaming off to take care of a brother or sister, four or five days at a time. She never stayed long, maybe because she didn't trust Rae Ann.

John Thompson and Rae Ann were still out partying when we kids went to bed, JT squished in between Miriam and me in Gram's bed because he was scared of the dark. The next thing I knew the window glass was tinged orange with the sunrise and from the porch I could hear grown-up voices, talking and laughing, drunk as rodeo stars. There was a loud smash of wood splitting. We had no idea what it was, but it turned out to be the front door. Inside Rae Ann's voice changed. She quieted down and squeezed out words, tight and edged with icicles. It wasn't until the rocking chair creaked that I figured out Gram must have come home while they were out and locked the front door. In her best church voice Gram ordered John Thompson to leave.

When she didn't back down, he threatened to take Rae Ann and us kids too. Next thing I knew Rae Ann came in the bedroom and started throwing stuff into a suitcase. JT jumped in Mim's arms. I ran to Gram, but she didn't say a thing. She didn't rock the chair. She didn't even blink. Through the broken door I could see John Thompson prowling around his big old car with that ugly look on his face. I tried to think of something to say to change Gram's mind, but she sat there stone-faced, letting me blubber and carry on. Finally when Rae Ann came out with the suitcase—dragging Mim by the arm, JT clinging on for dear life—Gram whispered to me, "Don't move. He's bluffing."

But just as if he'd heard, he huffed around the hood of the car, skipped three steps, and came running through the open door. He grabbed me where I was hanging onto Gram, hefted me off the ground, shoved me into the back seat between the other kids and gunned it.

We drove around for hours; all the streets looked the same. Then gradually the streets disappeared. We tore through a long stretch of open country. From the front seat the wind carried back bits and pieces of conversation, but I couldn't stay awake. JT slept too. I remember how the sun shone in a bright circle of light over our heads, pouring down steamy heat like a teapot pours water. My dress stuck to the car seat. When JT woke up and started to cry, I put his thumb in his mouth. At one point I asked Miriam if we were still in Twyman's Mill, which was silly because if you drove for ten minutes, you'd be out of Twyman's Mill. She must have thought it was silly too because she didn't even bother to answer.

After a bunch of squealy turns followed by cuss words, John Thompson parked by a row of houses that looked like gingerbread cottages at the Christmas bazaar. Greensboro. 'Course I didn't know that till later. When he asked Rae Ann if this was the right house, she said she'd never been there. They argued some more, and then he shoved her out of the car anyway. She went up to the strange house while we sat there baking in the sun. I was dying to ask Mim the right house for what, but he'd have hit me for sure. After a long time I heard voices and banging, a pan maybe.

That's when John Thompson made us get out, told us to straighten our dresses and pull up our socks. Halfway up the cracked cement walk, prodding the three of us in front of him, the yelling started. Rae Ann came out, followed by a tall man with wavy hair, the man in the photograph. With his fist shaking in her face, she was inching back down the front walk with her back to us, still arguing. John Thompson dragged us backwards too. Just after Rae Ann tripped, the tall man bellowed how he didn't care if she'd had us five years or twenty-five, he wasn't taking care of any more kids.

Behind him in the doorway stood a girl who didn't look much older than Miriam. She had a baby in her arms and two little kids stuck to her like an extra layer of leggings. Once the angry man slammed back inside, pushing past her, she moved out of sight too.

John Thompson and my mother whispered there in a huddle in the front yard. Miriam and I sat JT between us on the curb and hummed. JT climbed into my lap. Every once in a while a car would whiz past, and the dirt and trash from the street would swirl into the air. I closed my eyes against the grit. When I opened them, my father was standing on the stoop with a shotgun. He yelled extra loud so anyone could hear.

"I swear to God, if you leave those kids here, I'll shoot'em."

Miriam sprang up, looking for somewhere to hide. I rocked JT and hummed louder. While John Thompson argued with my father, Rae Ann bawled. The second the angry voices stopped, footsteps came down the walkway. With my eyes squeezed tight, I waited for the gun to go off. But when the car engine roared instead, Miriam and I both screamed. That exact second Rae Ann grabbed JT and leaped into the car. Mim and I stood there by that curb, our faces to the street, waiting, waiting for the gun to go off.

We didn't talk. We didn't move. After a long while a door slammed and I turned around, thinking my father had finally gone in, but it was my father coming out, without the gun, in a suit and tie. Without a word he walked right by us, climbed into his car, and drove away.

Once he was gone, the girl with the baby invited us to come inside. She turned out to be his second wife, Melanie. She told us a bunch of stuff. How the twins were his by some army general's daughter who'd decided against marrying him. How he worked for an aluminum siding company and had a desk job, a good job. I helped with the twins and Mim did some cooking, so he let us stay. I think he kind of liked it, free labor.

In spite of rude old John Thompson though, I actually wanted to go home. I missed Gram. I missed JT. I missed the way he called for me and the way his feet padded on the bare floor. I missed the way it felt when he buried his face in my neck while I sang. At my father's we weren't allowed to sing, not even to the twins at bedtime because he said the songs would make them dream.

I'd always thought dreaming was good. In my dreams people weren't ugly to each other. There were no clinic babies without parents. All the John Thompsons in the world worked far away and never had time to drink whiskey or take anyone's mother dancing. If Campbell and I wanted to camp out in the backyard together, no one would say we couldn't because whites and blacks shouldn't mix. And Cam could read me stories all day long, instead of just when we snuck out after bedtime to the tree fort. In your dreams the world was forever the way you wanted it to be.

Sometimes at my father's house after we said good night, he and Melanie would sit outside on the stoop and talk, nice and quiet. I would tell the twins stories made up from my dreams. I invented games too. Jumping on the bed was a favorite. It's like floating on the ocean, swooping up one wave and flying down the other side.

One night, though, my father caught us jumping. He slapped me and I hit him back. And repeated all the words I'd heard from John Thompson. That didn't go over real well. When my father yanked me down off the bed, I sucked in my breath and made my body as big as I could, ready to fight. I told him I didn't have to stay there, that I was going home to Twyman's Mill. I said I'd walk if I had to or hitchhike. The very next day he called in sick and drove me home. Just me. His car spit and coughed like an old tuberculosis patient and the whole way he muttered on and on about Rae Ann and the other women who'd used him, how hard it was to get ahead with women wanting this and that. In front of Gram though, he got all polite, lowered his voice, and apologized for not being able to keep me. I was too wild is what he said.

Gram sent me inside, but I listened anyway. Through the mail slot. The top half of his face and Gram's apron strap on her neck showed where she stood on the bottom step. She said as long as it had been since he'd been at the house, she was surprised he remembered where it was. He said he wasn't sure he was welcome. She just snorted and said it was the first time she'd known him to care what other people thought.

They talked about money for us kids. He admitted he'd made mistakes, but that if he'd sent money to Rae Ann, she'd've spent it on rouge and fancy magazines. He understood my mother all right. He sounded like a pleasant enough man with too many worries. Then I remembered he'd left my mother when he knew another baby was coming—me. Why should I try to make him like me? If he didn't like who I was, he could go back where he came from.

Chapter Twenty-Two
JEAN

Lacy's train was due to arrive in DC late Saturday afternoon before Monday's court date. I'd argued with her for two weeks about not waiting until Sunday to come. Despite the expense, an extra night to become familiar with her surroundings seemed like good insurance, as nervous as she was.

I scheduled an hour to pack the file and two hours to drive north. Peter and I said a lukewarm good-bye on the office phone. He had lobbied for me to get her situated and come home on Sunday night after she'd gone to sleep. Fine was trying the case. With Stephen's ups and downs, Peter liked the idea of a second adult close by if there were problems while he was at work.

We had argued. Lacy was too unstable to leave alone in a strange city. It was her only day in court. He said he understood but his voice was distant. I knew I'd disappointed him again. I was close to tears when I hung up, abruptly rather than prolong the dispute.

Following the road through Confederate battlefield country with the sun infusing the car with the honey-like sweetness of late fall, I was reminded of the weekend just before Peter's father died. The sense of separation from him that I felt over Lacy's lawsuit felt similar to that earlier time.

We had planned a camping overnight with the kids. Elly might have been three, talking non-stop. Although it was August, the usual dog days were on break. In the Blue Ridge Mountains it's fifteen degrees cooler anyway. Peter was teaching summer school then. That summer, with his dad in and out of the hospital, he'd taken a break.

The family time we'd anticipated in June evaporated when my trial schedule choked on a huge custody battle. The separated couple both had business degrees, both worked at high-pressure jobs. Although the wife did a lot of her paperwork from a home office, she flew to New York two days every week. Why they'd had children in the first place none of us involved in the case could figure out.

Of course the husband filed for custody. With his consulting firm in town, he'd been the one who dealt with the babysitter on the days his wife was out of town. He'd handled the school conferences and most of the doctors' appointments. After a three day hearing with teachers and psychologists, the judge announced he'd rule in two weeks. I needed a break badly. The car was packed, kids buckled in, when the Sheriff called. My client had shot her husband in front of the children and she was asking for me.

Peter went off with our three to the campsite and I was to come along as soon as I'd arranged a criminal lawyer for her.

"What about swimming to the island?" Eight year-old Stephen asked me.

"You have to set up the tent today. We'll swim in the morning."

"You promise?"

"Promise."

Peter gave me the evil eye to cement the reminder.

"Love you guys," I said as they drove off. Peter's hand out the window and the four of them hooting our family joke, "We love you, we love you," all the way down the drive. We had teased the kids that way when we dropped them off at the elementary school, but that summer day I felt more ashamed than embarrassed. Of myself for letting the woman talk me out of being with my family.

The jailor was beside himself. "She hasn't stopped talking. Stream of consciousness mostly."

"No confession?"

He grimaced. "No jury in the world would convict her. She's crazy."

"Grief-stricken, more like. She's lost her children for good now."

Getting back to the camp-out turned out to be impossible. The criminal lawyer she hired, on the advice of her best friend, was on vacation. As she came out of shock, she panicked, swinging between false self-righteousness and severe bouts of suicidal depression. I missed the camping weekend and spent most of the next two weeks running back and forth to the jail each time she threatened another meltdown. In the middle of all that Peter's father came home from his last heart attack with Hospice and died. I stayed with the children while Peter was with his mother.

Of all the kids Stephen took Grandpa Driscoll's death the hardest. They had played endless hours of checkers together and Stephen was old enough to remember his tall tales. The night of the funeral Stephen ran away. Looking back, he was making a clear statement that he didn't like the adult world. He wasn't ready to grow up and he refused to have it forced on him. Without Peter to consult, I dumped the other two children at a friend's and started the search. By the time I found Stephen in the town picnic shelter, two miles from the house, but within a stone's throw of his elementary school, it was two in the morning. His brain was in overdrive. Exhausted and scared, he was shivering in the pitch black corner of the open air shelter and talking to the noises from the woods.

I held him like a baby, rocking and mumbling reassurances until he was calmer and heavy with sleep. About the time I got him home and into bed, Peter arrived, sure there'd been a fire or some other disaster. He had left three frantic messages on the home phone, wondering where his family was, and without any reply, had decided finally not to wait any longer. We argued in whispers, afraid to risk waking Stephen. Separated by our own fears, it was a hard time for all of us. We didn't talk much when we should have talked more.

Looking back, I'm sure that the absence of safe conversation about death and loss contributed to Stephen's conviction that the world was not a predictable place so what did it matter what you did with your life. And my promises to the contrary, unconsciously I was part of his disappointment. How could I know what part of that time had stuck with him?

After I picked up Lacy at the train station on Capitol Hill, at her request we rode around the White House three times, just in case the President decided to take a walk, which he didn't. We did the whole loop from the Lincoln Memorial to the Supreme Court with Lacy chatting away.

"They ought to make every school kid come here and see this stuff. How can you not be proud of this country? We started from nothing." She made me stop on the lakeside drive to the Jefferson Memorial. "I bet this is more beautiful than Paris." She sighed. "You've probably been to Paris six times."

"Once, a long time ago."

"It can't be as gorgeous as this. Look, there's a puppy dog. Poor thing, on a leash. Snowball would be wild. All these hydrants."

"Don't forget we're going to meet Fine at ten tomorrow morning. He needs to go through the testimony with you to be sure everything's in order before trial on Monday."

"Yuck, I have no interest in seeing that worm."

"You have to keep sight of two things. All this rigmarole is for Danny. And Fine's on our side."

"I'm not so sure."

Sunday morning the front desk clerk rang my room at ten of nine. I'd already walked to the closest church and found coffee and a bagel on the way back. Copies of the Training Center records, complete with neat color-coded exhibit numbers, were splayed on my bed. I was still looking through the miscellaneous records box from the pediatrician's, hoping for a consultation note with the Fairfax doctors that would add to the medical substantiation of seizures as opposed to aspiration, the medical word for choking. It had been Fine's idea for me to keep looking. In our planning sessions, he anticipated the government's argument would focus on aspiration since it was not one of the automatic Table explanations that would yield the presumed connection to the vaccine. Although he had explained it to me in layman's terms more than once, treating me as if I were very stupid indeed, I had let it pass.

"A gentleman is here to see you," the clerk reported from the lobby.

"The worm," I said to myself. "Efficient worm." When I buzzed Lacy's room to warn her, there was no answer. Before heading down I knocked on the connecting door.

"Hey," her voice was muffled.

"Rise and shine. It's time for Fine." I poked my head into her room.

"Good morning," but there was no bounce in her voice.

"You're still in your PJ's."

"So?"

"The man doesn't take kindly to waiting."

"You go. Tell him I'm under the weather."

"Don't flake out on me now, Lacy. This is it. We have one chance to convince the Special Master."

"What if the Special Whatever doesn't like me? What if I get flustered and say the wrong thing? I can't do this."

I noticed her suitcase just inside her door. "You haven't unpacked?"

"Yes, I did."

I strode over and lifted it. It was heavy.

"I packed it again. I'm going home."

"Oh, no, you're not. You dragged us all up here, made me sit through those horrid telephone calls and conferences with Fine, convinced me to read all those medical articles and Congressional transcripts. After all that you can't give up."

She sank onto the bed. "I have two beautiful children who need me. Danny has Jenny. I've lived this long not knowing. Let's just leave well enough alone."

I sat next to her, our shoulders touching. The sun slid around the corner of the hotel, raining brilliance on the marble and glass of the city. I blinked at the brightness. I knew exactly how she felt. I had a good law practice. Most of my clients paid their bills. My children walked to school. My patient husband did more than half of the cooking. But leaving well enough alone hadn't worked. Stephen was on probation. Peter thought I was avoiding my responsibility as a mother. I'd missed Andrew's soccer games and Elly's recitals because I was too busy defending fathers who refused to send money to feed their children. And here I was smack in the middle of a case about which I had no trial experience at all.

"That's not Lacy Stonington talking. It's not even Lacy Kellam talking. Have you forgotten McIntosh sneaking away from you after admitting he knew Danny was the DPT baby? Or the woman at the training center asking you why Danny's face was chapped?"

Lacy's breathing settled around us in the quiet room. "I miss Mosste."

"I know, but he knew you could do this. We all know you can do it. Look at how you dragged all of us into this. By the sheer force of your conviction."

She looked pensive still, though not as dejected. "Moss said not to think about coming home unless I showed Washington what kind of women they grew in North Carolina."

"I like that man."

"If all this hadn't happened, Moss might never have found me. Isn't it crazy how good things come out of bad?"

Who was I to disagree? It worked for her. It worked for other people. Somehow though, thinking of Peter and Stephen and the mess I'd left at home, it was hard to see how it could work for me.

"I'll think about the priest telling me Danny was a sinner. And Scott sleeping with me when he knew he had the clap."

"There you go. I'll keep Fine busy. Ten minutes. Come down as soon as you're dressed."

She saluted.

"I'm not joking, Lacy. No more than ten minutes."

After four hours with Fine, she was on the verge of falling apart again. Her answers grew softer and softer. Like a drill sergeant Fine would repeat the question, pick apart her answer, question her conclusions. Every other question he reminded her she shouldn't volunteer anything. When she interrupted his question to answer, he ragged her. "Wait for the whole question. Can you do that simple thing? Just wait until I'm done asking the question."

She managed to raise her eyes to his, but he was relentless.

"I'm going to keep after you until you do it right."

Insisting that he had a better grasp of the medical issues, he ignored my requests to use the examination questions Lacy and I had practiced more than once in a gentler setting. At two o'clock I plead exhaustion without mentioning her. We broke for lunch. He never would have done it for her.

He ordered room service and kept working. With Lacy withdrawn and silent, I made excuses not to join him. I couldn't leave her alone. Bundled in front of the television — the air conditioning refused to take a break — she picked at her lunch. If she dozed off, I'd be lucky.

Once I thought she was asleep, I sneaked out and buzzed Fine. "Can I do something to help?"

"What's the matter with Lacy?"

It had taken me the better part of the year to convince him she was more comfortable being called by her first name. The way he spit it out, though, had no feeling in it at all. He might as well have kept on with 'Mrs. Stonington.'

"She's worn out," I explained. "This is her first time in court. Ever. She's not used to this kind of intensity."

He mumbled about handholding clients until I interrupted. "A quiet dinner and a good night's rest, she'll be ready for tomorrow."

"Better be. Dr. Gainesboro hates to lose." It seemed to me a gross misstatement, but I didn't call him on it.

Chapter Twenty-Three
JEAN

Fine caught me in the hotel lobby at eight o'clock the next morning. I was sneaking in with Lacy's take-out breakfast in a brown paper bag. I knew he had stayed at the Carlisle — much nicer and much more expensive. His silk rep tie was perfectly knotted under the whitest white button-down; his dark gray suit ever so stylishly cut to broadcast here was a man of talent and success. My ten-year old Joe Banks suit felt a little outdated.

Aftershave and toothpaste all mixed up with a hint of last night's brandy hit me broadside. I sidestepped towards the elevator.

"Where is she?" he spouted. "This Special Master is a stickler for promptness." And before I could answer, he hissed, "Is she sick?"

"She overslept."

"Acting suspiciously like someone who's not telling the truth."

"Give her a break." I felt the red rise in my face to volcano temperatures. "She has to admit to a roomful of people she gave up on her son, let him down. Or maybe even be accused of contributing to his problems. She has to face a man who walked out on her when she was nineteen and beautiful. She has to compete with two world-renowned pediatric neurologists and a rabid prosecutor with twenty-four dismissals under her belt. This is Lacy's last chance to do something to help the baby she lost twenty-two years ago. For once, think about it from her point of view."

Fine gazed at my flushed face and bowed his head as if in appreciation for a stellar performance. After the briefest hesitation, he pulled back the cuff of his shirt and flashed his Rolex. I braced for another lecture, but whatever he'd been about to say, he didn't.

Once the elevator door closed and I was alone, I wondered, for the first time, if finally he might be feeling a smidgeon of sympathy. A sense of humor was too much to ask for.

Lacy wasn't ready. While I was gone, she'd taken a shower and put on some make-up. It was an improvement over the woman I'd found half an hour earlier huddled in the chair staring at a blank television. Two dresses lay spread out on the bed. One had a V-neck and poufy sleeves, more partyish than churchy. The other was navy blue with tiny polka dots and a matching belt. Pretty drab. Or tailored and subdued, if you were late for court and thinking positively.

"I can't decide," Lacy said.

"Who are you trying to impress?"

She took the question seriously. If I were going to snap her out of her funk, I'd have to try harder.

"Listen to me. All Special Master Walters wants is to hear a mother tell her story. You'll never see the other two attorneys again. And I love you no matter what."

"Scott?"

"Scott won't even look at you. He's an adulterer and a deserter, remember?"

"I want him to be sorry he left."

"He already is. That's why he came for the hearing."

She reverted to silence, sitting down again in the chair. I spread out the breakfast and patted her shoulder. "We've got twenty minutes to get there. Three blocks of serious walking with morning rush hour. Please stop worrying. Just get dressed and come. You'll feel better once you're outside in the fresh air."

"I'm going to forget everything."

"No, you won't. This is your life. You know this."

"Even the part about the clap."

I looked stern. "Only if they ask you. I'll knock in five minutes."

At the courthouse Fine was pacing. It was not quite ten. When a couple appeared at the far end of the corridor, Lacy ducked behind me as we went into the courtroom.

"Will there be people watching?" she asked.

"Not many. This is not late-breaking news."

After I finished my normal routine of showing a client how to approach the witness chair and take the oath, Fine took her arm and indicated the chair between us.

"You sit here. Don't talk unless I ask you a question. No squeals. No squirming. Got it?"

"Yes, sir," she said with a lilt I had missed these last two days. I heard the insubordination, but Fine didn't. Or pretended not to. Squaring her shoulders against the chair, she kept both feet on the floor and made faces to his back while he read over his notes. Maybe I hadn't been considering the chemistry between them in the right light.

Lacy tapped my notes. "Can I go the ladies' room?"

Before she could ask for permission to be excused, Special Master Walters came from a small door in the wall behind the bench. He had the square jaw and block shape of a fighter. My shoulders sagged. I had hoped for wire rims and a bow tie.

When he entered, the two lawyers at the other counsel table stood up, still conferring in whispers. Ms. Kordoba was younger than I'd expected for a seasoned justice department lawyer. Her long black hair was twisted into a tight bun. I wondered if her scalp hurt. Under a very sheik black suit, she wore a brilliant yellow silk blouse. Two peacocks, I thought seeing Fine's reflection in her patent leather shoes.

Reaching behind him, she shook my hand. They obviously knew each other already, though I wasn't sure that was a good thing. After she waved a silent introduction of her assistant, a young man in a nondescript dark suit who followed her with his eyes, there was another round of hand shaking. Special Master Walters spoke to the bailiff, a pleasant greeting it appeared from across the room, and he then climbed up the narrow stairs to the judge's bench.

"Counsel, approach," Walters said after the bailiff had opened court.

When Fine moved forward, Lacy prodded my side. "Go."

"Only one of us can. Fine's the lead."

"What if I don't want him to be the lead?"

"Tough."

"Okay," she smiled sweetly. After a minute of silence where her head swiveled to the other counsel table, she pointed to Kordoba's back. "Is that the Greek witch?"

I regretted telling Lacy Fine's nickname for the government lawyer. Frowning at her to be quiet, I concentrated on the low murmur from the bench. If you're accustomed to being in charge, it's hard to sit back and wait for directions. Particularly from someone as terse and judgmental as Fine. I reminded myself this was for Danny, for every baby who'd had a DPT shot, for my own children. It didn't help much.

When Fine returned, I looked at him expectantly. He sighed. He wasn't used to co-counsel either. "Walters wanted us to know he didn't care whether we stood or sat. No special protocol. He doesn't care about theatrics, just substance."

I raised my eyebrows at the unusual preface. One expects Federal judges to do things more formally than country judges, not less.

"And," Fine continued, "this morning he wants to hear first about the onset of symptoms. We both waived opening argument."

"Streamlined justice."

While Fine adjusted the cuff length of each sleeve under his suit jacket, he nodded his agreement. He couldn't quite hide the sneer. Great, we had a lawyer who thought he was smarter than the judge. In my experience that trap was often fatal. Most people who'd been elevated from mere lawyership to judge status had an ego. I hoped Fine had sense enough to be deferential when it counted.

"First witness for the Petitioner," Special Master Walters announced. Fine called Scott Kellam. Because of the bench conference Lacy's attention had been diverted and she'd missed Scott's entrance. I was just as glad. His itsy bitsy wife turned out to be busty in a middle-aged way, but striving very obviously to recall her youth. Her dress would have looked good on a twenty-year old.

At the announcement of Scott's name, Lacy stiffened. She remained face forward. Any onlooker might have thought she was deferring to the formality of the occasion, too intimidated to look elsewhere. Fine seemed pleased with her, but I knew her better. She was angry. I put my hand on hers and gave it a quick pat. She smiled, but barely.

Scott's navy blue suit looked a little tight through the arms. The blue was too bright to be good quality, but the suit itself was nondescript enough to make him a credible witness. When he sat down, white socks showed at his pant legs. He stared past counsel table fixedly. I turned to see why and saw his buxom wife nodding encouragement. More support than he deserved, but maybe she was under orders too.

"Name and address, please," Fine projected.

After two mumbled repetitions by Scott of his address, the court interrupted. "If you would speak slowly, Mr. Kellam, and directly into the microphone, we could have this properly recorded."

When Lacy cleared her throat, Fine gave her a scouring look. I was sure he thought she was snickering. Much as she had predicted, Scott did not remember the exact date of the DPT shot. He did not recall any problem in the days following the shot except Lacy's preoccupation with the baby's fussiness, which he dismissed with a mystified shrug at Fine, as if another man would sympathize. Her frantic calls to him at work on July 2nd made more of an impression. He'd been busy completing a report for the new metro station when he received her initial messages that the baby was having trouble breathing. He did not remember whether the message was oral or written or which company person delivered it. With more clarity he stated they connected the second and third time she called.

He guessed that the first two calls occurred while he was out in the field, but was certain that the last call came before his lunch break. Immediately, and he repeated immediately, he went to the hospital, arriving in time to see his infant son in an emergency room alcove all by the purest chance. He described a hospital stretcher, covered with wires and tubes, and the tracheotomy tube in Danny's throat.

For his examination Fine was standing two feet in front of the witness chair, where he could see both his client and the witness. A heavy-duty reminder to any witness to speak truthfully and distinctly. Fine drew aim and boomed, "The medical record says, 'Mrs. Kellam had a problem this p.m. after the feeding.' P.M. meaning afternoon. Do you know who would have told the hospital personnel that?"

"No," Scott replied, but not as confidently as his earlier answers.

I watched Kordoba making a notation on her legal pad. Fine made a corresponding dip of his head. A mental reminder, I suspected. Trying to be helpful, I wrote it down in case he forgot. Foolish, really. Fine's attack head-on of the error in the hospital summary was tactically brilliant, so Kordoba's notation didn't make me nervous.

Fine pressed, "Is that 'p.m.' correct, to your knowledge?"

"No, it isn't."

Unexpectedly Fine crossed back to counsel table. "Could I have a minute with my client, Your Honor?"

The interruption was a surprise. He put his head down next to Lacy's. "When this man talks, I want you to look at him. This is the father of your injured son, and I want the court to see you two as a team. Understood?"

Lacy pursed her lips and turned to look at me.

"Mrs. Kellam," Fine hissed.

"Stonington," I whispered, and to Lacy, "Do what he says."

Like a five-year old she faced front and raised her face to the level of the witness chair, with her eyes closed. When she opened them, there were tears.

Fine made a military cut and returned to his examination posture just back from the line of vision between Scott and Lacy. "All right. You've said the 'p.m.' is a mistake. Now why is that?"

Scott stuttered. "It . . . I, Danny was already strapped on the hospital bed and they were working on him when I got there. Before my lunch break. It had to have been his morning feeding."

"How is that you are so sure of the time of your arrival?"

"Well, I just . . ." After he paused, he bowed his head. Lacy's hands stopped trembling and for several seconds her body remained stiff until his answer. "I just remember very well."

"This was a traumatic event for you?"

"Yes."

"How long were you at the hospital that day?"

"Until ten or so at night."

Choking, Lacy covered her mouth with her hand and pretended to sneeze. Fine ignored her, rattling out the next question.

"When did you leave?"

"When the doctor suggested I take Lacy, ah, Mrs. Kellam, home. Danny was in a coma. There was nothing they could do at that point."

"How many children did you and Mrs. Kellam have?"

"Just one."

"That's all for this witness."

I couldn't have done better myself, but Lacy was not as impressed. She started mumbling until Fine put his hand on hers and squeezed. After freeing her hand, she shook it in a pantomime of pain.

By the time Ms. Kordoba stood for cross-examination, Scott was already halfway out of the witness chair.

"Just a minute, Mr. Kellam," Special Master Walters said, "You must resume your seat for the time being. The Government now has the opportunity to ask you a few questions. You may take all the time you wish to compose yourself. You may ask for any question to be repeated. But I'll remind you you must speak loudly enough for the recording equipment."

With obvious disappointment Scott sank back down.

The judge continued, "And if you need a break, that's not a problem. None of this is meant to create any embarrassment. We are reliving moments that were unpleasant for you . . . and your wife then." When he beamed at the new Mrs. Kellam, I could hear

Lacy grind her teeth. "The Court is not unmindful of how disconcerting this is for a parent."

To my total amazement Fine leaned over and patted Lacy's shoulder. What a showman. The shock of it saved her from flinching and saved Fine, but it was a trick that wouldn't work a second time.

Ms. Kordoba walked to the rail by the jury box, though it was empty in this case. Leaning conversationally, she spoke very quietly. "Why is it, Mr. Kellam, that you didn't rush to the hospital after the first call from your wife?"

"I don't really know." He was frantically looking in Lacy's direction, though she never raised her head. "I'm not sure where I was when they forwarded the message."

"There must have been a reason it took three calls from her to persuade you to leave an important job like yours, with an employer who was anxiously awaiting your report, and drive an hour across town to the hospital."

Fine whipped up to a standing position. "Counsel is testifying, Your Honor."

Kordoba was too quick, "Mr. Kellam, why didn't you leave work after the first call?"

The judge shrugged; no harm, no foul.

"I don't really remember," Scott said. "She was kind of an hysterical girl. She always was. The first time she called I wasn't convinced that something drastic was wrong."

Fine sputtered too late. "Your Honor, counsel is badgering the witness. I object."

Lacy, to her credit, was silent.

Chapter Twenty-Four
JEAN

Once the judge disappeared for the break, Lacy let loose. "I can't believe him. He was at that hospital all day long and didn't stay with me? What a creep."

"Maybe he . . ." I tried.

"What kind of person would let their wife sit by herself all day long while their baby was having seizures? He was probably working on paperwork for his blessed project, eating dinner, schmoozing with the nurses. How dare he come here and pretend to cry like that?"

"If you'd told her ahead of time what he was going to say . . ." I said to Fine.

"I assumed she knew," he said. "How about coffee?"

"I hate coffee," she answered, but it distracted her enough to interrupt the tirade.

"Come on, let's take a walk," I offered.

"Five minutes," Fine repeated the Judge's announcement for the benefit of his inept co-counsel.

"Thanks," I muttered, taking Lacy's arm.

In the hall she started in again. "Fine knew Scott was there all that time. He knew. Why didn't he warn me?"

With the high ceilings and marble floors the words careened like fire engines. I pulled her aside and let Fine go past to the snack cart. The Kellams were already sipping their drinks. Even from the opposite side of the hall I could see that Scott's hand was shaking. Fine stopped to speak to them. Holding Lacy's elbow, I steered her in the other direction towards the stairs.

"Did it ever occur to you that Scott might have left you and Danny back then because he felt guilty? Sick to his stomach kind of guilty?"

Lacy looked at me with wide eyes and leaned back against the wall. "Don't be mad at me."

"I'm not, but you have to accept that everyone deals with trauma differently. Scott ran, maybe too quickly. And you stuck it out. Maybe too long."

"You think if I'd let Danny go sooner he might have gotten better?"

"No," I answered with vehemence, sorry to have cast any additional doubt. From the open courtroom door Fine motioned for us to return. I tapped Lacy's arm. "They're ready." We started back. "I can't very well crusade for Fine to think about someone else's point of view, if you won't. We need the Special Master to see you as the sympathetic party here. Bitterness, no matter how much you think it's justified, won't do that."

"I'll be good," she said.

Kordoba was still at the jury rail as if she'd never left. When the judge motioned Scott forward, he returned to the chair. She followed him, two steps behind like a shadow.

"You're still under oath, Mr. Kellam," the Special Master said.

"Returning to July 2nd, 1969." When Kordoba paused, everyone sat up a little straighter. I had no idea what else she thought she could get him to admit, but Fine didn't seem too worried. Unimpressed with her theatrics—or at least trying to convince us of that—he twirled his pencil and stared out the window.

"Your wife," Kordoba spit out the word as if it were a stretch to call Lacy that. I understood the prosecutor's win record, but liked her even less. This was not the user-friendly assistance for injured children envisioned by the politicians. "Your wife was there in the emergency room waiting area when you arrived?"

"Yes, she was."

"And she had already talked to the hospital staff, answered their questions, explained the circumstances that had brought her to the hospital that day?"

"I suppose."

"As far as you knew, the hospital personnel had no independent information about the events of that day before the child arrived and was placed in their care?"

"No."

"And what information did you give them about your son's behavior before he arrived at the hospital?"

"I wasn't there, I didn't know what had happened."

"When you left for work earlier that morning . . . when was that, that you normally left for your job?"

"Six-forty-five."

"Your son was awake when you left?"

"Usually," Scott strung out the word more slowly than his previous answers, worried about where she was headed.

"You've testified at depositions, Mr. Kellam, that he was awake and fine on July 2nd, 1969."

Lacy beat on my arm, "What depositions?"

"Later," I whispered.

Kordoba's disdain dripped from her voice, "And you testified as recently as this morning that you remembered nothing being wrong with him in the days immediately following the vaccination. Were you telling the truth on those occasions?"

"Of course I was telling the truth. But I meant until that afternoon when he was in the hospital."

Kordoba stepped towards the center of the court and spun on the ball of her right foot almost as neatly as a ballerina. "Please note for the record that Mr. Kellam has clarified his testimony and said 'afternoon.' "

Hopping up, Fine started to speak, thought better of it, and sat down. While he glared at Scott, I held Lacy's arm against the chair arm to keep her seated.

Kordoba's voice railed, "I'm done with this witness, Your Honor."

Fine was on his feet. "Petitioner calls Lacy Kellam."

"Stonington," I corrected.

He ignored me.

Special Master Walters spoke gently, "Come up, Mrs. Stonington, and have a seat. The Clerk will administer the oath."

Lacy waited to rise until Scott had passed through the gate. Once she'd been sworn, Fine stood and kept his eye on her as he pivoted back to his center court position. But before he spoke, she did.

"Mrs. Driscoll has my questions."

"No, I do," Fine answered, that steely tone I knew so well.

"Jean said . . ."

"She's agreed to the change."

Special Master Walters was visibly upset. "Mrs. Stonington. You will not speak until your counsel asks you a question. You have very competent counsel and I will not have this hearing turned into a free for all."

Clamping her lips together, Lacy sat back, her hands clasped together in her lap. I nodded my head.

Fine started again. "Tell us about your baby boy."

Before Fine had finished the sentence, Kordoba was out of her seat. "I object. This is a limited hearing on the issue of whether we have a Table injury. Mr. Fine is well aware of our time constraints, and I object to such a broad question."

"What your counsel means," the Special Master explained, directing his next remarks to Lacy in a much quieter tone, "is that we need to hear the state of your son's health before the DPT shot. Immediately before." He looked at Miss Kordoba, as if for approval. "In three sentences or less."

The government attorney smiled very briefly and sat down, crossing her legs and raising her eyes to Fine as if she were flirting. There was a short silence while their eyes locked until Fine waved his hand in an impatient circle in Lacy's face.

Special Master Walters leaned closer to Lacy, "Ma'am, let me state something that may or may not be obvious to you. These proceedings are adversarial. As problematic as that may be, it is to date the best system we've devised. The purpose is not to make you or any other witness feel inconvenienced, though that may sometimes happen in an adversarial process.

"If you wish to take a break, or ask counsel to repeat a question, that's your privilege as far as I'm concerned. Everyone wants you to feel comfortable. You should listen to the whole question before you answer. All of us are here to find out what happened, when, how, and where. If there's anything you don't understand, feel free to inquire directly of the court."

"Thank you, your Eminence, Special Master, sir," Lacy said.

"Sir is sufficient." Special Master Walters eyeballed Fine. Neither man looked happy. I prayed that Lacy would not ask the judge, at that point, to explain any of the technical words. The pep talk I appreciated, but I could hear an irreverent Lacy voice in my head calling into question the desire of either Fine or Kordoba to make her comfortable. Quite the contrary.

"All right, Mr. Fine." Walters ordered.

Fine tried a third time. "You caused, or asked, your pediatrician to give your three month old son a DPT vaccination?"

Lacy visibly gulped and whispered, "No, sir."

"Speak up," Fine barked. "We're making a record here."

"No, sir. I didn't ask for the shot. They gave it to him as part of the check-up."

"Yes, yes, but it happened. Correct?"

"Yes, sir."

"When did it happen?"

"What?"

"The shot. When did the doctor administer the shot?"

Lacy looked blank.

Anger and confusion passed across his face. "Administer means to give the shot to the baby."

"Oh, it was 1969. The last day of June. I can't remember whether there are 30 or 31 days in June. I'm sorry."

"It doesn't matter." Fine flung down his legal pad and strode back to the witness chair. "Up until the time and day of the shot, what was the state of your baby's health?"

"He was perfect. He weighed fourteen pounds and they were all amazed how much he had grown."

Fine took her item by item through the two days of fussiness and fever, arriving at the morning of July 2nd, with painfully obvious patience that slipped a little more with each convoluted answer. After she described Danny's jaw clamping down on her finger, Special Master Walters took over.

"What did you do when that happened?"

"I couldn't get my finger out."

"Did you call for help?" And when she didn't answer, "The authorities? The rescue squad?"

"I never thought of a rescue squad. In the mountains where I grew up, they don't have rescue squads. They have black hearses that come to get you."

Someone laughed. I couldn't tell where the laughter came from, but when the judge frowned, the laughing stopped instantly. He asked Lacy to continue and didn't stop her while she talked about finding the resident manager and their arrival at the hospital.

This part she and I had practiced five or six times. Every time we'd done it she'd forgotten one of Fine's bulleted points. With her eyes on Fine as he deliberately stood statue-like so as not to distract, her recitation took fifteen minutes and was perfect. Fear sometimes works wonders.

"Dr. Stith was Danny's pediatrician?" Fine added.

Lacy nodded, and then caught the court reporter's stare and remembered to say yes out loud.

"And where is Pediatrician Stith today?"

"Dead."

"Is that why you were unable to get all of the pediatrician's records?"

"And because they had two floods in their storage basement."

Kordoba's pen began beating the pad. Without a pause Fine switched back to more important matters, almost as if he agreed with her.

"Turning back to July 2nd, what time did you arrive at the emergency room?"

"Middle of the morning."

When Fine frowned, she added, "Nine-thirty, maybe ten."

"And earlier that week, what time of the day was the shot administered?"

"Danny's appointment was at three o'clock Monday afternoon."

When Walters peered over his glasses at the attorneys, I thought it was too good to be true. He'd obviously seen the statutory 72 hour window proved sufficiently to signal counsel he wanted to move to the next issue.

"Your witness," Fine said to Kordoba, with his back to her as he gave Lacy a rare smile.

Kordoba rustled papers. Pulling a folder out of her briefcase, she handed it to her assistant and gave him some hurried instructions. He plowed through the folder, scanning and turning pages rapidly.

Fine, without looking up from his own notes, whispered, "What's all that about?"

"Don't know," I said.

Taking a sheath of papers from her assistant, Kordoba strode up to the witness bar and laid them on the wooden rail.

"These are medical records you submitted through your lawyer?" she asked, unable to resist a small backward glance at Fine who was now rifling through his own papers, which he moved to his lap, but stopped the instant she looked back.

Lacy spoke firmly, "They came from the State Training School."

"Do you know whose handwriting that is?" When Kordoba bent and pointed to something specific, Fine turned to me.

"What's she talking about?" he asked.

"Beats me. Five or six doctors at the state hospital over the years have looked at those records. Any one of them could have marked up their copy. Can't you ask Kordoba to identify which one she's asking about? For the record?"

"I don't want the court to think we're concerned." He was a pro.

The judge interrupted Lacy's rambling answer. "That's not your handwriting?"

"No, sir. I never saw that before."

Special Master Walters spoke across Lacy's head to the government lawyer. "The document appears to be part of perhaps a larger set of documents."

Lacy answered, thinking the question was meant for her. "I wouldn't know. The state doctors wrote to all Danny's earlier doctors. They kept everything. That was the only place we could find any of the papers."

Walters squared his shoulders. "How did you come into possession of these records?"

"I telephoned the training center after I saw the television show."

Fine's shoulders dipped. "She could have gone all day and not mentioned that," he said more to himself than to me.

Without any visible acknowledgement though, Special Master Walters continued, "Did you ask if they had additional records?"

"I just wanted the ones from the emergency room, anything that could show you'all what had happened, other than me telling you. Something that would show you I was telling the truth."

"Okay. Did you obtain these records or did your counsel?"

"I tried first, and then it got so complicated. I didn't know what we needed exactly, so I called Jean."

"Your lawyer, Ms. Driscoll?"

"Yes, sir."

"Mrs. Stonington, is there any possibility that the shot was not administered on June 30, 1969?"

"No, sir."

The court sat back. After half a minute Kordoba looked up as if she hadn't realized there was no one speaking. Blinking, she resumed her cross-examination.

"Danny was born in mid-April?"

"April 10th."

"After your leave, you returned to work?"

"Yes."

"In your affidavit filed with this court you said you worked nights. Your starting time was?"

"Six."

"So you set the appointment early enough to allow sufficient time to return home and make dinner?"

"I set all the appointments like that."

"If the appointment had been at noon or even in the morning, wouldn't that have given you more time to settle the baby before you had to catch the bus for work?"

"Yes, but—"

"Then your appointment might have been that morning?"

"It was in the afternoon."

"Your first week back at work? Your first day? Weren't you worried about getting there on time?"

"I didn't go to work that day."

"Mrs. Kellam, in your answer to our deposition question you stated you returned to work after maternity leave." The prosecutor's words hung heavily in the air between them.

"That's true." Lacy looked at me and raised her shoulders as if I too must see humor in the repetition for no good reason that she could see.

"But June 30 is seven weeks after your son was born. According to your own testimony you would have been back at work then."

"I didn't work that day."

Kordoba was confused, but I didn't feel sorry for her. She obviously had no children of her own and her cursory understanding of maternity issues had made her assume things a good trial lawyer should never assume.

She persisted. "I asked you if you returned to work after maternity leave and you said yes."

"I did go back to work after maternity leave."

"The Post Office manual states that maternity leave is six weeks from the delivery date."

"You checked the manual?"

When Kordoba set down her pad and walked up to the witness chair, she almost bounced on those heels. I recognized that swagger, a litigator's joy at discovering a remedy to an unexpected problem with an adverse witness. Even then she thought being smarter than Lacy had allowed her to fix the hole she was in.

"I'm just trying to get this straight. Your leave was up on June 30 so why didn't you go back to work on June 30?"

"Because Juice gave me—"

"Juice?"

"My boss at the post office. That was his nickname."

"Oh," the government attorney drawled it in pointed sarcasm. "Good to know someone didn't give him that name at birth."

Lacy furrowed her eyebrows and glared at Ms. Kordoba. I was relieved the Judge couldn't see and glad for the reminder to neuter my own expression.

"So, Mrs. Stonington, why didn't you go back to work on June 30 as required by the official policy set out in the manual?"

"Juice knew I had the doctor's appointment. He didn't put me on the schedule for that day."

"So you're changing your answer now and admitting that, except for the doctor's appointment, that was your first day back?"

"No. Juice gave me a couple of extra days because Scott and I had planned a trip home that week. I thought if he had just a little more time with Danny, he might feel more comfortable with him. Plus my sister had offered to watch Danny so Scott and I could go out to dinner. Wednesday was our anniversary."

This was the first time I'd heard of any anniversary trip. I could see from Lacy's downcast eyes that the memory of it had upset her. She hadn't been so totally absorbed in her baby to lose sight of the growing rift with her husband. In all the talk of a sick baby the picture of a young woman, alone all day, far from family, in love with a man focused on getting ahead, had been lost, but here was another loss that Lacy had dealt with on her own. I wondered if Scott knew what he had lost.

Ms. Kordoba, concerned with saving the point she had been trying to make, wasn't giving up. "You never mentioned this trip in any of our depositions. Didn't it ever cross your mind that exposing a baby to every germ in the world could be the reason he got sick?"

"We didn't go. Scott's boss moved up the deadline for his report."

It took Kordoba a minute to control her obvious frustration, but, with her back to Lacy she closed her eyes as if she were counting to ten, pulled her face back into a semblance of calm, and returned to the jury rail where she leveled a look at Lacy that would have chilled a serial killer.

"So you returned to work on July 1 instead of June 30 when the trip was canceled?"

"I couldn't leave Danny with that fever."

She marched back to counsel table and flung herself in the chair. Her associate edged his chair away. "Mrs. Stonington, let's stop playing games. When exactly did you go back to work?"

Lacy managed a weak smile. "One year, seven months, and sixteen days after the first seizure. When he had to go to the state hospital for good."

Kordoba had fallen into a trap so neat that I had to restrain myself from congratulating Lacy on the spot. Jabbing at the pad in front of her assistant as if to shift the blame, Kordoba took a long minute to recover. When she finally stood, she held the pad to her chest as if it were a life jacket.

"You've said June 30 was the first well-baby visit. You testified and wrote in your sworn affidavit that your baby was perfectly healthy and that his pediatrician was not in the least worried about the fussiness in the days following that examination. Aren't those your words? Until July 2nd, one day was just like the next with your baby, isn't that the truth?"

Fine started to object, but I laid a hand on his arm.

"Let her answer," I said, remembering the power of her late evening revelations in my office.

"When you've waited all your life for something," Lacy's voice trembled a little, "each day is different and each day is special. And then—"

Kordoba cut her off. "I'm sure we all appreciate that insight, but . . ."

Special Master Walters cleared his throat. "Now, Ms. Kordoba, I told this lady she had to wait for you to finish your questions. You're going to give her the same courtesy and let her finish her answer. Go ahead, Mrs. Kel . . . ah, Stonington."

Lacy spoke as if she had a frog in her throat. "And then when something awful happens and your baby's not the same, you go back over every minute before things changed. The appointment was at three o'clock and afterwards he was fussy. I won't ever forget that."

"Then why," Kordoba paused, and even Fine went rigid, recognizing trouble in her tone, but not knowing how or what. "Why do these medical records, a compilation from all of Danny's doctors, not just the hospital admission record, recite 4:30 pm as his admission time?"

Lacy's 'I don't know,' was barely audible, but the court did not ask her to repeat it for the recording machine.

Although Kordoba quickly lowered her head, I could see her smile as she carried the documents to the court reporter for identification.

I stood up. "Can the witness take a break, Your Honor?"

Fine growled, "She doesn't need one. Let's keep going."

The judge pursed his lips and hesitated.

"It's okay with us," Kordoba added.

"Ten minutes, then." Walters exited through the door behind the bench.

Lacy scrambled down and streamed past counsel table. She left the wooden gate swinging. On the far side of the gate Fine stood to his full height, facing me.

"Don't ever do that again. The last thing we needed was for the court to sit and contemplate that last bit for ten more minutes."

When he came back in with Lacy, his hand gesturing wildly as he talked, Ms. Kordoba was still smiling. It felt personal, as if the humor was at my expense.

"The government may resume its cross," the Special Master said.

Kordoba smiled back. "Just one or two little things, Your Honor."

Fine harrumphed and I grimaced. It was an old litigator's trick to emphasize for the trier of fact that the case has been well made thus far.

Kordoba wrinkled her forehead and leaned back against the jury railing. "I'm confused about your statement in the affidavit that the child clamped on your finger. Do you mind if we go over that?"

Lacy nodded her head. She couldn't know how superfluous her agreement was.

"You say he was making a gasping noise, like he couldn't get enough air?"

"He made a noise when he first stopped breathing. Like a dead siren."

"And you say here that you thought he was choking?"

Lacy was still nodding slowly, trying to get a handle on why the government attorney was repeating things.

"You have to answer audibly for the tape recorder," the court reminded her.

"Sorry. Yes, I did think that."

"You thought he was choking on his breakfast? Cereal and applesauce, I think you said?"

"Yes, but . . ."

Kordoba interrupted, "So you stuck your finger in his throat?"

"Yes, but . . ."

"Your finger is bigger than the airway of a three month old baby?"

"I don't know. I . . ."

"Surely you don't need a medical degree, Mrs. Kellam, to know that your finger," Kordoba waved her index finger in the air to a non-existent jury, "is three or four times, no, let's be conservative, say double the size of the baby's airway. Wouldn't you agree?"

Gripping the rail in front of her, Lacy looked past her to me. "I guess it is."

"I'm done with this witness," Kordoba swished past Fine as she sat down, immediately conferring with her assistant. Probably congratulating herself.

Chapter Twenty-Five
JEAN

The lunch break gave us some time to re-group. Kordoba's emphasis on 'choking' in Lacy's testimony meant the government had something else planned. It frightened me and apparently Fine too.

He handed me his marked up version of the medical opinion from their expert. "Go over this again carefully." And to Lacy, "Get some lunch and don't speak to any of the other witnesses."

"I need to talk to Jean," she choked out, on the verge of tears, but Fine shooed her out the door. I waited to speak until she was gone and I was alone with Fine.

"Do you think Walters is with us on the 72 hours?" I asked as he arranged his papers in a single pile with the pad, upside down on top.

"He was." Kicking the gate open, he left. The man needed serious therapy.

After I finished my notes for him on Kordoba's medical expert, twenty minutes remained before the afternoon session. The government had no witnesses on the issue of the timing. Our witnesses had done it for them, and since none of the treating physicians were available, everyone was stuck with the records. I was still puzzling over where the 4:30 pm notation had come from and how it had percolated into all the doctor's notes. Barring surprises, the afternoon testimony, though, should be much less stressful since the medical experts from both sides had submitted detailed written opinions.

Attached to Fine's copy of the report from the government's doctor, I saw his curriculum vitae for the first time. Ten pages long, Doctor Stearns had written dozens of articles and served on numerous boards, including, I noted, the Advisory Board for the government's Center for Disease Control. Among his research kudos were a dozen grants, two specifically on the DPT vaccine, both in excess of two million dollars. Research grants meant greater credibility for any doctor, and two awards of that size were unusual.

Who had that kind of money for research grants? The government might, because they'd mandated the vaccine and needed to justify the law. But the drug manufacturers who sold the vaccine had a much more mercenary reason. In this case they both were looking for the same result. The new information sank like a brick in my stomach. It would be foolish to bite the hand that feeds you and I was sure the good doctor was not foolish. I left a note for Fine to check out the resumé.

Worried about Lacy's state of mind, I went hunting for her. She wasn't in the hallway. With a few minutes to spare, I found a payphone and called Peter. When his secretary ran him down in the lunchroom, he was slurping his Slim Fast and reviewing one of the eleven newspapers he read every day.

"How's it going?" he asked.

"I was going to ask you the same thing. Stephen's okay?"

"Seems to be. The counselor's making him think hard about some of his ideas, even gave him some stuff to read from addicts. Scary. He had a bad chemistry grade, but his other courses are rocking along." I could hear phones ringing in the background.

"Busy day?"

"Meetings, lunch with a new professor. Beats working."

Since the switch to teaching, Peter loved going to work. Inspiring students to delve into the forgotten lessons of history was like an adventure for him after the carefully prescripted world of investments and banking. And his tennis game had improved greatly.

"How about my girl?" I asked.

"Elly says I can't iron like you can."

"Oh, so now you're ironing for her?"

"She had a history test."

"Uh-huh. Maybe I should stay a few extra days."

"Andrew's eaten up with the World Cup soccer games, so he's hard to mobilize."

"I'm sorry I didn't call this morning before we started. Lacy's been up and down and all over the map, but she tells it the same every time."

"So the case is going well?"

"I didn't say that. This issue of the 72 hours is a bugaboo. We slide back and forth." It was an attempt to convince myself that it wasn't as bad as it had come across that morning.

"That doesn't sound like you're going to finish today."

"No, and that's worrying Lacy no end. Another night in the hotel on her budget. And away from Moss. I wish she'd let us summon Doctor Snowden. Even seeing him in the hall during the breaks would have reassured her, I think."

Fine, his suit coat flying, sped by the phone booth and disappeared up the stairs, two at a time.

"Oops, there's Fine," I said, "My master calls."

"Obnoxious as ever?"

"Worse. Not only is he smarter and quicker than the rest of us, but he'll tell you so."

"This is tough for you, isn't it?"

"He's actually growing on me."

"I wish I were there to see that."

"I'll tell you all about it when I get home." In spite of his sense of humor the tension between us lingered. Like the old days when the telephone operator listened in, neither of us was being completely genuine.

In the upstairs hallway the Kellams stood glued together at the top of the stairs, almost like teenagers in love. It was hardly what I'd expected from my phone conversation with them. Even though they were making good use of the time, they looked a little put out at having to stick around. According to the hallway clock, we had eight more minutes of the lunch recess.

"Did Fine ask for me?" I asked Scott.

"No," he said, handing me a Chick Fil-A bag.

"What's that?"

"Lunch."

Shocked, I took it and began unwrapping while I thanked him. "Where's Lacy?"

"Powder room."

The sandwich in hand, I went to check on her. Before I opened the door, it swung wide and Kordoba streamed out, her heels clicking on the marble floor. She passed without acknowledging me.

"Lacy?" As I rounded the corner, she slid down the wall into a heap on the floor. She was tugging at her dress to cover her legs and she was crying, though not totally out of control.

"Was Kordoba arguing with you just now?" I asked.

She managed a barely audible 'no.' Although the tears dripped onto her lap, she made no effort to wipe them. I ran the cold water and handed her a damp paper towel.

"We're losing," she mumbled.

"No, we're not. It's too early for that." She didn't laugh. I chattered on, "The court knows how memory works. Wait till this afternoon. We've got them cold on the medical issues."

"I blew it though, didn't I?"

"What do you mean? You told the truth."

"If the judge guy thinks I choked Danny, then all that mess about the shot and the time of day doesn't make any difference."

"Dr. Gainsboro will explain that. It's in his report."

"I . . . Fine thinks . . . " she couldn't finish.

"Don't worry about him. It's the Special Master who has to believe you."

Her hands fiddled with her belt. I was worried. We needed her to listen. She might have to testify again.

I stroked her hair. "Are you sure Kordoba didn't say something she shouldn't have? She's not supposed to talk to you unless one of your attorneys is present."

"She was trying to apologize, I think," Lacy said, her voice a quiet echo in the empty bathroom.

Too surprised to speak, I offered her my hand to stand. After a few hiccups and a swipe to her cheeks with the paper towel, she straightened her belt and fluffed out her dress.

"I was right," she said. "She doesn't have any children."

"How do you know that?"

"She told me. Said I shouldn't get so emotional, lots of the other mothers' babies had died."

A hard tremor of rage shot through me. If Kordoba could be that cold after hearing so many of these cases, she was more ruthless than I imagined. I could report that comment to the Judge. Even if he didn't sanction her, it would make her look bad. But my losing my temper in front of the Judge wouldn't help Lacy. I could hear Peter. *Aren't you a little too close to this one?*

"What does she know? She's a witch, anyway." It was a weak attempt to make Lacy laugh.

She was working on a smile. "No, she had a sex change operation. She and Fine were twins separated at birth." After pinching her cheeks, she shot a half-hearted grin at the mirror. "I look better than that floozy Scott's married to now, don't you think?"

With his very sturdy briefcase at his feet, Dr. Gainesboro identified his report and outlined the medical facts he'd relied on for his opinion that Danny had not aspirated. Rather his brain, after the first seizure, had stopped telling him to breathe. Carefully choosing his words, Dr. Gainesboro reiterated that the lack of struggling movements, the absence of vomit in Danny's mouth or in the tracheal tube, and the hospital x-rays of two fully expanded lungs, all were proof against aspiration.

The doctor quoted Lacy's affidavit, nodding politely in her direction when he mentioned her name the way he would have offered credits to a colleague delivering a scientific paper. Her statement that Danny did not move voluntarily after the initial sucking-in sound and that his jaw remained clamped for five minutes was, in Dr. Gainesboro's considered opinion, further substantiation for a grand mal seizure. Seizures were what we needed for a Table Injury.

During the government's cross-examination Kordoba harped on the hospital admission record, one page of the group of documents that had caused Lacy such problems on cross-examination.

"Doctor," Kordoba started, but paused as if she expected someone to pop up and object to the title itself. "The only contemporaneous record we have from medical personnel states 'Probable aspiration.' Isn't it true that none of the physicians who treated this child initially used the word seizure? In fact they don't mention seizures until days later?"

The doctor's answer came immediately. "Yes, and yes." Although Kordoba turned her back to the witness chair to signal that was the answer she wanted, Gainsboro continued. "That omission is unusual and very significant. It shows that they were not considering it, did not even think of it or they would have noted that the symptoms did suggest seizures." He shook his silver head, definitely highlighted by a professional. He and Fine probably shared the same hairdresser. "It's understandable," he said kindly. "They're not pediatric neurologists."

Fine knew his experts all right. It was the kind of bulls-eye plaintiffs' lawyers love.

Without another question from Kordoba, Gainsboro proceeded, "But more importantly, they do recite that the apoxia is of unknown etiology. If they had determined it to be aspiration, they would have so noted. But the evidence did not conclusively support that theory either. For reasons I have previously stated and so they couldn't."

Buttoning and then unbuttoning her jacket, Kordoba looked like she was weighing the odds at breaking him. "Doctor," she finally said, "I understand you have testified in a great many vaccine cases for parents, isn't that correct?"

"It depends on what you mean by 'a great many.' I have testified before today, yes."

If that's all Kordoba had, we might get by.

Special Master Walters acknowledged the end of our evidence with a break. He announced five minutes, disappeared through the door behind the bench, and reappeared in four, sending signals to both lawyers by flipping open the file and staring into the courtroom. Dr. Stearns, the government's expert, brought no briefcase with him to the stand. During the short recess between doctors, I had tried to explain to Fine about the research grants listed on Dr. Stearns' resume.

"All these doctors supervise grants," he replied.

"But I'll bet these are from the exact same manufacturers who asked for the compensation fund in the first place. They're specific grants to Dr. Stearns, not to his hospital. He wouldn't include them on his personal vitae if they didn't reflect on his individual medical reputation."

"Why would he put them on the vitae for a DPT case if there's something fishy going on?"

"He probably never looked at it. His secretary just fished it out of the file and attached it, like she does to every opinion he writes."

Fine grunted, but didn't look up from his pad.

I thrust the report, resume page up, into his hands. "I know he didn't list who funded the grants, but who else could it be?"

Fine flipped through the three pages of credits, perusing the list. "I'm not prepared to cross-examine him on his research findings. Are you?"

"But wouldn't we have grounds for a recess? I just saw the resume today."

"They sent it months ago." Twisting his tie into place, he looked up, daring me to question his failure to explore the issue when he'd first had access to the information.

Kordoba continued to harp on the 'possible aspiration' notation, almost leading Stearns through his testimony. When Fine did not object to anything, I started writing notes to him on my pad and drawing big arrows. He ignored me. Although Lacy sat up as if she were listening, she didn't react much. Her glances at the clock and the door were long and lingering. She was tired. I wasn't sure how much she understood. Most of what Dr. Stearns said was technical.

After Kordoba sat and the Judge cleared his throat. Fine mumbled something, ripped several pages off his pad, and handed them to me.

"You do it."

"What?"

"Cross-examine him about the grants."

After sucking in my breath at the shock, I stood and gathered the pages from Fine in fluttering hands. Despite all my urging, I was not sure I could do this. Much less do it so that it helped Lacy. I turned and glanced back at counsel table. Fine was looking down at his pad, and Lacy was beaming. This was crazy, Peter was right. I had no business being here in Federal court no matter how much I cared about Lacy.

As I approached the witness, Dr. Stearns slid back in the chair. I must have looked mad, but it worked. He was on the defensive.

"We have conceded, Dr. Stearns, for purposes of this hearing that you are an expert on pediatric neurology." It was legal mumbo-jumbo, filler. I needed time to get my mind straight.

"Thank you."

"We have read your submission with great care."

Dr. Stearns nodded and smiled politely.

"Would you say that you have done the same in your review of the medical evidence and your rendition of the written opinion?"

"Yes."

Perhaps perplexed at the uncharacteristic pleasantries, Kordoba and her assistant were whispering again.

"Outside of this case, before you looked at this particular child's records, you have some specialized knowledge of this particular vaccine, do you not, Doctor?"

"I'm not sure what you mean."

"Haven't you published in this field?"

"Oh, yes." He unclasped his hands in his lap.

"That, or I should say those, publications stem from some specific research."

"All publication should, if it's meaningful."

"And I have no doubt your research, as an expert, could only be meaningful."

Kordoba scraped her chair back from counsel table, but didn't rise. While the compliments must be wearing thin on her, I was starting to enjoy myself.

"This research, did it cover a span of years?"

"To which particular project are you referring?" He eyed me with a thoughtful expression, more than the usual wariness at opposing counsel.

Ah, I thought, as he stared at the report in my hand, maybe the good doctor was more compromised than even I had guessed.

"Well," I made a huge display of analyzing the report, without turning to the final pages, which were the resume.

When Kordoba hit her assistant on the arm, he scrambled for their copy in the piles of documents on their table. I glanced up at the witness, back to the report, and then out the window, suggesting that I'd picked out the information randomly.

"How about, for example, the 1987 project funded by Mechle?"

While Stearns was stumbling over the answer to the number of years he worked on the 1987 Mechle grant, the Special Master leaned over to the Clerk. After whispers back and forth, he took the report she handed him, the court's copy of the opinion and turned to the back pages. He looked confused.

Apparently Kordoba was not as familiar with it. She raced to the bench. "I've let this go on, Your Honor, assuming Counsel had some valid purpose, but it's clear she doesn't. She's fishing and the government objects. It's not the way we try cases here."

It was an ugly dig, but when I happened to glance at Fine, he was grinning. It reminded me that lawyers hurl insults when they are floundering.

As if the Special Justice were in pain, he blinked and held up his hand. "Ms. Kordoba." He cut her off. "Without proper foundation I wouldn't normally allow it. However since Dr. Stearns seems to recall the study in question, I'd like to hear what he has to say."

I stepped in front of Kordoba and in my calmest voice, said, "Excuse me, Ms. Kordoba, my witness."

She was forced to step back to avoid being bumped. As she retreated to counsel table, I wondered if her palms were sweaty. She probably realized by now there was worse coming. All trial attorneys recognize that feeling. The witness you thought was safe prepares to utter an unknown answer and your voice separates from your body out of panic.

"Dr. Stearns?" I repeated.

"What was the question?"

"How many years did the first Mechle project cover?"

His lips drew together to form the 'th' for three, but at the last minute he hesitated. "For an exact answer I'd need to review my papers."

"Certainly."

Everyone watched while Dr. Stearns tore back to his seat in the courtroom, fumbled with the locks on his briefcase, and rifled through its sheaths of paper.

"Perhaps a five minute recess," Kordoba suggested.

My mouth was open to object, but Special Justice Masters raised his hand, palm open. "The court doesn't mind waiting."

Back in the witness chair Dr. Stearns balanced the files on his knees while he pulled a handkerchief from his pocket and patted his forehead in tiny sharp swipes, returning his hand to his lap in between and glancing around the courtroom, but never making eye contact. Kordoba poured a glass of water and cleared her throat. She kept looking at Stearns, probably trying to warn him to stay cool, but his eyes were locked on the papers.

"I'm sorry," Stearns said. "Can you repeat the question?"

"Sure. What years did you receive money under the '87 Mechle grant?"

"That was an independent grant, combined with several other grants."

"I didn't ask you about the organization of the funding. I asked you about the timing."

Kordoba popped up, "Counsel is arguing with the witness."

Special Master Walters muttered, "Overruled."

"I think—this is only from memory—it was a two year project."

"So it would be 1987 and 1988?"

"That fits, but it would be in the findings." Stearns shuffled his papers and added, "Maybe it was '86 and '87. If the study date is '87, that might be right."

"You're having trouble remembering a grant that took up two years of your time less than three years ago?"

Kordoba crisply stepped out from behind the table, as if coming out of a fog into sunshine. "Your Honor, Ms. Driscoll is testifying," and, after the judge failed to respond as quickly as she would have liked, "I object."

Because the Special Master was reading the last page of the report, a minute went by before he spoke. When he did, he nodded in my direction. "No need to belabor a point well made, Counselor."

I began again. "Do you happen to remember the protocol for the Mechle study?"

"As I recall—keep in mind I've been involved in dozens of studies like these—"

"Dozens of Mechle grants?"

Kordoba practically screamed her objection and the Judge instructed me to let the witness finish his answer, but the upturn at the corner of his lips looked suspiciously like the beginnings of a smile.

When the doctor continued, his face remained blank and he didn't meet my eyes. "As I recall the team reviewed reports from hundreds of vaccinating doctors and compiled statistics which were then analyzed for different factors."

"Adverse reactions to the DPT vaccine were reported?"

"Yes, although it was a simulated model." Stearns' answer was muffled because he was once again examining the papers in his lap.

"And did the reported risk factors include seizures?"

"Among other reactions."

"You mean, seizures AND those other reactions."

As he nodded, he shifted in the chair, crossing and uncrossing his knees as he grasped the paperwork. I couldn't help shooting a triumphant look at Kordoba before I turned back to the witness chair.

"They're recording, Doctor. You have to speak your answers."

"Yes," he breathed heavily, "all of those reactions."

Standing at the rail by the witness chair, I leaned ever so slightly closer to him, enunciating painfully. "In your research findings for the 1987 Mechle grant, what did you conclude about the percentage risk factor for the DPT?"

"There was very little correlation."

"Surprised?"

"Excuse me?"

"Never mind." I stepped back and leaned against the empty jury box, assuming a pose that was impressively casual considering I was the lion and my prey had just realized he was lunch. "Doctor, you said 'simulated model.' That means not real cases, just actuarial games?"

"Actuarial statistics are very real figures, Ms., ah . . ."

"Driscoll."

"Ms. Driscoll. This kind of research stems from a very accepted methodology in the scientific field."

"I don't think there are many mothers who would accept actuarial statistics instead of live babies in the delivery room, though, do you?"

Dr. Stearns did not answer, but it gave Kordoba the time she needed to look more closely at the resume. She walked rapidly towards the bench. "Your Honor, there is no mention of Mechle on Dr. Stearns' list of research grants. Counsel has not laid a proper foundation. We ask that those questions and answers be struck and disregarded."

Special Master Walters shook his head as he spoke. "The witness already answered the question in the affirmative. He's had ample opportunity to correct that information if it was erroneous," The judge glanced at me. "Do you have more questions for this witness, Ms. Driscoll?"

"One more, if I might. What companies manufactured the DPT vaccine during the years of your studies?"

"We didn't track it by manufacturers."

"No? Well, I'll ask it this way. Why would a particular drug company, say Mechle, why would they care to fund research about risk factors for a vaccine they didn't manufacture?"

Dr. Stearns gazed wide-eyed at Kordoba. Pretending not to notice, she examined her own notes in great detail. Finally he said, "I don't understand the question."

"As an expert in this area, are you telling this court that you don't know who manufactured the vaccine that is the subject of your opinion, the vaccine that is at issue in this lawsuit in which you are appearing as an expert, the vaccine that is alleged to have caused Danny Kellam's seizures and his subsequent apoxia and thereafter his severe retardation?" My voice echoed across the still courtroom, bouncing back at me. Lacy was riveted and facing forward with enthusiasm for once.

The doctor coughed lightly. "It's in my report I'm sure."

"Never mind. Let's try this question. How much money did Mechle give your particular team for research on the DPT vaccination project?"

"I'm not the funding person."

"Convenient. How about . . . over one million dollars?"

"Research projects on a national scale are expensive to run."

"It could have been five million, you're not sure?"

"You seem to know more than I do."

"The question calls for a yes or no."

When the doctor didn't answer, Special Masters Walters put the report down and peered over the edge of the desk. "You will answer."

"What was the question, sir?"

"Did Mechle give you one million dollars for the DPT research project?"

Dr. Stearns's 'yes' was a whisper.

I had trouble keeping myself from saying thank you.

When the court called for closing argument, Fine surprised everyone by asking for rebuttal time.

The Special Master cleared his throat. "It's after four now, Mr. Fine. How long do you expect this rebuttal evidence to take?"

Kordoba couldn't wait her turn. "They haven't subpoenaed any rebuttal witnesses. Absent notice to us, they can't call any."

Fine looked at her over his glasses. "In discovery we listed potential witnesses. I think," he paused for effect, "that meets the Federal rule."

It was a technical point, but he was right and she knew it. Like a rooster he strutted forward with the list of witnesses for Walters to see. I was mentally scrambling, trying to recall the other names. None of them was here at the courthouse. The hearing had been scheduled for one day on the court's docket. Whether the absent witnesses could make it to Washington overnight was a separate question altogether. The list included a few of Lacy's relatives from North Carolina, her friend Cameron, Scott's parents, office staff from both Fairfax physicians' offices in case records needed to be verified as business records, and Snowden. As Lacy's personal physician, he knew the most, which wasn't saying much. 79 years old, a non-treating physician for the injured child, his inclusion on the list didn't bring me much hope.

By the time Walter's secretary had checked his schedule and he had dismissed us with a reminder to be ready to go at nine, Kordoba had packed up her briefcase and was at the door. Her assistant could barely keep up.

"Good night," Fine called after them.

Lacy shuddered.

"Dr. Gainesboro did well," I said, hoping to avoid an explosion from Fine.

He looked daggers at me. "Driscoll, my room at eight p.m. Make it nine. I've got calls to make. And dinner reservations."

When I do trial strategizing before big divorce cases, I sit down with the depositions marked, the statute of what I need to prove, my typed list of witness questions, and an empty pad. The exhibits I spread out along the top of the table. Mostly so I don't forget them, but partly for inspiration.

In Lacy's case the exhibits were few because we'd been so unlucky with the old records. I did have her black and white photo of Danny at three months and several later photos that tried to mask the unnatural twist of his limbs and the droop of his head that had become more pronounced with age. From one of Lacy's more recent trips to visit him at the state residential hospital, I had a photo of him with his mother. Holding her small hand in his great gnarled one, he sat in his wheelchair with his oversized sneakers and his kneepads. Although his neck was in the brace, his head was still cock-eyed.

During an emotional dinner with Lacy, I carried the conversation with painstaking care to avoid babies and the day's testimony. After dinner, although I was exhausted, I walked her back to the hotel and tried to reach Peter and the kids on the phone in the lobby. Busy signal after busy signal. Maybe they'd left the phone off the hook by mistake. With teenagers it wasn't a very likely scenario, but my mind was full of doctors and hospital records and I didn't dwell on it long.

The Washington sidewalks were still busy with men and women in suits as I walked over to Fine's hotel. The lobby's walnut paneling was worth admiring and I was tempted to ask what it cost to stay there. Good thing Lacy's case was on a contingency. She could never have afforded Fine's taste in hotels. Because he was late coming from whatever fancy restaurant he'd chosen, I had to show every piece of identification and bribe the bellman into unlocking the living room portion of Fine's suite so I could sit down. On the desk there I laid out the paperwork in my usual manner, adding the photos. It was almost ten by the time I sat down on the sofa, in slacks and a sweater. Although I tried to imagine something cold and energizing because I was falling asleep, it didn't work.

When I woke up, only one light was on in the room. The floor lamp had been dragged to the desk. Someone had draped a blanket over me, shoulder high. Fine, with his hands in his hair, was sitting at the desk.

I struggled to sit up. "I'm sorry, Mr. Fine, I couldn't stay awake."

When he didn't answer—too deep in concentration—I adjusted the blanket around my shoulders and walked over behind his chair. His legal pad was covered with handwriting.

He put his finger on the most recent photo of Danny. "Why does he look like that?"

"Like what?"

In the photo Lacy's expression was hard to read, not unhappy, not grinning either, but she was intent on her son. Danny's fingers, curled spastically at that perpetually awkward angle, covered part of his face, but he was definitely smiling.

"Happy," Fine murmured.

If Lacy had been here, she would have said, that's the power of love, but it would have been like speaking Farsi to Fine.

"That's a question for Lacy. Want me to work on some of this stuff?"

"No, you go to bed. There's not much to do really."

"I don't mind. I can do witness summaries for closing."

"Thank you, no."

"Rebuttal?"

"I've taken care of it." It was a clear dismissal from the man in charge.

The next morning Kordoba was raring to go. When Fine announced that Scott Kellam was the first witness, she practically flew out of her chair.

"Your Honor, the government renews its objection to this kind of rebuttal testimony. It's repetitive. With all due respect to the Kellams, do we have to hear this sad story one more time?"

Walters spit back, "We won't know if it's repetitive until we hear it. Petitioner may proceed." The pugilistic side of him, kept under wraps? Or merely impatience over a second day crowding his calendar, I couldn't tell.

When Fine stood for his examination, his suit jacket fell into perfect form around his trim shape. His tie hung exactly between the lapels. His hair held the part. While he walked forward, shoulders square, eyes bright, he was saying, I am a professional. I was the only one who knew he'd been up past midnight, studying the medical opinions, re-working and re-writing his questions.

As Scott sat in the witness chair again, a tremor passed over his face. I could feel his dread. He'd assumed he was done, had gotten off relatively unscathed, and now he was being recalled. Even though Fine was, in essence, on his side, the inference that Scott had done something wrong resurfaced. The lawyer's anger over Scott's slip the day before lingered in the strident way he moved across the wooden floor and stood within inches of the witness box.

"You've told us how clearly that day in the hospital remains in your mind after all these years, Mr. Kellam," Fine began.

Kordoba was on her feet, bending forward over the table. "Is there a question in there, Your Honor? Mr. Kellam's testimony stands as it reads."

"Mr. Fine," the judge spoke evenly, "You are an experienced practitioner. Please refrain from re-stating the evidence." Special Master Walters had satisfied both lawyers and made his own point as well by not using the word testimony. The evidence was the evidence and neither lawyer was going to make him remember it differently.

Vaguely in the direction of the judge, Fine gave one of his conciliatory nods, but stayed facing Scott. "I believe you testified that in June of 1969 your wife was on maternity leave?"

"Mr. Fine," the judge repeated.

"I apologize, Your Honor, just trying to lay a foundation. Was your wife a lazy person, Mr. Kellam? Your first wife?"

Next to me Lacy straightened and tensed her legs as if she were ready to square off if he inferred anything else about her character. In big letters I wrote on my pad, CALM DOWN.

"No, she wasn't lazy," Scott answered.

"She took care of the apartment and Danny single-handedly?"

"Well, I was at work all day."

"Fair to say she had a lot of energy and enthusiasm for that baby?"

"Oh, yes. He was everything to her."

Even Lacy must have heard the forlorn tone in his answer because she slumped back in the chair. When Fine cleared his throat, she was examining her hands. Forgotten was Fine's admonition to watch Scott. I wondered if she were still dwelling on the way things might have been if Danny had not stopped breathing that day.

"What did your wife generally do during the day? What kind of chores?"

"Objection," Kordoba said, "If he was working, he wasn't in a position to know what she did."

Raising his hand to preclude Fine from response, Special Master Walters said, "I think if he returns and finds those things done, he can testify that she did them. There's been no mention of a maid. And these are not wealthy people."

Kordoba sat, more put out than she should have revealed. Her pen snapped repeatedly against her pad. Not a patient person. Fine repeated the question.

"Laundry, at least one load a day. Babies . . ." Scott shrugged, implying an acceptance without understanding. "She washed and waxed the floors, ironed clothes, vacuumed, went grocery shopping, took Danny for walks in the stroller. We only had the one car. I hadn't gotten a raise yet."

"So she was up and about all day, not reading French novels in bed?"

"No, no, Lacy didn't read much."

I knew it would feel like a slur to Lacy, but it was truthful and he was being cooperative. "Shhh," I whispered to her before she could grumble.

"I presume she was dressed in street clothes when she did these kinds of chores, the grocery store, the laundry?"

"Of course."

Disgusted at the waste of time, Kordoba flung down her pen. It skittered across the table and dropped to the floor. Fine, the ultimate and complete gentleman, picked it up and handed it to her with a flourish. She snatched it from him.

"When you arrived at the hospital on July 2nd, 1969, Mr. Kellam, what was your wife wearing?"

Kordoba was back at it. "I object. What possible relevance can what she wore have to whether there was a table injury or not? Mr. Fine is stalling."

"Counselor Fine, are you stalling?" the Special Master asked with the hint of a smile.

"Absolutely not, sir. If the court will allow the question, the relevance will be obvious."

"Read back the question for the witness, please," Walters said, but Fine simply repeated it.

"When you first saw your wife at the hospital on July 2nd, what was she wearing?"

"If he recalls." Kordoba interjected, scrambling to recover her concentration.

"If you recall," Fine conceded with so much politeness I wondered if he hadn't meant from the beginning to bait her.

Special Master Walters frowned in Kordoba's direction. "Mr. Kellam, hold up just a minute before answering, please." Adjusting his robe as if cameras were whirring, Walters sat up very straight in his chair. He waited until both lawyers were looking at him and until the courtroom was completely silent.

"This hearing is to determine whether we have the onset of a table injury to a three month old. I understand counsels' enthusiasm for their clients' respective positions, but I will not have my courtroom become a coliseum, fight-to-the-death kind of circus. This is rebuttal, and I don't want any more interruptions from the government or sarcasm from the Petitioner. Understood?" He stared at Ms. Kordoba who tried to look apologetic.

"You may answer," the court ordered, turning back to the witness.

Scott spoke loud and clear, "She was wearing her nightgown. A red nightgown."

"She was still in her nightgown when you arrived at the hospital," Fine said. "Okay. That's all."

Kordoba muttered something from her seat.

The Special Master cleared his throat. "Ms. Kordoba, did you want to examine this witness?"

"No questions," she said. While Scott stood and practically raced back to his third wife, Kordoba readjusted the piles in front of her with sharp, decisive movements as if she could now return to more important issues, but she didn't fool anyone.

Chapter Twenty-Six
JEAN

Fine rose slowly from counsel table, with a show of reviewing his notes as if he hadn't bothered during the recess. As slowly, he walked over to the window to give Lacy a chance to relax and settle into the witness chair. Rain fell past the window in a steady drizzle as if someone had forgotten the faucet. My mind drifted. The basement door at home ought to be latched firmly to avoid flooding and I hadn't been able to reach anyone there by phone to remind them. Peter was not in his office, though normally he kept office hours religiously. I'd left a message with the department secretary, but his departure from routine bothered me. Like mothers everywhere when they're not at home, I could only hope everyone was doing what they were supposed to be doing in my absence.

On my right Kordoba conferred with her assistant. I surmised from her random glances at our table she meant for us to see that she felt the entire procedure was a total waste of time. Was I the only one that understood how much was riding on this?

"Mrs. Stonington," Fine started, "how is it that twenty-two years after the fact you recall the time of your appointment for Danny's vaccination on June 30?"

"Scott was supposed to be home from work at 4:30, and I wanted him to be there in case I needed help with Danny while I was fixing dinner."

"You anticipated problems?"

"Oh, no." She looked a little surprised. These were not questions we had practiced.

Fine snorted impatiently. "Why were you worried about him being there then?"

"Snowden had warned me that babies get fussy after shots. Since it was Danny's first shot, I planned it so I could get over there and back on the bus by the time Scott came home. I did the other appointments like that too before Scott . . ."

While Fine cleared his throat loudly, I cringed. A dozen times he'd instructed her not to mention Scott's desertion. He wanted the court to see them as a unit.

She recovered quickly, "I set them all that way."

Kordoba slapped her pad down on the table. "This question was asked and answered yesterday, Your Honor."

Special Master Walters eyed Fine.

"If the Court will bear with me, I'm almost at the rebuttal matters."

"Counsel should be aware I have a very good memory. Repetition does not increase your chances."

Fine bowed his head to acknowledge the Court's polite hint. "Mrs. Stonington, you said 'Snowden' warned you?" He voiced surprise, but he knew from our sessions exactly who Snowden was. "Who is Snowden?"

Lacy misunderstood, assuming Fine hadn't been paying attention. "My friend. My doctor. I liked him better than the pediatrician." She said the last, turning to Special Master Walters.

Kordoba pushed back her chair. "Your Honor, we object to Doctor Snowden testifying."

Fine shook his head at Kordoba as if she were a misbehaving child. "A little premature." And then after a pause, much more softly, so that only I heard. "Just a little." It was the second time he'd treated me like a colleague and it felt good.

When Kordoba remained silent, Fine bent his head to his notes. Special Master Walters looked confused, as if he hadn't expected either of these experienced attorneys to violate procedure.

"Ms. Kordoba," he asked, "is this Doctor Snowden not on their witness list?"

"Yes, sir, he is. And Mr. Fine is absolutely correct. Snowden has only been mentioned, not called to testify. So I will save my argument for the appropriate time."

Before continuing his examination Fine bowed as if he'd been toying with her from the outset. "Mrs. Stonington, when you first brought Danny to the emergency room on July 2nd, what did the nursing staff do?"

"They took him away from me."

"Is that when they performed the tracheotomy?"

"The throat tube thingy?"

Fine's cheeks rose under his eyes in distaste as if he were being asked to eat grubs. "Exactly. The throat tube thingy."

"Yes, they did that in the emergency room, and a bunch of other stuff. The nurse told me later they were having trouble getting him to breathe. It was late afternoon when they moved him upstairs."

The judge sat up. "Well, I'm happy to hear what Mrs. Stonington has to say about all this, but if the statement here in the admission record is that he stopped breathing ten minutes before coming to the emergency room, and we already know . . ." he pulled Kordoba's training center paperwork from the exhibits, "there is a time and date on this. It says 4:30 p.m., and it says, 'Informant, mother.'"

He sighed and put the papers down deliberately. "All right, go ahead, Mr. Fine."

For a good minute Fine did not continue. He placed his hand against his tie, deep in thought. Lacy was shrinking into the chair as if she were literally afraid of the question. He'd made it clear to us from the outset that he hated to lose, but it was more than that. I wondered if he felt what I did. If he regretted what had come before, his impatience, his harsh words?

It seemed to me, sitting in that handsome courtroom, a historic place where American lawyers and judges had battled over the truth for almost two hundred years, that the law had played a trick on Lacy. After a lifetime of silence, she'd bared her soul, made her plea in her own words to strangers with more power than she had ever had or wanted. Not only was she going to lose based on the tiniest human error, but she no longer had the insulation of innocence, of not knowing why.

The technicalities of a law written by the very ones who were avoiding responsibility meant more here in this place than the clear and simple fact that before that DPT shot on June 30, 1969 Danny Kellam was a gurgling healthy baby and afterwards he was . . . a tragic double.

In Lacy's eyes I saw the reflection of a deep and abiding love for her firstborn son. In the turn of Danny's head at her voice caught in a photo one cloudy March day two decades later, I had seen him acknowledge that love in the only way he knew how. But no one else—not the lawyers, not the judge, not the politicians who'd set up the circular path to 'assistance' or the businessmen who sold the medicine that had hurt him instead of helped him—would ever comprehend the depth of that love. Nor would they understand no matter how they twisted the truth that the love wasn't wasted.

Still, it was a failure of epic proportions. And worse yet, it would be repeated in thousands more cases after Danny's if Adriana Kordoba and the Justice Department had their way.

Fine took a deep breath, "How long were you at the emergency room before anyone came and took a statement from you?"

"Hours."

Fine cleared his throat ominously.

Her knuckles were white above the rail where she gripped it with both hands. "Three, four, I don't know. I called Scott again from there and when I put the phone down he was standing in the doorway, big as life."

"And how long after Mr. Kellam came," Fine continued without much enthusiasm, "was it before the doctor came?"

"Doctor McIntosh didn't get there until dinnertime."

"Doctor McIntosh is . . .?"

"Doctor Stith's partner."

"Did he take the medical history or did a nurse?"

"I don't know."

"You don't know who took the information from you?" Fine's voice was chilled. This was what I had been afraid of with Lacy. Things could unravel so quickly.

"It was a person in a white coat."

"That's all the questions I have." When Fine forgot his usual Ringmaster's flourish to turn the witness over to Kordoba, she sprang up with too much enthusiasm. Even he continued to watch her instead of presenting his usual nonchalant face to the world. His eyes followed her the way a cat keeps one eye on the door in case it opens and he can dart out in that instant. Fine was wishing, I guessed, that he were somewhere else.

Balancing on the edge of her table, Kordoba sent a casual glance at Lacy before speaking; a thinly veiled sneer camouflaged with a smile. I imagined how insignificant that kind of look might make a person feel, even a person with education and legal training. My entire body tensed, ready to spring up and defend Lacy if Kordoba attacked her.

"Mrs. Kellam, I mean Stonington," she drawled, "in all this testing and taking x-rays and reviewing records, did any of these doctors ask you about hereditary conditions that might have affected Danny's ability to breath?"

Fine sat up straight and poked me with his elbow, but I was already paying close attention.

Lacy looked perplexed. "What kind of conditions?"

"HE-RE-DI-TEAR-E," Kordoba repeated, "Like when your grandfather has red hair and freckles and you do also."

Lacy asked, "You mean did anyone in Danny's family have the same reaction to a DPT shot?"

It was a gut response and so was Fine's belly laugh. Maybe he did have a sense of humor.

Kordoba recovered. "No, I mean did anyone ask you if someone related to Danny had a medical condition that affected breathing?"

"I don't remember a question like that."

"So you didn't tell any of the doctors or nurses or, ah . . . people in white coats that breathing difficulties ran in your family?"

"They . . . I don't know—"

"You didn't tell them because they didn't ask? Or because you didn't think it was relevant?"

"Objection," Fine said, as if he had an inkling where she was headed. "This witness is not a medical expert. Her opinion on medical issues is not admissable." To me, he hissed under his breath, "What the hell is she talking about?"

Kordoba pressed. "I'm not asking for a medical opinion, only what a reasonable person, a concerned parent with a related medical condition, would do when her child stopped breathing with no explanation."

Fine practically spurted the words. "Objection, no foundation. We've heard no evidence that there's a family history of breathing problems. Hypothetical questions are only permitted to experts."

In that instant it seemed as if Kordoba had been waiting for two days to catch Fine in this exact position. Her nails glittered against the polished walnut table where she remained coolly leaning against it.

"I'm trying to put on that evidence, Your Honor, if counsel could hold his laundry-list of objections."

"Would the government like to make a proffer?" Without waiting for an answer, Walters was moving to the door. "In chambers. You may come too, Mrs. Driscoll."

When the judge released us, Lacy was still seated in the witness chair. She looked as if she'd shrunk several inches like Alice in Wonderland.

"You could've taken a break while we were gone," I whispered.

"I didn't know. Are we okay?"

"Everyone's tired. Just a little bit longer." There was no way I could prepare her for what was coming. When Special Justice Walters took the bench, I retreated to counsel table, my pen and pad ready.

"Ms. Kordoba, you may continue your examination."

"When you were five, Mrs. Stonington, did you or did you not receive weekly shots at a doctor's office in Twyman's Mill for breathing difficulties?"

Lacy's entire body deflated. Her chin fell below the witness rail. While her medical history was an idea that had not occurred to any of us, Kordoba's announcement of it must have struck Lacy as particularly damning, the more so since it was obvious she had never before connected the two things. She had lived with twenty-one years of guilt already.

"I . . . I, ah, went to the clinic for shots. For about two years. Gram called them allergy shots."

"You were allergic to breathing?"

When she didn't answer, I wondered if Kordoba had any idea how scared Lacy was. The new Mrs. Kellam started to titter, but Scott elbowed her silent. No one else laughed. I hoped Kordoba felt the chill. I hoped she'd rot in hell.

Shaking papers in Lacy's face, she shot out the next question. "Isn't it true those shots were meant to clear your lungs?"

"No one ever told me that." Her face was as white as I'd seen it. "I was little—"

Kordoba interrupted. "Isn't it true, Mrs. Kellam, that you started the shots after a bout with rheumatic fever?" She didn't give Lacy time to answer. "An illness that affects your heart and your lungs, the same organs that failed your son on July 2, 1969?"

Fine was objecting, I was objecting, Kordoba was rattling off questions and slapping the wooden rail in front of Lacy.

"Silence," the court ordered. The sudden stillness silted in around us so that the only motion was Kordoba's last drop of the papers against the wooden rail.

"Am I supposed to answer, your Eminence, sir?" Lacy squeaked.

"No," Walters said crossly.

After another conference in chambers Kordoba admitted she had no witness to establish the new medical records she had been waving in Lacy's face. Without a medical expert or the keeper of the records, the government's 'alleged' evidence of hereditary breathing difficulties would not be admitted. Kordoba returned to her table, walking like a fashion model with one heel missing. It hardly mattered. The possibility had been raised, even without the substantiation. The Special Master offered to let Kordoba complete her cross-examination on the issues Fine had raised in rebuttal, but she was shuffling notes and opening folder after folder, having trouble staying focused.

She held up the page for Lacy to read. "Mrs. Stonington, you've had a chance to reflect on the written records made at the hospital."

In slow motion Lacy nodded.

"You have to answer audibly for the court reporter," Fine said, adding as an afterthought in an exhausted tone, "out loud."

Kordoba thundered, "The hospital records state Danny was admitted at 4:30 p.m. after his feeding, do they not?"

"You told us that's what they said."

"Despite those records, you've now decided that you arrived in the morning?"

"I haven't just decided—"

Special Master Walters interrupted, "It would help us all, Mrs. Stonington, if you had any specific recollection of the exact time you arrived with Danny."

Lacy straightened and turned to face the court. Closing my eyes, I thought, here it comes. She's not really sure and she's going to tell him that. Fine was holding his breath. Lacy kept her eyes on the judge and spoke evenly. She never wavered.

"It was late afternoon when they moved Danny to the fourth floor. He had tubes all over him, including the one coming out of this throat. That had to have taken them a long time. I'd been sitting in the emergency room since breakfast and I hadn't eaten any lunch. It felt like a week, but I know it was hours. When they finally told me I could go up, I looked at the clock. It said 4:30. I'd been there all day."

She hesitated for the briefest moment, shot a quick startled look behind me as if she'd seen a ghost, and turned back to the judge. I clenched my teeth and waited.

"I may not be very smart," she leaned closer to the bench, "and most of the words in those papers are gibberish to me. I don't know whether you believe me or not, but I want you to see my face so you remember it when you rule."

Chapter Twenty-Seven
JEAN

"Are you through yet?" Kordoba hissed at Fine once the Judge had excused himself to make a pre-arranged conference call on another matter. Lacy went out before I could speak with her, her shoulders slouched and her head bowed. She'd whispered an apology as she passed the counsel table. The Kellams had been excused. The courtroom was almost empty.

Fine didn't answer Kordoba. He wouldn't talk to me. I left the two of them to each other, a little like leaving two tigers in one cage. All the way to the hallway door I could feel their eyes on my back.

Now what? I said to myself. Courtroom drama was fine, but we were out of evidence. Even if Snowden had come, as mad as Kordoba was, even if she lost the objection to his not being the treating physician, the Judge wasn't going to let in much of what Lacy's obstetrician knew because it was hearsay, volunteered by Lacy or pulled from the treating pediatricians. Snowden, after all, had been on vacation on July 2nd, 1969.

When I heard Lacy's shriek, I raced down the corridor, convinced she'd finally lost her temper with her ex-husband.

"Oh, my God. Thank God. I love you," Lacy repeated from Moss's arms halfway down the stairs. "You came."

"Ay-yah."

"Oh, Mosste," she said, "You shouldn't have. We'll be penniless. They'll fire us both and we'll have to beg on the street corner." She turned and yelled up at me, "In Henryville that means a quick death. All those duty-stricken Southern Baptists." Then back to him, "They'll bury us side by side. After they wax your mustache and sparkle up that white coffin you picked out at Snyder's Funeral Home. Is there enough in the cookie jar for a gravestone? 'Devoted Husband, Fruitcake Wife.'"

In between hugs he removed his ten-gallon hat, never letting go of her.

"How d'you get here?" she asked, out of breath. "Isn't he sweet?" she said to me when they reached the second floor.

"The truck," he answered.

"But the timing belt?"

"The guys at work passed the hat."

"Oh, man. I love those guys. I'll have to make them apple cobbler every Friday for a year."

"I reckon."

In the hallway group, an elderly gentleman stood watching and smiling. Snowden, I guessed, from his age. At breakfast Fine had grilled Lacy about her friend Snowden. She admitted she'd spoken with the aging doctor by phone the night before she'd left home. He had no way to get to court, hadn't driven himself in thirteen years, and his recollections were hazy. Before court opened Tuesday morning Fine insisted she telephone again and convince him to take a taxi at Fine's expense.

Once Fine left for the courthouse Lacy fretted, worried that the trip would be too much for her old friend. Shorter than I'd expected, Doctor Snowden was about as broad as he was tall. I was dying to speak with him, but decided to give Lacy a chance for a short reunion before I complicated things with legalese. If he'd been the steady friend she'd described in all our office conversations, his presence ought to calm her down.

When Fine walked by and saw Moss with Lacy balanced on one arm and his ten-gallon hat in his hands, he paused and whispered to me, "Why is that man here?"

"He loves her." That stumped him.

On the payphone at the end of the hallway I tried home again. A strange man answered.

"Who is this? Where is my husband?"

He interrupted my question. "Is this Mrs. Jean Driscoll? Have you talked to your son Stephen in the last twenty-four hours, ma'am?"

"No, of course, not. I'm in the middle of a trial here in Washington. My husband's supposed to be there with the children. What's happened?"

"Your son Stephen didn't come home from school yesterday afternoon. Mr. Driscoll's at State Police headquarters filing a missing person's report."

"That's more than 24 hours ago. No one called me."

"Mr. Driscoll didn't want to interrupt."

"Andrew and Elly?"

"They're fine. They're here, doing homework actually. Their dad made that very clear."

"It'll take me almost two hours to get there."

"I won't tell you what to do, ma'am, but there's nothing more you can do here at this point. The APB'll be out momentarily and there are two officers talking to his school friends."

In the background I could hear Elly talking to someone close by. "Who's there?"

"Mr. Driscoll's back. I'll let you two talk."

Peter's voice was strained, as if he'd been lecturing non-stop for days. "He's vanished. Bryan too. God, how I'd like to throttle that kid."

"What did Bryan's mother say?"

"She had no clue. She left for work yesterday before Bryan got up for school. Both boys reported to homerooms. Several kids saw them together, and one of the girls who likes Bryan says he's been really grouchy lately, talking about how different California is. Way cool, she says. Don't you love it?"

"Can you call his other friends to see if he's contacted any of them?"

"Police say they're more likely to tell the truth if an officer makes those calls. We're supposed to keep the phone line open and stay close in case he telephones."

"I'm coming home. Fine can handle closing argument."

"Sweetheart, if you're almost done, just come when you're finished."

"What if Stephen calls and I'm not there?"

"They're pretty sure the two boys are together. They took their backpacks, some food from Bryan's house. And they're seventeen. Just come when the case is over."

To deal with the crazy pounding in my head, I ducked into the bathroom. I needed time to think. I ran water into my hands and splashed my face. Wild drips streaked the mirror and the wall. They didn't teach you how to deal with this kind of thing in law school. Or in parenting classes. The image of Stephen sleeping in an alley somewhere rose behind me like a specter. I wanted to finish here and get home. The distance between us seemed monumental and I realized it was mostly my fault. When had I last spent an hour with any one of my children, listening to what they thought was important instead of lecturing them on my priorities? With a damp paper towel against my cheeks, I looked at myself in the mirror and didn't like what I saw.

Kordoba came out of one of the stalls and moved to the adjacent sink to wash her hands. Everything about her was in order, her hair coiffed, her suit unwrinkled.

"Look, Adriana—"

She cleared her throat and her forehead tightened into a frown. Had I stepped over some line by trying to be collegial?

I started again. "I understand you don't have children of your own." I hoped I didn't sound as desperate as I felt.

"Careers get in the way."

As if mine were insignificant. "I'm sorry."

"Don't be. I like what I do."

"And you're very good at it."

She ran a brush through her hair, keeping an eye on me through the mirror. I must have looked like a wild woman. Although she and I both recognized the futility of this, Lacy's breathless plea from our very first meeting at my office stuck with me. And if Stephen turned up hurt because of my being here, I was going to make it worthwhile.

My voice cracked. "Why are you fighting this one so hard? It's a little case, really. No huge medical bills to repay. Kid's in the state hospital, no future care formulas to speak of."

Without responding, Kordoba leaned against the sink and smoothed the eye shadow over her right eye. It was a callow gesture and it made me mad.

"Can't you try to look at it from Lacy's point of view? Imagine as a mother, loving that baby, laughing and playing with him, waiting for him to say Mama, trying so hard to make him roll over, sit up. Walking to doctor's appointments where they never told you anything, for months and months. Being alone, unsure, terrified that he wasn't getting well because of something you did or failed to do. Giving up everything for that baby. Losing the man who had rescued you from abuse and poverty, losing your dream of a happy family. And then having to give up the baby." I took a breath. "Take a goddamn minute and try to imagine what it was like for her. What it is like for her."

She raised her hands to clap, but must have seen the outrage in my face. "You're very eloquent. Your law school obviously taught different skills than mine."

"Aren't you even a little bit concerned about doing justice?"

"If you wanted justice, you should have gone to divinity school."

"That's pretty low. You sure fooled Lacy with that *apology*." When she blinked and paused, I wondered, if like Fine, she was regretting that lapse.

Sticking the brush back in her handbag, she stepped toward the door. "If you feel that strongly," she said, "why didn't you accept the deal?"

"What deal?"

"The one Fine and I worked on last night at dinner."

I was seething. Fine shrunk in my eyes to almost non-existent. "What did you offer him?"

"$10,000 clear to your little gold digger for medical expenses. No proof necessary. Plus the attorneys' fees. He insisted."

How could he think that Lacy could live with a deal? Especially a deal where the manufacturer didn't acknowledge responsibility? Kordoba was gone before I could speak or move.

I threw the paper towel into the metal bin. In the hallway, as I approached, the group grew quiet. Beyond Lacy and Doctor Snowden stood a very frail-looking woman half his size whom I hadn't noticed before. Next to him she could have been a midget. Her skin, wrinkled in a dozen swirling patterns, reminded me of the creamiest hot chocolate.

I moved closer to Lacy. "Do you have a minute?" I said, edging Stephen from my mind.

She ignored me and took the old man's hand. "Snowden, this is my friend. And my lawyer."

"Jean Driscoll," I muttered and shook his other hand. "Lacy, I . . ."

"And this," Lacy swiveled on the balls of her feet like a child on Christmas Eve, "is Mary." She put her head next to Mary's ear and said more loudly, "You never told me your last name."

"Jefferson," she said in a much sterner voice than I had expected from such a small person. Her handshake was surprisingly firm. The name rang a bell, but I couldn't quite place it.

I pulled Lacy aside, "Fine's been trying to make a deal."

But she didn't respond. "You need to talk to Mary Jefferson."

"Later."

"No," she was fierce, "Now." She tucked Mary's arm into mine. With Snowden on one arm and Moss on the other, she left us in the hallway. When Ms. Jefferson began to speak, I had to lean inward to hear.

After the bailiff announced the resumption of court, I walked Mary Jefferson in and maneuvered her right behind Fine where he sat immobilized before a pile of beautifully typed notes at counsel table. Precise as ever, he must have faxed the handwritten notes from the night before to his secretary early with instructions to fax them back typed. He didn't turn around, even when I stretched over the rail.

I spoke quickly and quietly over his shoulder. "You really had me going during the Kellam cross. I thought you might actually care. But you're so busy making deals you don't have time for a real witness."

He waived me away, refusing to even look at me. I blistered him with my eyes. "Hamilton." I flung out his first name like a glove. "You need to put Ms. Jefferson on the stand."

"It's too late for dramatics. A deal would have saved Lacy this embarrassment. I've done everything possible."

Lacy interrupted, her voice strong and clear. "Do what Jean says."

Curious about the controversy at our table, Kordoba spun around, but there was nothing else to say. As Fine glared at me, we took our seats. He went back to his pad. Lacy ignored everyone and shifted to a sideways position in the wooden chair, just far enough so she could see Moss out of the corner of her eye. With his cowboy hat on the bench next to him, he kept his eyes on her. She was so right about him; he was all hers. While we waited for the Special Master, Moss whistled Amazing Grace under his breath until the bailiff came over and told him he'd have to leave if he couldn't behave appropriately. He only smiled back and resumed the slow stroking of his long white mustache.

"Please, if you care even a little bit about her," I whispered to Fine.

"It won't make a difference," he whispered back.

Once the bailiff re-opened court, Special Justice Walters gathered up the exhibits while he addressed the lawyers. "I'm assuming since we've heard from everyone at least once, we're ready for closing argument. Counsel for the Petitioner?"

"Actually, sir," I shot up and moved away from Fine so he couldn't stop me. "We have one remaining witness."

"That Snowden man?" Walters asked.

"Dr. Snowden is available if the court would like to question him. As Lacy's obstetrician, he could corroborate Danny's good health immediately before the shot, but I don't think that's in dispute." At the rustling and muttering from the government's table, I paused without turning around. "Ms. Kordoba might want to be heard on that. I don't mean to put words in her mouth."

She was already standing. "Doctor Snowden wasn't present during these events. Whatever he knows he only knows by reason of hearsay." She flourished the pages in her hand and sat down. "The government is ready to present closing argument."

"Petitioner calls Mary Jefferson," I said.

"Objection." Kordoba was sputtering, but back on her feet. "Ms. Jefferson is merely an employee of Dr. Snowden's. Presumably she heard the same hearsay the doctor did. If he can't testify, then neither can she. And she hasn't been deposed."

I waited patiently for her to finish. "If the court please, Ms. Kordoba can hardly claim surprise. Mary Jefferson was included on our list of potential witnesses from the outset. The government chose not to depose her. That's their business, but she has independent knowledge of these matters. Until late yesterday, we didn't know we would need her. She is, nevertheless, here and ready to testify."

I would have added 'on the timing issue,' but Fine yanked my jacket, and to avoid stumbling, I fell back into the chair. Mary Jefferson was already standing at the rail with her hand on the gate and the other on her hat as if a sudden breeze might blow it off. When Kordoba dropped back into her chair in defeat, the bailiff offered his arm and walked Ms. Jefferson to the witness chair, where he waited until she was settled. After he explained something in whispers, she undid the hat pin and set the hat on her lap.

I nudged Fine. He nudged me back.

"You got her up there."

After I stood, I rested my hand on Lacy's shoulder. Slight as she was, she sat herself up, straight and steady, to bear the extra weight.

"Ms. Jefferson," I enunciated. "You're a little hard of hearing?"

"Sometimes I hear good, sometimes not."

"Do you know Doctor Samuel Snowden?"

"Laws, yes, we worked together for near on forty years. I was his nurse. He was a great big fella first time I set eyes on him. Right out of school. He's shrunk a little, but . . . don't we all?"

Half the courtroom laughed, but not Fine or Kordoba.

I waited until the laughter died down. "Do you still work with Dr. Snowden?"

"Goodness, no. When I retired, he retired."

The courtroom tittered again. Even Special Justice Walters bowed his head to hide a smile.

The nurse continued, "I suppose Doc might tell it differently."

"When was that, Ms. Jefferson? That you retired?"

"Ten years ago."

"During the time that you and Doctor Snowden worked together, did you ever have occasion to meet Lacy Kellam?"

"Miss Lacy was famous in our office."

"Famous?"

"Miss Lacy came back from the dead."

"She what?"At the unexpected statement I made the mistake of turning towards the window to collect myself and caught Fine's 'I told you so' expression.

Mary Jefferson kept on. "Miss Lacy had a twin sister and they were both stillborn, but Miss Lacy came back. She's a fighter. She told that story to anyone who'd listen. What a talker, that girl."

Thrusting his legal pad in front of his face, Walters struggled to control a smile. Kordoba must have decided this testimony was insignificant. Buried in her notes, she was writing on index cards what I presumed was her closing argument.

I cleared my throat and started again. "Did you know her baby, Daniel Boyd Kellam?"

"If you knew Lacy, you knew her Danny. You never saw such a proud momma."

"Ms. Jefferson, I would like you now to tell this Court if you ever remember talking to Lacy around about the time her son Danny got so sick?"

When Kordoba stood, she stood so fast, the papers and cards went flying. Although her assistant scrambled to gather them together, she paid no attention to the swirl and scurry at her feet. "Around about? Your Honor, this is a court of law, not Ms. Jefferson's front porch. I know Ms. Driscoll is from the country, but we've been here a long time on this one and . . ."

Lacy could hardly contain herself. Moss actually guffawed, and even Fine's mouth curled upwards at the corner.

"I'll rephrase the question," I offered. "Nurse Jefferson, tell the court what you know about Lacy's baby getting sick in June of 1969."

Ms. Jefferson nodded to me, but turned to the Judge. Frowning, she looked at him as if he ought to do something about the bad manners of the interrupting lawyer. When she continued to stare at him, he waved his hand to signal that she should speak. She rewarded him with a wide smile. Shifting her body back to face me, she spoke louder as if the confusion were simply a matter of her audience not being able to hear. I could see how any new mother would instinctively rely on her.

"When Doc went on vacation, he always turned his clients over to another doctor. In case of emergency, you know how they do. But I liked to work those days he was away. Put things back in the right places, you know."

"Your Honor," Kordoba complained.

"I'll allow a little leeway. This witness is not accustomed to courtrooms."

"What did he say?" Nurse Jefferson asked me.

"He says you can tell us in your own words what you know about Lacy Kellam's baby during Doctor Snowden's vacation in 1969."

"I was trying to do just that." She shot a disapproving look at the government lawyer. "Lacy called the office, poor thing, crying and all worked up. Her Danny wasn't moving. Not breathing, not crying, nothing. I told her, take that baby over to Fairfax Hospital right away and I'll call the pediatrician. That was first thing in the morning, right after I got there, about eight-thirty."

"Plaintiff rests, Your Honor."

Kordoba was rigid in her chair; her associate blithering away in her ear to no avail. I couldn't even feel sorry for her at this last minute reversal of a point she thought she'd hammered home yesterday. She stood, more out of habit, I thought, than a decision to act. In the silence Nurse Jefferson had risen, but as Kordoba approached the witness chair, she sat back down and smiled with all the graciousness of a schoolmarm for the new student. Kordoba's voice was strained and too loud in the still courtroom.

"How is that after thousands of work days and millions of telephone calls from frantic mothers you just happen to recall the time that one patient out of hundreds called your office twenty two years ago?"

Nurse Jefferson gripped the rail with both hands and leaned over it. "Young lady, I'm not in the habit of forgetting things. People who're born dead and come back are special people. Doc Snowden knew that. That's why he treated Lacy the way he did. Her Danny's heart stopped more than once, but he's still alive twenty-two years later. Must be a reason." She was staring at the Judge. "I'm not one to go stepping on God's toes, but if the mother's special, her child's bound to be special too. Don't you think?"

After a short throat clearing and a quick glance at the lawyers, the Judge spoke. "You know, Ms. Jefferson. I'm not inclined to step on God's toes either."

Chapter Twenty-Eight
JEAN

Without going into details, I told Lacy I'd talk with her later and left them all in the courtroom. Scott had come up without his wife, apologizing in mumbles to Lacy who was grinning like a little girl being offered an ice cream sundae. Fine was watching as if he'd never seen a man apologize, but he managed to offer his hand to me as I passed.

"Counselor," he said, "You were right. I would have missed that." It was the first time he'd offered to shake hands.

Halfway down the wide marble stairs, Lacy caught up with me. "You're leaving without saying good-bye?"

"I didn't want you to worry. Stephen's gone missing."

"What . . .Jean . . .why didn't you say something?" Her eyes clouded with tears. "When, how long have you known?"

"It's not important. Peter's there. And the police. I've got to go . . ."

She called after me, "I love you." And I didn't mind that a lobby full of people stared as I hurried away.

I drove eighty-six miles in eighty-six minutes. The State troopers must have been staking out someone very important because they certainly weren't on the Virginia highways I was traveling.

While the scenery blurred, my imagination raced ahead of me. Scenario after scenario spun out with the disappearing roadway. Stephen, racing through a warehouse to escape the dealer he'd tried to turn down. Stephen and Bryan, hitchhiking across Montana in a snowstorm to reach the California paradise that existed only in Bryan's memory. Stephen, holed up in a flophouse putting evil substances into his body. Sobs caught in my chest and I had to pull onto the shoulder. That sweeping feeling of desolation I'd felt as I walked across the empty training center lawn crashed around me. How had Lacy carried it with her as she raised Diana and Carson, as she made those solitary visits twice a year to see the blankness in Danny's eyes? It must have taken incredible reserve for her to live through the last two days of testimony and the last year and a half of constant reminders, an emotional barrage I was just beginning to fathom.

When I finally made the top of our hill, there were no police cruisers in the driveway. Before I had the car door fully open, Elly crashed into me. Andrew stood at arms length, gripping the door as if he might drown without it. His grin was as intense. When I looked up to see if Peter was right behind them, Stephen appeared on the porch, then disappeared into the house. I sat back on the car's front seat and let my breath ratchet down to normal.

"You were gone so long," Elly said, patting my shoulder as if she wasn't sure I was real. "Dad let us have pizza all three nights."

Andrew elbowed her aside. "Don't be mad." Those serious dark eyes.

"Pizza is nutritional," I conceded.

"I mean at Stephen," Andrew interrupted. "He was helping Bryan. Like you were helping Mrs. Stonington. And he came home on his own."

"On his own from where?"

Peter appeared with my suitcase and the hanging bag from the trunk. "Better let him tell you. It's quite a story."

"You believe him?"

"Mostly."

Inside the kitchen the counters were clear, the sink empty. No pizza boxes littered the table. I was impressed. "Where is he?" I asked. Peter smiled his old tennis victory smile and pointed upstairs.

So much can happen in seventy-two hours. Ask Lacy, so much can happen in a minute. For days I'd been running on adrenaline, but now that I was home I felt the strain of being so focused, so invested. It had been a long time since I'd felt that way about anything, much less a client. I hugged Elly and roughed up Andrew's hair. They looked so much taller. Elly's bangs were dogging her eyelids.

"You guys are so great. I know I don't tell you enough. If I ever lost one of you, I . . . I . . .I don't know how I'd go on." Andrew was rolling his eyes in Peter's direction and I could tell he thought I'd lost my marbles. "But if either of you ever runs off without telling us where you're going—"

After I put down my briefcase, I went looking for my other son. No matter what he'd done or I hadn't, I needed to tell him that I loved him.

Afterword

On the Monday following the 1992 hearing in Special Court of Claims #90-00104V, *Lacy Kellam Stonington, on behalf of her son, Daniel Boyd Kellam, versus Secretary, Department of Health and Human Services*, the Court held a telephone conference. Issues related to the triggering of a Table Injury had been raised in another case and were scheduled to be decided by the Fourth Circuit Court of Appeals. Special Master Walters believed the ruling would be precedent for the Kellam case.

While we waited for the Hellebrand decision with a page-long list of other families in similar cases, Lacy became quite an expert on the DPT vaccine. She scoured magazines and mailed me articles. She began a letter writing campaign. She wrote to her state delegate, John J. Butch Davies, explaining that the trust fund had accumulated 600 million dollars, but was limited to compensating injuries from vaccinations after the inception of the Act. Children injured prior to October 1, 1988 relied on congressional appropriations for recovery and in late 1992, the money ran out.

Lacy wrote, '*I know children need to be vaccinated against diseases, . . . but there are thousands of vaccine victims like my son Danny in this country who have sacrificed their opportunity to lead a normal life as a productive citizen. In 1986 Congress promised to help these children who made the sacrifice. It's not happening.*

'I don't see my son every day, but there isn't a day that goes by that I don't think or even wonder what if this hadn't happened and what he would be like at 23. . . .One child hurt by a vaccine is one child too many.'

Delegate Davies forwarded Lacy's letter to Congressman Allen, Congressmen Bliley, Senator Robb, Senator Warner, and the Secretary of Health and Human Services with a cover letter of his own requesting assistance. Four letters came back to her, assuring her they would do what they could. No reply from the government.

In the summer of 1994 Lacy wrote me to say that Jenny's daughter had drowned in a neighbor's unattended swimming pool. The news cast a long shadow from Narden to Henryville and beyond. I remembered the notations on Danny's hospital record of visits the little girl had made. I wrote Jenny a note to tell her how saddened I was and how much her continuing care and love for Danny was appreciated.

After a brilliant set of essays, all filed uncharacteristically early, Stephen was accepted the following April to college. We struggled through a summer of attempts at complete independence, accompanied by arguments about calling home when plans changed and paying for your own gas. By August he was packed and Peter and I were ready for him to go.

The fall of 1994 beat all the records for rain. The farmers gloried in it without knowing that seven months later a 500-year flood would sweep away most of the Piedmont's best topsoil, two centuries' worth of investment by her farmers. In Henryville Lacy switched jobs again and became a pharmacist's assistant. She learned how to enter prescriptions in the computer and run the billing program. Her daughter Diana moved west, married, and 'did make-up' for the rich and famous. Carson worked on his community college degree. Lacy assured me Moss was thriving as a part-time farmer: hay and Christmas trees being his preferred harvest.

At the office Jillian moved to a part-time schedule to devote herself to her family and to give her wrists a chance to heal. I began doing more bankruptcy work in Federal court, telling husbands and wives who called that I'd changed the focus of my practice. Federal court, I'd learned from Lacy's case, meant more advance work, but shorter trials. Bankruptcy cases meant less emotion and easier nights. In October Peter and I took two weeks and went to Spain to visit friends whose rooftop deck overlooked the Mediterranean. Contemplating the same blue sky and wide seas that had inspired Leonardo da Vinci and Columbus lent an ageless quality to our earthbound years that helped me appreciate Lacy's ability to transform her loss into something positive.

In November Fine wrote to say he had received a new offer of settlement. As much as I hated to, I telephoned him before calling Lacy.

"Why now?" I asked him.

"Two other decisions just came down from the Fourth Circuit. They solve our medical record problem because the occurrence of the encephalopathy is a presumed Table Injury. Shifts the burden of proof. The Special Master's already as much as said that the government's theory of aspiration isn't supported by the records. Kordoba's trying to settle to minimize the damages."

"What about funding?"

"Congress just passed a special appropriation. We need to move on this before the money's gone."

Before I could reach Lacy, she left a message at home for me to call. Andrew talked with her.

"She's pretty funny, but she talks so fast I missed half the jokes."

"Did she sound upset?"

"No."

When I called her back, she opened with, "I love you."

"I miss you. Nothing very exciting has happened here since. How's Moss?"

"Still making me laugh. The other day I was talking like I do at the pharmacy and when Mosste came in, Mr. Neidermier told him I was the same in the evening as in the morning. Crazy."

"That's why everyone loves you."

"Is something happening with the court?" she asked.

"You're a fortune teller now."

"No, but Jenny says they've been snooping around down there. Kordoba called the hospital administrator."

I bristled. "They shouldn't be able to get anything without filing in court and copying us. Privacy Act covers all that."

"Maybe Fine got the papers and didn't think it was important enough to tell you."

"What else does Jenny say?"

"Danny has pneumonia. He's in the infirmary there."

"That explains it."

"What? Something has happened."

"They're offering a lump sum and an annuity. No more court, no second expert, no more briefs."

"There was more court?"

"Not for you. But apparently in the other case, a decision on the medical issue helps us. Fine expects the Special Master will rule any day now."

"I don't want to settle."

"I told him that."

"He didn't know it already?"

On February 8, 1995 the Department of Health and Human Services under Secretary Donna Shalala published final rule changes in the Federal Register (Volume 60, Number 26) that eliminated the presumption of eligibility based on historical vaccine reaction symptoms. Seizure disorders, like the ones Danny Kellam suffered, were removed as a Table Injury. It would be ten times as hard to prove the connection for other injured children. News reports noted that the fund had accumulated $825 million in reserves from the parents' surcharges, but neglected to add that less than 20 % of the claims made since 1988 had been paid. The safe acellular version of the vaccine, used in Sweden and Japan for almost two decades, had still not been approved for use in the United States, much less required. In other vaccine compensation cases evidence had been introduced that American manufacturers had abandoned the "safe" vaccine because of the cost.

When the final ruling came in the spring, Fine sent Lacy a copy the same day he mailed mine. She called me first.

"I can't understand this junk. Did we win?"

"We did."

"Why does it take twenty pages to say that?"

"Lawyers."

"What do we do now?"

"Hire another expert to show what it will cost to take care of Danny."

"His Highness Fine knows someone, I expect."

"He does. He asked me to get your permission."

"He's scared of me, isn't he?"

"Maybe so."

"We showed that witch lawyer something."

"You did that." We were both chuckling.

"How are your kids?" she asked.

"They're great. I think. Stephen's at college, writing symphonies, and Andrew's still playing soccer."

"After this new guy files his opinion, do I have to go back to court?"

"No. You're done."

"And if we win that part?"

"Oh, we will. It's just a question of how much money."

"Fine'll be in his element."

"What will you do with the money, Lace?"

"I just want enough to buy Danny a new wheelchair."

"You can buy him a new bed, music videos, a radio, whatever you think he'd like."

"Can I send Jenny flowers?"

"Bouquets."

"Guess what I did this week?"

I could see her grin through the phone. "I couldn't begin to guess."

"They had this show on television, Katie and Matt."

I groaned. "The Today Show?"

"Yeah, they were talking about crib death. The symptoms, other explanations, you know. I called to tell them about the DPT shot, but the receptionist switched me to an answering machine. I called right back and said, 'Don't give me that machine. I want to talk to Matt.'

"They put me on hold again and just as I was about to hang up, a man came on the line. Guess who it was?"

Acknowledgements

During the ten years it took to move this story from inspiration to reality my family and friends showered me with continuous encouragement, detailed editing suggestions, and periodic doses of the hard cruel facts about being a writer in the twenty-first century. Professor Pat Skarda, my first real writing teacher, a person of unequalled humor and succinctness, taught me the value of persistence. My patient husband learned how to cook. My critique group adjusted to my tardiness and my rants. My first agent, Candy Tufts, a fellow Smith College graduate, suggested I write short stories, it would teach me how to choose my words more carefully.

The story itself would never have moved beyond a figment of my imagination if it hadn't been for the real mother and son who lived the story and for whom there will never be any happy ending. An expanded National Vaccine Information Center, with Barbara Loe Fisher's constant vigilance, offered continuous updates and insights into medical and regulatory changes as did the Center for Disease Control. Special thanks to my mother who taught me many things, the most significant of which is that there is beauty in everything if only you take the time to look.

[1] *HR Report No. 908, 99th Con.2d Sess. 3 (1986) where presumptive causation is included in the statute to facilitate the contemplated easy recovery.*

Discussion Points for Book Clubs

1. What role does adversity play in Lacy's perceptions of the world and of her ability to direct or alter the events in her life?

2. What do Lacy's memories of her childhood tell us about her as a person? How do they inform her role as a mother?

3. What ethical or moral obligation do doctors have to tell the whole truth to the families of their patients? Was there any justification for the doctors' withholding information from Lacy based on their perception that she wasn't strong enough to handle the truth?

4. If career choice is based in part on personality, how does Jean's dissatisfaction with her job affect the way she views herself as a person? As a mother?

5. What are the pros and cons of one parent revealing to another child's parent(s) information about their child's participation in dangerous or illegal activities?

6. How is the portrayal of Hamilton Fine important to the development of Jean's character? To her realizations about balance between career and family? How about Adriana Kordoba's effect on Jean's self-analysis?

7. How do the contrasts between Lacy and Jean contribute to the reader's understanding of the challenges working mothers face?

8. When is it that Lacy finally realizes she can change the world around her? Are there other times in her journey when there is a glimmer of that possibility?

9. At what point is the risk from a vaccine too great to encourage its use? Who should make that decision and what part should parents play in that decision?

10. Consider the challenges Lacy and Scott Kellam faced when Danny was injured by the vaccine and how the manufacturers and the government might have assisted in meeting those challenges.